THE GANGSTER

MAGIC & STEAM: BOOK TWO

C.S. POE

This is a work of fiction. Names, characters, places, and incidents either are the product of the author's imagination or are used fictitiously, and any resemblance to actual persons, living or dead, business establishments, events, or locales is entirely coincidental.

The Gangster
Copyright © 2021 by C.S. Poe

All rights reserved. No part of this book may be reproduced in any form, stored in any retrieval system, or transmitted in any form by any means—electronic, mechanical, photocopy, recording, or otherwise—without prior written permission of the publisher, except as provided by United States of America copyright law. For permission requests and all other inquiries, contact: contact@cspoe.com

Published by Emporium Press
https://www.cspoe.com
contact@cspoe.com

Cover Art by Reese Dante
Cover content is for illustrative purposes only and any person depicted on the cover is a model.

Edited by Tricia Kristufek
Copyedited by Andrea Zimmerman
Proofread by Lyrical Lines

Published 2021.
Printed in the United States of America

Trade Paperback ISBN: 978-1-952133-26-8
Digital eBook ISBN: 978-1-952133-25-1

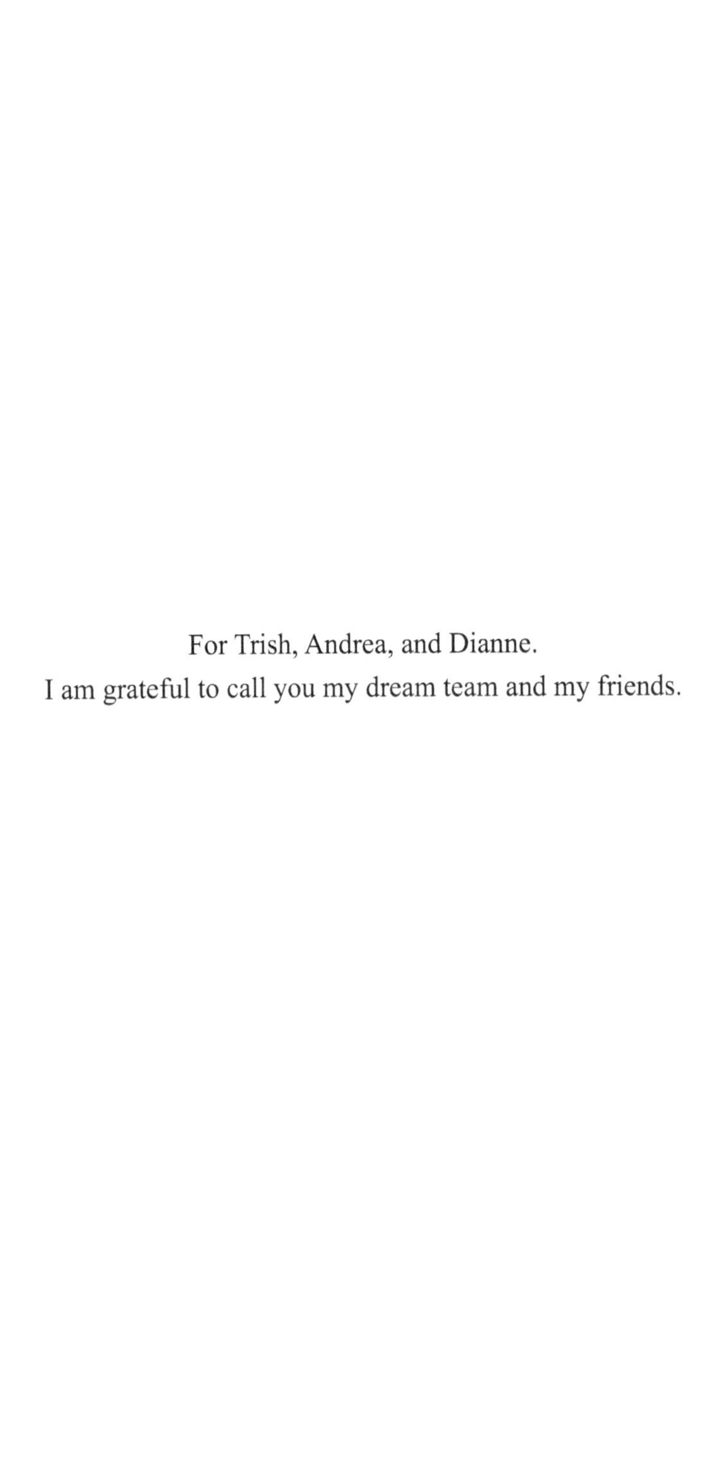

For Trish, Andrea, and Dianne.

I am grateful to call you my dream team and my friends.

I

"Stop!" I shouted as I gave chase to Fat Frank Fishback through the chaotic fray of Manhattan's Lower East Side.

Fishback—who was, in actuality, all arms and legs—skidded and slipped on the frozen cobblestones, righted himself, and made a sharp left toward a dilapidated tenement listing hard to one side. He shoved a big-boned woman from the open doorway and disappeared into the unsound structure.

"Sonofa—" I raced in the same direction, moved past the startled woman, and called a curt apology over my shoulder as I barged unwelcomed and unannounced through someone else's home.

The interior was dark, and despite the night of winter already upon us, no lamps had been powered on. Steam piping had been installed throughout the Five Points earlier in the year, but it was obvious these people were too poor even for steam energy to light their home. The odds of finding an illegal syphon installed somewhere on the property in order to suck the teat of the city's steam grid were quite good.

The installation in the slums had created a point of serious contention with government officials and the Old Money of New York City. Strongly worded letters had been published in the newspapers proclaiming it a waste of taxpayer dollars to light the streets of the wretched. As if these folks *chose* to live in squalor.

But despite the opposition, City Hall went forward with the investment. Funding had passed in January, and it became a matter of New York wishing to assert its dominance over other major metropolitans in the United States. The desire to proclaim itself superior to the likes of Boston or D.C. was a hell of a driving force. The mayor had used Grand Central Depot as his selling point—if tourists felt like they'd entered the city through the doors of a palace, then even the most unfortunate among us must have access to the latest advances in steam technology.

Access and means being two entirely different points, of course.

But I digress.

I wasn't here to chastise a too-full tenement of occupants barely earning enough to keep bread on the dinner table. I was here for Fishback. Nothing more.

I dodged the shadow of a resident coming out of a room, his curses now joining with the woman's—a symphony of fury and protests left unanswered in my wake. I raced along an extended narrow hall, shoved off the far wall in order to make the tight turn down a second dark passage, shot up a short flight of stairs, and finally caught sight of Fishback when he opened a door exiting onto a side alley, his rail-thin body briefly illuminated by the kaleidoscope of urban nightlights.

"Stop right now!" I hollered.

Fishback gave me a triumphant expression, stepped outside, and slammed the door shut.

I didn't slow my run, merely held an arm out, palm

forward, and dipped into the ever-present elemental magic that encompassed Earth. The stream of raw energy churned and whipped at my request for its power, filled my body, and then erupted in a gale of wind. The *whoosh* of bitterly cold air blew the door off one rusted hinge and left it sagging like a broken wing. I ran outside, onto a set of rickety wooden stairs, hoisted myself over the banister, and jumped to the alley below.

I landed on the balls of my feet, shoes barely scratching a whisper from the cobblestones as magic aided me safely to the ground. But the door's now-unfortunate state had been what startled Fishback. He straightened from the bent-over position he'd been in and spun around to face me. His chest heaved as he fought for breath the winter air had stolen. Fishback's gaze flicked to the door and staircase behind me, and then his face blanched. His eyes grew wide. Panicked. Like a cornered animal ready to bite and scratch and claw until one of us was dead.

I had no illusions about my person. A man just shy of thirty, brown hair mottled with gray, a height and build hardly bigger than most women's, and no weapon on hand. So no, it wasn't my appearance that scared Fishback, a gangster known for squeezing the life out of coppers with his bare hands.

It was the technicality that I was *not* a copper. Special Agent Gillian Hamilton, active caster with the Federal Bureau of Magic and Steam, *thank you very much*. And it was my magic that had put the fear of God into Fishback.

"Fishback—" I started.

He turned on one heel and ran for the mouth of the alley.

"I said *stop*," I yelled. I tugged the brim of my bowler down and started running again. "Federal Bureau of Magic and Steam, Fishback. You're under—"

A glass bottle whizzed in front of me from the tenement

on the left. I stumbled back a step to avoid being knocked out and turned my face away as it shattered against the outer wall of the building I'd just exited. Above me, the thrower shouted from an open window in a gravelly voice, "Magic pig in the alley!"

I broke into another sprint before a second bottle could hit its mark and slammed into the congested traffic of Baxter Street. All around me were unsupervised packs of children, stray dogs, wagons coming and going in either direction, and pushcarts *everywhere*, laws be damned, hawking the last of their oysters, knishes, and pickles before crowds dispersed for the evening. There were steam pipes crisscrossing building facades, rattling and pinging as residents powered on lamps and radiators. More metal tubing ran along the gutters of the streets, suppling steam energy to the yellow, red, and green streetlamps.

The voice from the window was still crying, "Magic pig! *Right there.*"

There'd been such volatile magic employed throughout the Great Rebellion that by the end of the war, Congress had enacted the Caster Regulation Act of 1865. On the surface, it aimed to bring the magic community out of hiding and make our intrinsic abilities legal to perform without fear of violence or jail time. But the finer details of the law required that every scholar—those who studied raw magic and documented the manmade spells—architect—the ones who fabricated the spells—and caster—those who performed the magic, such as myself—undergo mandatory documentation with the federal government. Keen and critical oversight of magic usage would protect soldiers and civilians alike from what happened during the war.

That's how the Federal Bureau of Magic and Steam was founded.

I'd come forward when I was eighteen and applied to the regulation, but due to my atypical caster level, the

Bureau jumped to offer me a job, a badge, and perhaps most importantly, respect. For the last decade, I had been doing my damnedest to represent the magic community, to educate citizens and eradicate detrimental old wives' tales, all while upholding law and order in the city.

It was, to say the least, an ongoing campaign.

I dodged between two pushcarts and stepped onto the road, only to be abruptly cut off as three men moved to stand in front of me. Fishback disappeared into the throng of people.

"Step aside," I ordered, pulling back the open lapels of my coats to show my badge.

They were all taller than me. Bulkier than me. With the sort of wicked smiles seen on men who used their fists to demand respect. The one on the left had his arms crossed over his barrel chest, with the stub of a smoking cigar clenched between his teeth. On the right was a man with a handlebar mustache and a badly set nose from a long-ago fight. In the middle was Tommy McCarthy, a known member of the Whyo gang that ran this neighborhood. He wore mechanical fighting gloves, the cogs spinning and pressure gauges releasing steam as he flexed his fingers.

"Look what we got here, boys," McCarthy said. He smiled widely, showing off a broken canine. "A copper on our streets."

"I'm not here for you, McCarthy."

"Know who I am, do you?" The steam whistled as he made a fist with one glove. "Scared, ain't ya?"

"No."

McCarthy blinked almost comically, glanced at Cigar Stub and Broken Nose, then tried to regain his footing by saying, "You *ought* to be."

"You're interfering with official matters pertaining to the Federal Bureau of Magic and Steam, and I *will* arrest you if you don't—"

"Arrest *me*?" McCarthy echoed with a bark of a laugh. "You ain't even tall enough to suck my cock," he replied, reaching down with one mechanical hand to cup himself through his trousers.

"I have no tolerance for your crude behavior. Step aside."

Broken Nose pushed back the folds of his coat and unholstered a Waterbury pistol. He pointed the three-barreled weapon at my head and cocked the hammer. "How about I put a few bullets through your brain instead?"

As the aether was galvanized, manufactured magic snapped and crackled in the air around me. A strong jolt shot up my spine and I shook it off. It was merely a physical response to the illegal spell reaching out to interact with my own magic. But seeing that Waterbury—

An unkillable, deadeye marksman.

His finger pulling the trigger.

And blowing Milo Ferguson's head off.

Those same fingers had held my chin just hours before while he whispered words that were seared into my bones like a cattle brand: *It'll remind me of you—*

No.

Thunder rumbled from overhead.

I raised a heavily scarred hand, palm looking as if it'd been used to press drying ferns, then snapped.

A bolt of lightning tore down from the sky and hit Broken Nose's pistol. The Waterbury exploded into a smoldering heap of scrap metal, and the ignited aether round knocked him off his feet like a horse had kicked him in the chest. The spark jumped to McCarthy's mechanical gloves—cogs and wheels flew every which way, pressure gauges went haywire, and steam valves burst. He dropped to his knees, screaming while tearing the gloves from his hands.

I looked at Cigar Stub, one hand still raised, electricity

pulsating in my hold.

He stumbled backward several steps before fleeing without a care for either of his two-bit gangster friends.

I rolled my eyes and lowered my arm. The magic grated against the damaged nerves in my hand, and I shook it a few times to quickly dissipate the spell. Ignoring startled, wary, and gawking onlookers on the street, I carefully picked my way around McCarthy and Broken Nose, both groaning on the ground. I broke into a run in the direction I'd seen Fishback go and was surprised to find him within a minute. His form was hunkered down on the stoop of a shop shuttered for the night. A nearby streetlamp was blinking erratically, the red color pulsating like we'd been enveloped in the city's heartbeat.

Fishback raised his head at the sound of my steps. He shot up and started to run.

Finally having a clear shot of the man, I held my arm out and sent a violent gust of bitterly cold winter wind after Fishback. It threw him to the ground and kept him pinned to the cobblestones. I approached from behind while removing a pair of handcuffs from my coat pocket.

"I'll weep the day a man listens to me on the first command."

I hadn't pegged Frank Fishback to be a crier.

It took an astonishing amount of degradation of one's own morality to become known for having perfected the art of strangulation. For the New York police force to fear a single man. For the mothers and wives of coppers walking the beat to ward against evil when the name *Fishback* was uttered.

And yet, here he was.

Crying.

Fishback sat behind the bars of a cell on the fourth floor of the New York field office at Twenty-Third and Fifth, where if he'd been on the north end of the building, he'd have had a beautiful view of Madison Square Park and Lady Liberty's dismembered right arm. Fishback's attire was still in a state of disarray from the arrest, and he had a shiner on his cheekbone from where I'd thrown him to the ground. But aside from those shuddering breaths and a wet nose he wiped on the back of his hand every few moments, Fishback had remained as silent as a mouse.

I stood in the narrow hallway opposite of the cells, window to my back where cold air leached through the old glass, staring at Fishback. I absently tapped the purple-tinted goggles hanging from my neck in beat to the *hiss* and *ping* of steam clanking through the building's heating system.

"How hard did you hit him?" Director Loren Moore asked in a thoughtful, almost curious tone. He stood to my left, as tall as an oak tree and built just as sturdy. He was over a decade my senior, with age-appropriate steel gray speckled into his ash-brown hair and well-groomed, if fashionably out-of-date, beard.

"I supplied ample warning to stop," I countered.

Moore lifted a pipe to his mouth, snapped his fingers over the bowl to light the tobacco with a flicker of fire magic, then took a few puffs. A heady cherry scent settled over us as Moore studied our guest. "Talk to us, Fishback."

Another quiet sob wracked Fishback's thin body. He shook his head while staring at the floor.

"You had a good thing going," Moore said, taking the pipe from between his teeth. "A real entrepreneur. Contracted by the Whyos to murder honest cops. How many counts, Hamilton?"

"Twelve, sir."

"*Twelve*," Moore said to Fishback. "Twelve times in two years you've pissed the police force off, and still they've not been able to organize themselves enough to touch a single hair on your head. So what happened?"

Fishback raised his head. He swallowed convulsively, his gaze darting back and forth between Moore and me.

"Was it the money?" Moore asked. "Is that why you started middle-manning the sales of magic ammunition? Not so smart, was it, Fishback? Because once word of magic involvement gets out on the streets, you become my problem." He made a gesture toward me. "And when I have a problem, I send for Agent Hamilton."

The compliment pooled in my belly and brought warmth to my cheeks. Loren Moore had been my director since the start. I'd spent years proving myself beneficial to the Bureau by taking on some of the worst backlogged cases that no other agent wanted to handle. My unrelenting hard work had been noticed—fairly early on, I think—but it had taken a few years before Moore began promoting me through the ranks. Now, I hadn't come into this career looking for an elevation in my status. I had just wanted to do some good. And while enforcing the law wouldn't minimize the skeletons in my closet any, it was a sort of… penance, if you will. And the relationship that had grown between myself and Loren Moore over the last several years was a bit like a weed sprouting between the cracks in cobblestones. Despite the odds, Moore trusted me, believed in me, respected me—and sometimes that was all that got me out of bed in the mornings.

I quite enjoyed Moore's company, and I do believe the same could be said for him, which was something, considering I am not the most likeable person. And while he *was* my superior, I truly believed that had I not worked under him, we might have been real friends. Although, when Moore praised me, I couldn't help but wonder if the weight of his words, the lingering silence in the moment, was wholly imagined, or if there was something unspoken he was hoping I'd pick up on. Moore was a bachelor, after all, but was he *confirmed*? Like me?

Huge tears poured down Fishback's cheeks, leaving streaks in the blood and dirt on his face.

"It rarely ends well when Hamilton returns to the office unhappy," Moore finished.

"It was for the money," Fishback blurted out. He looked at me, his breathing quickening. "Money. That's it. He said it was an easy job—that I'd make a hundred just by picking up a delivery and handing it off. A hundred dollars. *Shit*. The last mark I did for them Whyos was only fifty, and that was a hell of a lot more work."

"Yes, I imagine choking a man to death really works up a sweat," I replied, deadpan. "Where did the delivery originate?"

"Out West."

"That's over a million square miles, Fishback."

"I don't—California? Arizona? I ain't sure."

"Who hired you?" I tried.

Fishback gulped again. I feared he was one strong swallow away from taking his own tongue down his throat.

I took a few steps forward, wrapped a hand around one of the bars, and asked, "Would you rather a transfer to Sing Sing?"

"I wouldn't last the night, Mr. Hamilton," he protested.

"Agent."

"Wh-what?"

I expelled a huff. "Agent Hamilton."

"P-perhaps we can work out a deal, Agent Hamilton," Fishback suggested.

Breaching my personal space.

Sweet and herbal breath whispering against my ear.

His cobalt eyes recognizing a tendency—sensing a mutual attraction.

I heard those spoken words, but they weren't in Fishback's voice. It was low. Smoky. Masculine.

Every *tick* of cogs, I thought of him, and every *tock* of second hands brought him closer. I felt as if I were a man with a mechanical heart and Gunner the Deadly held the winding key. I touched the breast of my suit coat with my free hand, where I carried the travel receipt from Bartholomew Industries in the pocket. The handwritten message at the bottom was simple. Only a few words. But the weight of them, as carefully chosen as when he decided to speak or let a moment linger on in silence, had changed everything.

Meet me.

Yours,

Constantine G.

The infamous all-black-wearing, gunslinging, criminal-killing, airship-robbing outlaw had trusted me—*a lawman*, for heaven's sake—with something sacred.

Something that perhaps no living person on God's green Earth knew.

His name.

Constantine.

"Hamilton?" Moore's voice penetrated the fog of distress and zeal that'd been consuming me since returning from Arizona territory.

I startled and glanced at Moore. "Sorry, sir." I cleared my throat and turned to Fishback. "The only consideration I will make is holding you in our office overnight instead of an immediate transfer to Sing Sing. You've got this cell to yourself, a heated building, and"—I jutted a thumb at the window behind me—"perhaps you'll even catch a stray firework or two tonight."

"He'll find me here. *Kill me*," Fishback protested.

"Impossible," I answered. "This office is staffed around the clock. Our agents are some of the finest in the country, and we're on no one's books."

Fishback wiped his face on the sleeve of his coat.

"Who hired you?" I asked again.

"I ain't got his real name."

"Fishback—"

"It's the truth Mr.—ah, Agent Hamilton. I swear it. Only ever knew him as Tick Tock. New to the streets, but a true gangster if there ever was one. But I ain't even met the man. Only moved a handful of deliveries for him before you *intervened*."

Moore made a sound under his breath and another cloud of cherry smoke filled the hall.

I pushed my coats back and set my hands on my hips. "Why do you fear a man whom you've never met?"

Fishback stared at me like a dead man walking. "Tick Tock got an architect working for him, better than anyone in this building."

"I highly doubt—"

"Agent Hamilton," Fishback whispered. He was desperate. "I *know*. I middle-manned those crates myself. I met with a magical mechanical man who picked 'em up on Tick Tock's behalf. They weren't no aether bullets. They were fire."

II

December 31, 1881

"The incidents are related."

"Take a seat, Hamilton."

I draped my winter coat over the back of a chair positioned in front of Moore's desk, sat, crossed my legs, and let my bowler rest on my knee. The private office was aglow with warm yellow bulbs. Outside the window behind Moore's desk were tendrils of light from a green streetlamp four stories down and a blue safety light atop our building to warn any illegal, low-flying airships in the night. The illumination met in the middle, catching falling snow in a medley of color.

Moore shut the door, hung his suit coat on the brass rack beside it, then moved around me. Still standing, he tapped ash from his pipe into a glass tray atop the desk. "We have no evidence that this Tick Tock character is directly, or even indirectly, related to your incident in Shallow Grave."

I sighed audibly.

"But," Moore continued, setting his pipe down, "your

tone aside—"

His pause was enough to make me squirm.

"I do agree that the probability of two criminals simultaneously unlocking the secret to storing elemental magic in a tangible manner is not likely." He smiled, and there was an amused twinkle in his brown eyes.

"Yes, sir."

Moore turned and fetched a decanter from the shelf to the right of the window. "What's wrong, Hamilton?"

"I've lived a long life."

He pulled the stopper, poured a splash of amber liquid into two squat glasses, and offered one. "This'll help."

I thanked him as I reached out and accepted the crystal. Our fingers brushed in the exchange, and a single arc of electricity briefly joined us before snuffing out of existence in a plume of smoke. The sensation wasn't unpleasant, per se. It left a sort of drunk-just-under-the-surface feeling. Moore and I were each high-level casters, but thankfully not elemental opposites—fire and electricity, respectively. That sort of touch was still dangerous, though, and was meant to be avoided at all costs. Magics interacted with one another. There was no way of controlling an automatic function. It would be like asking a caster to simply stop breathing. That was why the Bureau paired us magically inclined with bruisers—agents who hadn't a single spell in their blood. It was why the new hires at our field office were given explicit instructions I'd heard repeated so many times, they'd long ago been memorized.

Special Agent Gillian Hamilton works alone. This is a safety measure put into place, and we cannot stress this enough, as a precaution for you. Should you find yourself in a situation that includes distress to Hamilton's physical well-being, do not touch him. Contact Director Moore on your Personal Discussion Device. You can find his code on page two of your manual.

That was one of the many reasons I was starving.

For Approval. Attention. Affection. I knew this about myself. Knew that in October, I was a skeleton—so deprived of human intimacy and all its subtle forms, I had been wasting away.

And then I had met Gunner.

Gunner had been impressed by me almost immediately. He'd approved of my abilities instead of shying away like everyone else, be them other agents or civilians. His attention had been flattering, thrilling. *God*, it had been almost terrifying, the way he'd studied me and picked up on such inconsequential details, such as the brand of my perfume. And the affection… the brush of his nose against mine, kisses so erotic that simply thinking of them took my breath away. And perhaps what had touched my neglected heart the most: the way he had cared for me while I was in a compromised state. Gunner had put me to bed and seen to my belongings, shown care to everything from my expensive Richmond Bros. shoes to the Everyday Man brand of my shirt cuffs.

I used to yearn for these moments with Moore—moments when he would pass me something and a thumb or finger would touch my own, or when he stepped a bit too close, perhaps even brushing my shoulder as he did. These moments were the catalyst in what, long ago, had me questioning the intentions of Moore's bachelorhood. But whether he was interested in men in the same manner as myself, or I was simply overthinking every minute action made by an older, attractive man, the point was, those shared seconds had been just enough to keep me alive over the years.

Hopeless for what I didn't deserve.

But shamelessly yearning anyway.

Until now.

Because that spark and smoke between us was nothing

when compared to merely the way Gunner looked at me from across a room.

"Hamilton."

I hastily took a sip of the whiskey. Smooth and malty, with a hint of caramel on its way down. "Excellent, thank you," I answered automatically.

"Dublin, twelve years. How're your hands?"

I glanced up. Moore had taken a seat. He watched me, smoothing his manicured beard with one hand. I looked at the glass in my hold. The crystal had caught the light of a nearby lamp and cast skittering prisms across the wooden floor. I switched hands and flexed the left absently. "It's nothing."

Milo Ferguson—Tinkerer—had very nearly blown my hands off in October. He'd utilized the first elemental bullet known to exist. The spell had gone haywire without a proper caster to control it, overpowered my own lightning magic, and absolutely torched my nerves from the inside out. A doctor in Tucson had performed what I considered a miracle and saved all ten fingers, but I hadn't dared admit to anyone that while I could feel the weight of the glass in my hand, I couldn't *feel* the glass.

"I wonder how stable that fire ammunition is," I said, putting an end to the silence. "Considering how volatile Ferguson's had been."

Moore hummed in acknowledgment. "The community feared this moment would come. Had any other agent gone to Shallow Grave, they wouldn't even be alive to investigate this."

I raised my brows.

"That's the truth and we both know it, Hamilton." Moore sipped his whiskey.

My cheeks flushed and I hoped he'd only think it was the alcohol.

"For two months we haven't gotten a single scrap of intelligence about who in the country might be behind the construction of the bullets Ferguson had on his person," Moore said, in an almost thinking-out-loud sense.

"Correct."

"Until tonight."

"Which could mean any number of things," I answered.

"I think it means only one."

"That is?"

"The prototype has been perfected." Moore leaned back in his chair and rested the tumbler against his knee. "Why else would we go from merely the two rounds Ferguson fired to the anonymous report of Fishback seen hauling an entire *case*?"

"If only I'd found him before he was able to ditch the evidence…."

"Yes, well, that'd have been preferable," Moore replied, "but I'm still looking forward to hanging this over Inspector Byrnes's head."

"Are you intentionally picking fights with the police?"

"Allow me this pleasure, Hamilton," Moore said around a chuckle. He had an easy laugh and a handsome smile. "Watching Byrnes's face turn as red as a radish makes me feel young."

I turned the crystal glass in my hold. "I suspect Tick Tock intentionally hired Fishback to middle-man his incoming packages. Tick Tock is a new-to-me gangster, in a city already overrun with gangs. But Fishback's an established name who'd lend legitimacy to Tick Tock."

"Makes sense," Moore answered. "I'd also add that Tick Tock must be a local boy."

I furrowed my brow. "Why do you say that? The packages are coming from, and I quote, out West. Tick Tock could be from anywhere and merely looking to establish roots in a heavily populated area."

"This mysterious *architect* is from out West," Moore corrected. "Fishback has made a career out of killing coppers in New York, and yet, he isn't on the national wanted list. He's hardly even known upstate."

I raised my tumbler and asked before taking a sip, "Police department ego?"

"Byrnes would be the laughingstock of this country if the likes of Boston or Philadelphia knew he couldn't apprehend a single man. And yet that's exactly who Tick Tock hired—a man who the police cower from. I'm certain it was intentional."

"I suppose you have a point."

"I like that you don't pull your punches."

"I pull."

"Even with me?"

"Of course."

Moore set his glass aside and threaded his fingers together in his lap. "I wish you wouldn't."

A palpable silence settled between us, and the rest of the building came to life in the absence of our conversation. Steam *ping, ping, ping*ed in the piping. A scholar laughed in the bullpen down the hall from Moore's office. Someone else popped the cork on a bottle of champagne, no doubt dipping into holiday celebrations early. I shifted focus to watch the magic in the room, glittering tendrils ebbing and flowing like the tides of the East River. But when the fiddleheads reached Moore, they unfurled and burst as if he was a lighthouse and the magic an ocean storm.

Moore cleared his throat and opened a desk drawer.

My vision snapped back to the magic-free plane.

"This is for you," Moore said as he set a small brown-paper-wrapped package before me.

I set my glass aside. "What is it?"

"A gift for the new year."

I'd begun to push forward in my chair, but paused. "Sir?"

Moore picked up his tumbler again and motioned to the package with the other hand. "Just open it, Hamilton."

I obediently took the package into both hands, set it on my lap, and tore the paper free. I worked the lid off the box and revealed a pair of polished black and gold goggles in a style often favored by casters. I picked them up and found a stamp in the leather identifying their origin: Odyssey Magic Wares. Custom builds and premium quality. I looked at Moore.

He finished the whiskey in his glass before saying, "So you can retire that junk you've been wearing the last two months."

The junk in question was the pair of purple-tinted goggles Gunner had left behind at the hospital in Tucson. Not that I would have referred to them as junk. They might not have been a high-end custom build, but they got the job done, and most importantly, they were a gift. At least, I allowed myself to think of them as such. Gunner had a motive, a reason, a strategy for every action he took in life. Leaving them had been intentional—they had been for me. And I had worn them each and every day, from dawn 'til dusk, since my return home.

But then the reality of what Director Moore said—*a gift for the new year*—sank in. Was it typical of a supervisor to present a token to an employee? I suppose if it were a means of thanking me for a year's work, that wouldn't be… unreasonable. I *was* one of his top agents, and I *had* been with the Bureau for a decade, after all. (Never mind what had happened to me while in Arizona.) So it was probable that that was what Moore meant by the gift. Because to even consider the alternative, that this costly item was being offered with the same intentions as Gunner's, was wildly inappropriate, no matter what I sometimes thought of Moore.

"Oh," I managed around the heartbeat lodged in my throat. "I mean, this is really too much."

"Hamilton—"

"I can't possibly accept this."

"Yes, you can."

I looked at Moore once again. He sat at a sideways angle, his body relaxed but face tense, as if I'd been called into his office for disciplinary action and not whiskey and holiday presents.

"It's very thoughtful, sir, but I feel I've performed my duties the same as—"

Moore made a small gesture with one hand. "This has nothing to do with the job. It's from me to you. That's all."

That's all.

Was it, though?

Yes. Of course. My God. I'd been isolating myself from human companionship for so long that I could hardly react appropriately to the well-meant intentions of another who, in my own words, I should have liked to call a true friend. Perhaps Moore felt the same. And this was what friends did for each other. Granted, I second-guessed literally every action of men because those with our inclinations couldn't be up-front. We couldn't flirt publicly or begin traditional courtships. So how on Earth were we supposed to communicate?

I hadn't a clue.

Gunner was far better at it all than I. In every aspect, up to and including spotting his opportunities for a tumble in bed. He'd said men like us recognized one another. That it was a survival instinct. Well, it'd taken Gunner undressing me with his eyes before I caught on to his interests mirroring those of my own, so I suppose that meant….

Moore was still staring at me.

I'm fucked, I thought. I couldn't figure this out. Did Moore mean something further by this gift, with a subtleness I was far too dense to pick up on, or was he simply being kind and was unwed because he'd long ago married his career?

"Thank you," I said quietly. "Ah, about Fishback—"

"He'll keep until morning. No, don't protest. It's New Year's Eve."

"I thought the papers had printed something along those lines…."

Moore smiled again and the tension in the air eased. At the mention, he dropped his hand onto the folded newspaper on his desktop. "Did you see the *Daily Cog*'s wedding announcements?"

I snorted before I could catch myself. "Sorry. No. I don't make it a habit to review the comings and goings of society."

"You ought to." Moore raised the paper and turned it so I could see the articles in question he'd left it open to. "Plenty of cases have been solved over the years because of a bit of newsprint."

"And so what's the case today?"

Moore turned the paper to himself to read the text aloud. "Only Son of Old Money Set to Wed New Money Beauty."

"Scandalous," I remarked blandly.

"Mr. and Mrs. Frederick Bligh Announce"—Moore kept reading—"New York, December 31, Henry Bligh, twenty-seven, the only surviving heir to the Bligh family fortune, is to marry the twenty-two-year-old daughter of Mr. and Mrs. William Olin of 635 West Thirty-Sixth Street in what is certain to be the affair that sets the stage for 1882."

"Bligh's getting married?" I pinched the bridge of my nose so I didn't roll my eyes in front of Moore.

Henry Bligh was a fellow special agent and caster—his

magic a level two on his best days, compared to my level five—with the New York field office. He was very handsome, very blond, and very, very rich. He was also a son of a bitch if there ever was one.

"This is why you need to read the papers."

"Rest assured, my life remains unchanged, even knowing that Bligh's blushing bride-to-be is about to cause an uproar on Millionaire's Row. Were the Astors invited?"

Moore glanced at the article once more. "Invitations to the wedding of the New Year include such prominent guests as Colonel and Mrs. John Astor, the Widow Vanderbilt, and former President Ulysses S. Grant."

"They'll have to sit Grant between the two just to keep the peace," I muttered.

Moore chuckled again and set the newspaper aside. "His wedding is going to bring attention to the Bureau in the coming weeks, Hamilton."

"Attention is nothing new for us."

"No, but an agent who's also a member of high society, and one getting married no less, is going to bring unwanted attention on our office— gossip, and the like. I request that you remain cordial with Bligh until after his honeymoon at the end of January and the papers find something new to discuss."

I couldn't very well tell my director what I really thought of Henry Bligh—that he was an insufferable and spoiled man, unbecoming of the badge he wore. I couldn't say that because Bligh only showed that side of himself to me. He came across as charming and witty with the rest of the staff, while painting all of them a picture of myself as a bootlicker. That I only managed to be held in such high regard by Moore because I'd relentlessly fussed over him for the better part of a decade and wormed my way into the position of senior agent.

Bligh was also the one to spearhead the rumors that I was

an immoral cocksucker who belonged on the Bowery. That I was a whore only worth the pocket change a man had on-hand. For nearly three years, he'd been doing this—jokes and lies at my expense—belittling my hard work and dedication to the Bureau while simultaneously undermining the basic respect I deserved.

Henry Bligh made a mockery of me.

And it broke my heart on the daily.

"Of course, sir," I said, the words ringing hollow in my ears. "If I may only say, I find it disconcerting that for a man preparing for what should be the happiest moment of his life, I hadn't even realized Bligh was courting. That's all."

Moore's expression was unbearably serious as he said simply, "Too many courtships these days are out of obligation, not love, Hamilton."

"Yes, sir."

With that, Moore poured himself a second glass of whiskey, motioned to myself, an offer I declined, then asked, "Do you have plans?"

"What's that?"

"For this evening."

Suddenly, the receipt in my breast pocket felt as if it were scorching right through my layers of clothing and Gunner's signature—*Constantine G.*—was branded to my flesh. "Yes." My God, did I imagine the corner of Moore's mouth turn down or was I projecting again? "A family friend is coming into the city for a visit," I added in a rush.

"Oh?" He seemed relieved. "From where?"

"Dodge City."

"Tomorrow, then?"

"Tonight," I corrected.

Moore's frown was back, but it was obvious and a little puzzled. He once again picked up the newspaper, unfolded it, and turned to the daily printout of the airship timetables. "Bartholomew Industries is the only airline out of Dodge City, isn't it?"

"Yes, why?"

"They've already landed."

I pulled my pocket watch from my waistcoat and studied the face. "They land at seven o'clock."

"Holiday schedule," Moore replied, tapping the paper with his index finger. "Airbright Passages and Ora Continental too—they've all been scheduled to arrive two hours early so the skies are clear for fireworks."

December 31, 1881

Grand Central Depot loomed at the cross streets of Forty-Second and Fourth Avenue. The building's first three floors created a perfect square, with entrances on the four cardinal points. The middle of the structure was open to the elements during daytime traffic and soared upward another seven stories. There were sixteen platforms in all, with local airships docking on the lowest three floors, cross-country on the next three, and the massive, international airlines that blotted out sunlight when they passed overhead arriving on the top story. The Depot boasted steam-powered chandeliers and gilded lifting apparatuses with an attendee inside to assist with passenger luggage. There was a ticket counter and schedule boards for airships coming and going all around the world—from Newark to Paris to Tokyo. It housed restaurants and shopping, a newsroom, billiards, a police headquarters, even an on-site doctor.

It was a true palace, in every sense of the word.

The Depot was nine years old now, but just as opulent

as the day it opened its doors to the world. I liked to imagine even Cornelius Vanderbilt had been impressed with the finished results. Or as impressed as the world's once-richest man could possibly be.

I threw open the southern door and rushed inside. The storefronts lining the expansive hallways were dark and shuttered. My shadow dogged me as I ran underneath chandeliers dimmed so low, they were barely enough illumination for the cleaning crew to work by. I entered the atrium of the Depot and slowed, tilting my head back. The telescopic stained-glass roof had been rolled over the docked airships and platforms for the evening, preventing unauthorized late-night landings. I could make out no one walking on the decks or staircases overhead, could hear no crews calling to one another. I couldn't even find a lamp in any of the captains' quarters. I turned and spun on one heel as I quickly took in the immense room, but the Depot was silent and empty.

The entirety of New York City was celebrating together, and there I stood—alone.

A man unmoored and with no darling to call his own.

I reached into the inner pocket of my suit coat and removed the travel receipt. I carefully unfolded the frayed, worn paper, my eyes dropping to the handwritten note at the bottom.

Yours,

Constantine G.

Perhaps not.

Perhaps he never had been mine.

Never would be.

Gunner had not been in communication with me since Shallow Grave. No calls to my PDD, no letters, not even a telegram. It would have been a relief to know that he thought of me as I did him, but of course, I hadn't really expected any messages. He was a wanted man and too smart to do something so senseless.

Too smart.

He really was.

Gunner had had two months to consider the ramifications of venturing out of the wild and lawless West. Standing here, albeit late, his decision was abundantly clear, and I was a fool to have honestly believed he'd have risked his literal neck for me. I was no prize. I knew that much—had long ago accepted the stark reality of being no one's—but in the resounding silence of the Depot, I heard my heart breaking all over again.

If, for only one night, I was hoping to pretend. To lie to myself about just one more thing.

I hastily wiped one cheek with a gloved hand, folded the receipt, and returned it to my pocket. I looked toward the bank of skeleton lifts, but the interiors were dark and the caged doors pulled closed. However, in the most western corner of the atrium, was a tightly wound spiral staircase that led all the way up to each of the airship platforms overhead. I walked toward it, the *tap, tap, tap* of my heels bouncing off the marble floors as if I were surrounded by an endless expanse of ballroom dancers.

I would go up to dock eleven and see for myself, confirm that Gunner had chosen safety and practicality, and then leave. I would return home to my bachelor apartment at The Buchanan and go to bed. I would tell Moore, when he inevitably inquired after my family friend, that something had come up and he'd been unable to visit. I would go on with my life.

I would, somehow, try to forget Gunner the Deadly.

I grabbed the ornate brass handrail, the cold biting through my gloves, and began to ascend. I kept to the balls of my feet to reduce the echo on the cast-iron steps and was halfway between the first and second floors when I heard it.

Not a voice from my memory, but a melody to my physical ears—that deep smokiness that gave rise to gooseflesh and made my very bones tremble as if the earth was giving way.

"Where are you going, my dear?"

The toe of my shoe caught; I stumbled forward and awkwardly grabbed at the railing with both hands. I jerked my head so quickly to look over the side of the staircase that had the banister not been there, I'd have certainly tumbled off the edge and broken my neck on the floor below.

Gunner the Deadly watched me from the ground. His mouth twitched in that there-and-gone smile, and his gemstone eyes, so blue that the sky should have been envious, glittered even in the dim lighting. America's most wanted man—legendary outlaw and vigilante who did more good than bad but had no interest in defending his name to the likes of law enforcement—was here. In New York City. For no other reason but that he had promised to call upon me on New Year's Eve.

"Come down here," he said in that low, almost monotone manner in which he spoke, but still his voice carried in the expansive atrium.

My heart had been hastily re-collecting its broken pieces in those seconds I stared at Gunner, patchworked itself back together, and with its first tentative beat, filled me with an emotion that, although foreign, I could still recognize at an instinctual level.

Happiness.

I hoisted myself up and over the staircase banister, a gust of magic-infused wind meeting me on my descent and aiding my landing with nothing more than the muffled *tip-tap* of my heels on the marble. I looked up at Gunner. He was in head-to-toe black, as per usual. The glint of a pocket watch chain on his waistcoat caught the glow from a chandelier—silver, not gold—and a pair of traveling goggles hung around his neck.

I couldn't tell if his illegal Waterbury was hidden in the folds of his thigh-length winter coat, but I had to simply assume it was. With the exception of a bowler on his head and not a Stetson, Gunner looked how I'd left him in Arizona. Well, he *did* seem impossibly more handsome, but that was not a factual assessment of his person.

"That's a clever little trick, Hamilton."

A smile tugged at my mouth, and then a nervous, breathless laugh escaped me. "It's not a trick. And it's Gillian."

"Gillian," he repeated, and hearing Gunner say my name made me feel as if stars were colliding inside me. His gaze roamed for a beat, and then he said, "You're shaking."

"Cold," I lied. "I'm late. I'm so sorry—"

Gunner bent, collected the handles of his carpet bag in one hand, then straightened. "Never mind that. Shall we go somewhere more accommodating?"

"Oh. Yes." I turned, inclined my head toward the south hall I'd entered from, and said, "This way."

Outside, it was still snowing, leaving a thick, wet, pristine layer that crunched loudly underfoot. No doubt the expanse of gray clouds that'd rolled in over the black sky was sending the organizers of the city's yearly fireworks exhibition into a panic. This immediate block was devoid of foot traffic and the usual congestion of touring automobiles and gaudy motorwagons—of which I was perfectly fine with. After nearly being blown up by the iron-and-silver monstrosity built by Milo Ferguson, I'd had a bit of an aversion to those sort of vehicles.

On the walk toward the Third Avenue El, we passed underneath a steam-powered lamppost and were briefly bathed in cherry-red illumination. Red suited Gunner, I thought. Not that I expected he'd ever have interest in the fashion of those who embraced Aestheticism, but the occasional bold splash of a colored necktie would look good on him.

"You're staring," Gunner said before he caught my eyes in a quick, sideways gaze.

"Oscar Wilde is coming to America," I blurted out, which was absolutely not what I had meant to say. "Just after the New Year."

"Yes, he's on a lecture tour."

"You know who Oscar Wilde is?"

Gunner looked at me again.

"Of course you do," I muttered, then fell silent. Two months of endless days and sleepless nights, I'd pined for this man, now so close I could touch him, hold him, kiss him, and I couldn't even say something socially acceptable to the moment. Not a *Gunner, how are you?* Or *How was your flight?* Not even *Had any run-ins with the law as of late?*

No. And why?

Because I was me. And "me" was a disaster.

At the end of the block were stairs leading up to the El platform. New York was such a frequently visited and densely populated environment that citizens had to be accepting of new methods of transportation constantly infiltrating the landscape. Airships were well and fine, but law prohibited their presence south of Forty-Second Street. Horse-drawn carriages had once been in vogue, but with the advent of steam technology, they were now a novelty at best and a nuisance at worst.

The desperate necessity for mass transit in the lower portion of the city had seen to the creation of the Manhattan Railway and the spectacular locomotives that ran its elevated rails above the streets. Powered by simple steam pneumatics installed underneath the tracks, the locomotives pulling the passenger cabs were propelled up and down the lengths of Second, Third, Sixth, and Ninth Avenues at all hours of the day, with the exception of no Sunday service on Second and

Ninth.

I was quite an admirer of the whole setup.

I took the first three steps, stopped abruptly, and turned. The addition of the stairs had brought me to eye level with Gunner, who'd been walking behind me, and it was an odd experience—looking at him straight on instead of up. I looked up at everyone, after all, but with Gunner, I found that I sort of… enjoyed it. Perhaps it was because he never used his six feet as a means to threaten or overpower.

"That wasn't what I meant to say."

Gunner asked, "Which part?"

"All the parts." I shook my head and asked, "No Stetson?"

"Hardly matches the trends of Broadway."

"But I'm certain you've got that Waterbury."

Gunner's mouth twitched and his eyes had that amused glint to them. He tugged back the lapels of both his winter and suit coat to show he'd gone with a black shoulder holster instead of a low-hanging hip holster. "What sort of man do you take me for?"

"One prepared for anything."

"I can't rest on my laurels, Gillian." Gunner hid the weapon. "I've a reputation to uphold."

"And you're number one on the wanted list again," I concluded.

"Are you flirting with me?" There was the smallest suggestion of a playful lilt to Gunner's voice.

"Simply stating the facts as they are."

"I do appreciate a man who strokes my ego." Gunner reached a hand toward my face, but I leaned back, allowing him to caress only air. "Let me touch you," he said, very calm and very matter-of-fact.

"Not here."

"Who's to see?" Gunner countered, taking a look over his shoulder at the empty stretch of sidewalk in our wake.

I inhaled a shaky breath. "There are over a million people in this city," I answered. "Anyone might see."

Gunner stared at me. It was that look of dissection, where he took me apart to study my blackened inner workings. "One million," he eventually repeated, and a plume of cold air escaped his mouth.

"That's right."

Gunner's gaze briefly flicked overhead at the rumble of an incoming train. He started up the stairs, brushed by me, and said, "I see little has changed during our brief separation."

The cold air on my face as Gunner moved by felt as if I'd been slapped. I turned and watched as he continued up toward the platform. "What does that mean?"

"You've been taking breaths that do nothing for you."

The Buchanan bachelor hotel stood on the corner of Twenty-Seventh and Fourth Avenue. It was an eight-story love letter to architect H.H. Richardson, the fellow responsible for Trinity Church in Boston. Romanesque revival in style, The Buchanan was built with a mixture of red brick and brownstone, and adorned with a polychromatic façade, arched windows, and a copper roof. The falling snow was sticking to the fire escape that ran down the building's front.

Gunner stopped at the curb and stared at the structure. "You live in a hotel?"

"It's an apartment hotel," I corrected. "No kitchen, but I have access to the restaurant on the top floor. It's becoming popular in the city—long-term living exclusive to unmarried men." I looked up at him and concluded, "Very private."

"How interesting." He took a step onto the street.

"Gunner?" I said, so quiet that I was certain the snow was louder and he hadn't heard me.

But Gunner turned.

"I want to apologize."

Gunner moved back to my side—too close—no, not close enough—and asked, "For?"

"Our conversation at the El." I lowered my head and stared at the snow collecting on the buttons of my shoes. It was easier to lay bare my cowardice when one of the most courageous men I knew wasn't boring a hole straight through my heart with just a look. "I realize that I was the one who made you come here—"

"No one makes me do anything," Gunner interrupted. "Even you."

"Right. Of course. I meant to say, I'm grateful you've come to New York. But that sort of expression of romance isn't—we can't. There are certain establishments on the Bowery where we could touch and be around others, but—"

"Gillian."

"Yes?"

"Stop staring at your shoes."

I swallowed hard and raised my head.

Gunner's face had softened around the edges. I'm not certain I'd have even noticed the change before that all-too-brief tumble in the sheets together, but after having witnessed Gunner's unguarded expressions during the throes of passion and sated bliss afterward... well, I'd memorized that look. Carried it with me. I'd been the one to do that to him, and it was incredible.

"Do you remember what I told you in Arizona?" Gunner asked.

"I remember everything."

He smiled. Just a little. Just enough. "Some men like us,

they find happiness. You'll be one of them, so long as you stop apologizing for your existence in this world." Gunner put his free hand briefly to his own chest and patted. "*This* doesn't change, but attitudes do. Starting with your own."

Twenty seconds ago, I had been Atlas, bearing the sky on my shoulders, a burden that was to be mine for all eternity. And then it was like someone had found me on the most western edge of the world and lifted enough weight that I was able to raise my head and see the stars for the first time.

"Gunner—"

With no warning, the atmosphere prickled around me, raised painful gooseflesh across my body, and then a faraway searing heat burrowed itself under my skin.

Fire.

I turned sharply to face east, studying the distant stairs to the El platform from where we'd disembarked at Third Avenue. I shifted my focus to study the thread-like appendages of magic as they flowed around a few pedestrians, but the energy didn't linger, didn't light them up like a lighthouse on the ocean's edge. Where had that artificial spark come from?

I quickly tugged my gloves off, shoved them into my coat pocket, and held one out, palm up. I allowed the tendrils of raw and unused magic to coil around my scarred fingers, then closed my fist over it and gave a tug. Like a bullet shot, the magic carried my own energy along two separate pathways in a dizzying rush before each fractured and splintered into a tangle of—something that made no sense. I could feel the whisks of a spell originating somewhere in the chaotic fray of the Five Points downtown. But the detonation was significantly closer. And manufactured for sure. There was a gaping wound in the atmosphere where the spell hadn't replaced the borrowed magic with the lifeforce of the caster.

"Gillian?"

I startled, lost the visual hold on the magic around me,

and turned to see Gunner had reached into his coat, hand resting on the butt of his Waterbury. "I'm okay." But even as I heard myself speak, I distantly registered how automatic the answer had been. How disingenuous I sounded. I was quite adept at lying, but this injury to the atmosphere was so sudden, so toxic, and so *perplexing* that I was too distracted to attempt sincerity.

What was I to do? I couldn't inform Moore. Not exactly, anyway. And I couldn't leave Gunner in order to ferret out the cause on my own—not when this evening had been so anticipated and he'd traveled so far.

"Gillian," Gunner said again, a bit more insistent.

I hesitated to shake the event off but flexed my hands a few times and did my best to ignore an after-current that rippled through me as if the heartbeat of the city had shuddered. "Come with me," I told Gunner before hastening across the street, snow crunching underfoot as I approached the front doors to the hotel.

"What was that?" Gunner questioned, his long legs and sure stride keeping an easy pace with me.

"Never mind it," I answered.

"Good evening, Mr. Hamilton," the doorman called as we approached.

"Dawson," I greeted the doorman, who wore a long coat and hat. We stopped before the door he held open, and I motioned to Gunner. "This is—John Gaylord. A friend of my family's." I glanced at Gunner in time to watch him tip the bowler he wore at a rakish angle toward Dawson. "He'll be a guest of mine for a few days."

Dawson didn't appear to find the story suspicious. He said to Gunner, "Welcome to The Buchanan, Mr. Gaylord."

"Thank you," Gunner answered.

"Happy New Year, Dawson," I said.

"And to you, sir."

I stepped into the lobby, shook my coat, and then walked down a short hallway. The lower portion of the walls were paneled with polished mahogany. Above that were living motifs built into the walls—an amalgamation of switches and screws and cogs, all moving in an unhurried harmony to depict murals of the New York skyline. The wall art transitioned from day to night in time with the gentle *ticktock* produced by the gleaming mechanisms. Rounding the corner, I took the stairs on the left. The handrail was cut from the same dark wood as the walls, and the iron-wrought balusters shone from a recent buffing.

"John Gaylord," Gunner murmured to my back.

"Quiet."

"If that name was any less inconspicuous, it'd be suspect."

He had a point, I supposed. With his six feet of perfectly sculpted masculinity, eyes like sapphire brooches seen on Millionaire's Row, and that husky commanding voice, Gunner stood out. Anyone with lingering appreciation for his uncommon aesthetic would have surely expected him to have an uncommon name to match.

But that name belonged to me.

The city could have John Gaylord.

Only *I* could have Constantine Gunner.

Upon reaching the fourth floor, I walked to the door closest to the stairs, removed a ring with a few skeleton keys from my coat pocket, and inserted one into the lock. I tapped a button on the key bow to activate the wards, and the tumblers audibly clicked into place. I pocketed the ring once more and pushed open the door. The first room was a small parlor, but seeing as I was an unattached man who was hardly home, that didn't much matter. A water closet was behind a closed door to the left, and the adjoining room to my right was the bedroom that overlooked Twenty-Seventh Street.

The steam radiators hissed and sputtered in the dark parlor. I flicked a wall switch and the overhead glass globe bathed the apartment in a warm tungsten glow.

Gunner stepped inside behind me, set his carpetbag on the floor, and I turned as he shut the door. He took the lapel of my winter coat in one hand and tugged me forward while he backed himself up against the door. Gunner raised his hand and knocked the bowler from my head.

"I had to buy a new hat because of you," I warned.

A smile tugged the corner of Gunner's mouth, and he guided my bare hands into the folds of his coats to rest on his slender hips. "You'll have to teach me a lesson."

"To never touch another man's hat."

Gunner rested his gloved hands on my shoulders. "Kiss me."

I rose up on my toes to meet Gunner as he leaned down, but his gaze flicked from me to the floor and he froze. Curious, I looked down as well. The snow that'd collected on both our shoes had melted and left a small puddle on the hardwood floor, but just to my right was an unaccounted for droplet.

Another.

And another.

I let go of Gunner's hips, took a step backward, and tilted my head to study the water. At the right angle, the overhead light caught the surface and the glimmering trail led all the way to one of the parlor windows. I spun toward Gunner again, who unholstered his Waterbury and cocked the pistol. I looked to my bedroom. The door had been partially closed, which was my intruder's mistake, because I never shut that door in winter.

I moved toward the room, stood to one side of the threshold, and pushed the door open the rest of the way. The bedroom was dark—curtains pulled taut across the windows to keep out the relentless glow of red and green streetlamps—

so it took half a second too long to make out the shape of furniture and the out-of-place mass at the foot of my bed.

The shadow charged forward without warning, grabbed my shoulder, hauled me forward and then back against the door. I heard the knob bust through the wall and my head knocked against the solid wood. A massive hand wrapped around my neck and squeezed. I grabbed the man's wrist with both hands and released an explosive fire spell. The stench of burned hair and seared flesh filled my nostrils as he screeched in pain and released me. I dodged to one side, and when the man doubled over, cradling his smoking wrist to his chest, I slammed my elbow down on the back of his neck.

The intruder grunted and fell to an unceremonious heap.

I took a deep breath, shoved my two-toned hair away from my face, and demanded, "Who are you?"

The man cocked his head up, and illumination from the parlor cut a harsh line of light across his face. His left eye was gone, replaced with the housing of a compass. The needle bobbed with his movements as if always trying to direct him north. His lower jaw was all brass and silver, cogs spinning and steam releasing from sockets as he bared sharpened silver teeth like those of a wild animal.

A mechanical man.

He climbed to his feet and raised a gun—no. The gun was his arm. His *arm* was a gleaming four-barreled piece of deadly weaponry. "Tick Tock kindly requests you look the other way in this matter regarding Fishback." His jaw snapped and the words had a metallic ring. "Enjoy the holiday, Mr. Hamilton."

I bristled. "It's *Agent*. And I will do no such thing."

He sneered, cocked his weapon, and manufactured magic was activated. It was a fire spell, but with a makeup so very different from my own. And once again, raw magic was ripped from the atmosphere, and the lifeforce around me felt battered and broken without a caster replacing the energy. The man's four-barreled pistol began to glow red.

A magical *mechanical man.*

I took a mental step back from the moment and let everything slow. The mechanical man bared his teeth again and roared. He pulled the trigger, and a sensation, much like that of an unwelcomed touch, clawed its way up my spine. Only one barrel released a magic bullet, and I shot a hand out in time to raise a shield of bright, shimmering water. The fire slammed into my magic and sounded a crash so loud that I was certain it shook the walls, before it was put out and only a haze of smoke remained. I'd begun to lower my hand when the man fired again—all three remaining bullets releasing at the same time.

Gunner grabbed the back of my collar and yanked hard. I was slammed into the floor and time jerked, lurching forward in a jumble of misplaced seconds as my senses recalibrated. I rolled onto my side, propped up on an arm, and looked behind me. The fire shots had missed me, gone through the open doorway, and set the wall beside the water closet on fire. Gunner had flattened himself against the front door, narrowly missing the explosion after pulling me out of its path. He raised his Waterbury and fired.

The mechanical man jerked as he was hit in the chest with a round of aether. He staggered a step, stumbled back against the foot of the bed, then managed to turn and trip toward the window. He yanked the curtains back, pulling the rod clean from the wall. Mechanical Man hoisted the windowpane up one-handed and began to climb out.

Gunner cocked the Waterbury for a second shot.

I looked back toward the water closet a second time, raised my hand, and cast another water spell, hammering the wall with it until the flames and smoke had dissipated and my apartment resembled a very disappointing aquarium.

Gunner fired again.

I rolled onto my backside as Mechanical Man climbed out of the window and onto the fire escape before taking another round to the back. He spun like a prima ballerina performing her final show, dipped against the railing—then fell.

There was a loud silence for one, two, three seconds, and then my PDD, still sitting atop the bureau where I'd forgotten it that morning, began emitting a series of tones. Two high pulses followed by three, short low beeps. 33678 was Director Moore. Except why would Moore be trying to reach me on a holiday he knew I had plans for—possibly the first in my adult life? It would have to be an absolute emergency.

But Moore would need to wait a moment.

I scrambled to my feet and ran into the bedroom. The tones on the PDD began for a second time as I climbed through the open window. Dark blood and broken gears painted the walkway. The sting of icy snow on my cheeks felt like a dull razor pulling at facial hair. I leaned over the railing and studied the scene below. Mechanical Man lay in the middle of the road, a tangle of broken bones and weaponry.

Gunner maneuvered his body through the window behind me before stepping close enough to put a hand on my shoulder.

"I'm fine," I answered before looking up. "Are you?"

But of course he was. He was Gunner the Deadly, not Gunner the Dead.

The PDD was emitting its third series of tones, and if I didn't know better, I'd say the device was becoming exasperated.

"What's going on, Gillian?"

I shook my head and looked to the road once more. "Something terrible."

IV

December 31, 1881

"Seems a might suspicious," the copper said for a second time from where we stood in the middle of the street.

Dawson had heard the *whomp* and *crack* of flesh and metal slamming into the cobblestone from his post inside the lobby, and thinking the body was that of a resident, had rushed to render aid. I'd left Gunner upstairs, raced to the ground floor, and gone outside to find the poor man looking terrified and grief-stricken.

"Mr. Hamilton," he exclaimed, running toward me. "There's—he must have—"

"I need you to find a police officer right away."

The request brought Dawson partially back to his senses. "On New Year's Eve? I can't imagine I'd find one who isn't warming his belly with a beer or three."

"I don't need them sober," I said, managing not to snap at him. "Anyone with a badge and a pulse will do."

In truth, I didn't actually need a metropolitan officer for

anything important. This stranger had broken into the private residence of a federal agent, so it was clearly my jurisdiction. (Never mind that he possessed and employed illegal magic.) But one of the agreements that kept the peace between agencies was that the Bureau needed to have the police formally offer the reins—so to speak.

And that's how I found myself in the company of Officer Kelly, who was already a sheet or two in the wind and likely wouldn't have remembered the words to "Auld Lang Syne" come midnight, if Dawson hadn't dragged him out of whatever watering hole he'd been hiding in.

I pushed my open coat lapels back, tugged up my trousers, and crouched down beside Mechanical Man. I put a thumb on his broken jaw and pulled his mouth open to study those hideous teeth.

"Mm-hmm… might suspicious."

I tipped my bowler back and looked up at Kelly. "Where in my account did I lose you?"

Kelly jabbed a finger downward, indicating Mechanical Man's chest. "Only aether tears a man apart like that." He gave me a wide, malicious smile. "A shame you federal sort think you're above your own laws."

"I'm a caster, you thickheaded brute."

Kelly crossed his massive arms, and his ill-fitting blue uniform pulled tight across his chest. "Sure looks like ammunition damage, not a spell."

I stood, hands on my hips. "Care to find out?"

"*Hamilton*," called a stern voice from the cross streets.

I recognized the speaker immediately, and my stomach felt as if it'd just plummeted off the edge of the fire escape like Mechanical Man. I lingered on Kelly a second longer, was successful in getting him to shift uncomfortably and be the first to look away, then turned to my left. "Sir," I answered as Moore stomped down the snow-covered street.

"I've been calling you, goddamn it," Moore barked. "What's the point of assigning you a PDD if you never carry it?"

I held both hands up. "Sir—"

"We've got a situation—" Moore cut himself short and seemed to finally acknowledge the mangled body at my side.

A plume of cold air escaped my lips as I said, "So have I."

Moore slowed but kept moving toward me. He studied Mechanical Man and then looked at me with a raised brow. He must have recalled Fishback's words just as I had.

A magical mechanical man.

I nodded once.

Moore directed his attention to Officer Kelly. "Director Loren Moore of the New York branch of the Federal Bureau of Magic and Steam. This death falls within our jurisdiction under directive S. 134.5: Unlawful retention and employment of illegal magic."

"S. 240 and S. 120 as well," I murmured before crouching beside the body again.

"S. 240: Unlawful ownership of an illegal magic firearm, and—120?"

"Yes, sir."

"S. 120: Trespassing on federal property, which includes an agent's place of residence," Moore concluded.

Kelly took off his helmet and scratched his forehead. "Aye, but those wounds—"

"Thank you for your attention, officer," Moore said. "You'll, of course, file an official report with your captain?" Moore removed his bowler and pulled his PDD headset up and over his ears. He flicked his arm and the handheld transducer slipped out from his sleeve. "Did you need me to repeat the jurisdiction codes?"

Kelly put his helmet back on and said gruffly, "No, sir. I got it. Good night." He hoisted his belt up his belly, turned, and began west on Twenty-Seventh.

I shifted weight to my right side and stared up at Moore from my position as he put in a request to the office for a prisoner transport at my cross streets—no dillydallying. "He must have scaled the secondary fire escape overlooking Fourth Avenue so as not to be seen by the doorman."

Moore tugged the headband to rest around his neck and put his hat back on. "And how did he come to be down here?"

I jutted a thumb upward. "He fell from the fire escape outside my window."

Moore stuffed his hands into his trouser pockets and began to walk a circle around me and Mechanical Man. The snow underfoot had that deadened crunch to it—consistency that made for a perfect snowball. Just the right amount of wet to stick a rock inside, pack it tight, and make the boy who never quite fit in walk home bleeding.

I heard the *smack* in memory, rubbed my left temple where my hair was shorn close, and said after a moment, "He utilized fire ammunition."

"How many bullets?"

"Four. One round." Magic was snapping erratically from the dead body, almost as if the manufactured spells left behind in the skin or the cogs or whatever it was that made this union of flesh and metal possible was dissipating before my eyes. Dying, almost. But Moore hadn't acknowledged it. I carefully lifted Mechanical Man's broken arm that seconded as the unregistered gun. "This is nearly identical to the weapon Milo Ferguson had."

"You're certain?"

"Absolutely." I yanked up the sleeve of his suit coat and shirt and winced. "Except Ferguson's wasn't fused to his body like some sort of hellfire abomination."

"This is Fishback's magical mechanical man."

"That was my assumption as well." I dropped his arm and leaned back on the heels of my shoes. "There must be a practical reason for the bonding of these elements to the man's body, instead of, for example, wearing something that is detachable."

"Why's that?"

"Well, looking like this, he'd be alienated from society." I waved one hand at the mangled body. "He certainly couldn't have taken a stroll through Union Square without causing a scene. So why allow such an assault to his person? It must be a key to utilizing tangible magic without a caster."

"Do you think he was forced into this?"

"I couldn't be certain. But he told me to look the other way and let Tick Tock handle Fishback. It confirms everything about Fishback's story—the fire ammunition, a new gangster, and of course, the magical mechanical man."

I wrapped a bare hand around Mechanical Man's jaw and could feel the elements in their raw form. But underneath that, there was an impression that wriggled away like a nightcrawler sensing the warmth of a lantern in the dark. I moved my hand back to the gun, where it connected at the elbow, and I followed a band of iron with the tip of my index finger. That same feeling was worked into the iron as well, but it slithered as I tried to hone in on its specifics.

When I raised my gaze, Moore was squatted on the opposite side of Mechanical Man, staring at me.

"There's something in these components."

"Magic?"

"It's difficult to tell. I suspect it dissipates after death. Interesting that some of these mechanical additions are built from silver and iron and he utilized manufactured fire magic."

"Highest melting point," Moore replied, his eyebrows

rising slightly.

"Less chance of damage to his person, since he's not a caster," I continued. "His artificial body parts must somehow work in conjunction with the magic bullets—a sort of counterbalance so the spell doesn't go haywire as it did with Ferguson."

"Could there be more mechanical men like this? Each built with specs that allow for the most advantage in using different manufactured spells?"

The question was perfectly reasonable. Logical, even. But the thought of perhaps a whole army of these monsters wielding magic without care, without training, and suited up in unique and horrifying ways in which to maximize the spell's output—it made my blood run cold.

"You mean to suggest that if he were using ice magic in those bullets, his mechanical parts might have been vanadium or nickel?"

Moore nodded. "So on and so forth." He looked to his right as the sound of a steam engine choked and sputtered in the cold air and a prisoner transport automobile rounded the corner. He stood and raised a hand to the driver.

"We need to talk to Fishback," I said, standing as well and beginning to count questions off on my fingers. "That architect's exact location and damn name, for starters. Is Tick Tock himself building these mechanical men? How many are there? Where's Tick Tock hiding out—same location as the delivery handoffs or someplace else? What about—?"

"That's why I was calling your PDD," Moore interrupted. "Fishback is dead."

V

December 31, 1881

Moore tromped across the snowy street to the sidewalk as the engine of the prisoner transport sputtered once or twice, and then the automobile was heading back to the field office with the remains of Mechanical Man. I'd been impatiently waiting for Moore to explain Fishback's sudden demise, but he'd remained stoically silent while the second agent assisted us in collecting my dead intruder. And now that we were left to our own devices, he was walking toward The Buchanan instead of continuing our conversation.

"Sir?" I called.

"I want to see the extent of the damage caused by his fire ammunition," Moore answered.

"W-wait, *what*?" I looked up at the fourth floor. Gunner had closed the windowpane at some point, but with the curtain rod hanging to one side, there was just enough spillover from the parlor to faintly outline my bedroom and mark my occupancy.

And his—*Gunner's*.

The director for the entirety of New York's Federal Bureau of Magic and Steam was bullying his way into my building, and unbeknownst to him, America's most wanted outlaw stood on the other side of my apartment door. Lord save me or strike me down, but don't linger.

This can't get any worse.

"But Fishback—" I protested loudly, racing after Moore.

"We'll discuss that in private," Moore said pointedly as Dawson opened the front door and he walked into the lobby.

I rushed inside, shoes squeaking on the floor as I followed Moore up the stairs. "Wait a moment—"

"And you'll have time to explain that aether damage too," he said without breaking stride.

Correction... this *was worse.*

"Aether," I repeated, not quite a question, because Moore would chew me up and spit out the bones for even attempting to feign ignorance, but still. I came close.

"Because one of my most talented agents, a veteran caster with confirmed control of aether spells—he wouldn't require the ownership and usage of a Waterbury, would he?"

Of course Moore recognized the weapon based on the wound pattern alone....

"No, sir," I answered obediently.

"So consider—which floor, Hamilton?"

"Fourth."

"So consider me *very* interested in your answer."

I had literal seconds to formulate a plan, concoct a believable story, and somehow convey to Gunner that he needed to hide—although how I was going to pull off that last one without being a mind reader was beyond me. I wasn't angry at Gunner for shooting Mechanical Man, since, after all, he'd saved my neck by doing so. But having to lie to

Moore about what was so *very clearly* damage dealt by an illegal firearm, and when I was well-known for not carrying a weapon on my person at all…. I grappled for one of my go-to half-truths, but my mind was churning up nothing but a scratchy hum, like a lightbulb about to pop.

My career was over.

I was going to be arrested for sheltering a wanted man.

Gunner's neck would be in a noose before the first firework was shot off.

And it was *all* my fault.

I moved around Moore at the fourth-floor landing and stepped to my unlocked door. "There's something I need to explain, sir." I eased the door open. The parlor was empty. Had Gunner heard our approach? I pushed it farther and invited Moore inside. "About the wound track. Of course I don't own a Waterbury."

Our shoes squelched loudly on the wet floor.

"Which is why—" Moore stopped speaking. He stared at the wall on our left, charred black with smoke stains near the ceiling. He reached out and pressed his fingertips to the wood. "Was this from all four bullets?"

I shut the front door. "No. He fired one at me first, which I deflected. The second shot was the remaining three bullets of the cylindered round."

Moore looked down, shifted one foot out of a puddle, and motioned to the floor. "And I gather that this is from you?"

"Yes, sir."

He glanced at the dark interior of my bedroom, then marched toward it.

I opened the door to the water closet, but it was empty. Which meant—dear God—Gunner was hiding in the bedroom. I ran after Moore, the heels of my shoes slapping loudly against the inch of water underfoot. He was already standing at the window, inspecting the rod yanked from the wall and then peering through the fogged-up glass at the fire escape. I dared a look at my closet—the door was slightly ajar. Moore certainly wouldn't have a reason to go pawing through my clothing, right?

"There's blood and cogs on the floor."

"Oh. *I mean*, yes." I moved around the foot of the bed to stand behind Moore. "He was wounded when he ran to the window, opened it one-handed, and climbed out."

"Where he then fell to his death?"

"He overbalanced."

Moore turned and looked down at me. "I've never known you to report a lie, Hamilton."

I opened my mouth, but my throat had seized up before any words escaped. If only Moore realized…. "He attacked me," I explained, in what I hoped was a cool and collected tone. "His death wasn't intentional, but I was in immediate danger and reacted accordingly."

The magic surrounding Moore responded to my explanation—a savage and pulsating flare-up. The energy that poured off him and encircled me caused the nerves in my left hand to spasm painfully, and it curled into an unintentional fist. I had to pull each finger back one by one.

"This is your last chance," Moore said with forced civility. He pointed a finger at me. "The full story."

I had prided myself on being a lawman since the day I'd received my badge, but it didn't negate the fact that… I lied. A great deal. Not about the law, mind you. And not about my cases—at least, not where the finer details mattered—not because I enjoyed lying, but because my survival was dependent on being respected but ultimately forgotten. Would Moore have understood if I sat him down and explained myself? Perhaps. But our relationship—that of a director and senior agent—did not leave room to consider this option.

With Moore, he expected me to be black-and-white at all times, and… I….

I could have told the truth. I could have been the coward and turned Gunner over in exchange for the continued and carefully constructed existence I'd created. But even the mere notion of Gunner's neck broken by a length of hemp in exchange for my *black-and-white* life was too much to bear.

So I took a slow, deep breath, squared my shoulders, and said with a gravity akin to my world dropping out from underneath me, "I have nothing further to report."

I'd seen Moore angry before, had even been the reason for it on more than one occasion, but I'd never experienced the man well and truly pissed. I hadn't expected the sudden burst of magic around him, the smoke pluming outward from his body and clothing in the same way the sky blackened when my emotions were twisted and toyed with. And I'd certainly not been prepared for having Moore grab a fistful of my coat and spin us so I was slammed up against the window.

"Don't *lie* to me, Hamilton," he shouted, ignoring the smoke and sparks growing between us.

A Waterbury was cocked, manufactured aether joining the already-chaotic magic atmosphere, and then the three barrels came into view—resting on the back of Moore's head.

"Let him go," Gunner said, voice low and alert.

Moore's gaze darted to his left, his focus shifting from me to Gunner at his back. Moore's expression had changed. Gone was the anger and betrayal, replaced with a wariness as he mentally catalogued clues and narrowed the list of suspects who would be so bold as to put a gun to his head. Moore let go of my coat, raised his hand as if to let Gunner see he was no longer a threat, but then spun, arm outstretched with a flame in his hand, pointed directly at Gunner's face while Gunner still held his Waterbury extended, finger on the trigger.

The parlor radiators pinged.

Moore's fire crackled.

I peeled my back off the frozen glass and skirted around Moore.

As I expected, my director recognized America's infamous outlaw immediately, even if he sounded like he didn't believe what he was seeing. "Gunner the Deadly?"

The corner of Gunner's mouth twitched. "You must be Loren Moore."

"I am."

"You're the reason outlaws don't bother with the East Coast anymore."

"And yet, here you are."

"Only for pleasure," Gunner corrected. "Speaking of, do you manhandle all of your agents, or merely the ones you're looking to bugger?"

I startled and shot Gunner a look. His expression was impassive, as usual. When I glanced at Moore, his face was an open book in comparison—surprise gave way to shock and then to alarm. Moore lowered his arm, extinguished the magic, and shifted his attention to me.

Dear God… I had been correct. Those goggles had been a gift meant to communicate a degree of romance. Moore had, after a decade, attempted to gauge my tendencies and interest earlier that night, and perhaps, if I were learned like Gunner, I would have reacted accordingly. But even if I'd truly understood his intentions back at the office, had trusted what my gut told me in that moment, what would I have said?

Moore was handsome, no argument there. He was successful. Accomplished. Confident. Even the threat of magical danger due to caster bodies touching, or the potential complications stemming from him being my director—both would have been secondary concerns in my mind. I'd have been excited to see where a tumble with Moore might have led.

If only I had known of his attraction before October.

Because while I made no attempt to lie to myself about what there was between Gunner and me—it was not a courtship, nor had there been any rules established regarding exclusivity—for as long as Gunner was willing to brave danger for me, I had no intentions of straying.

"Hamilton," Moore started, uncharacteristic apprehension in his voice.

"Sir, allow me a moment to explain what's going on." I put a hand on Gunner's still-extended arm. "Gunner, please."

Gunner didn't take his eyes off Moore as he lowered his Waterbury, spun the pistol, and holstered it under his left arm.

"I met Gunner while on assignment in Shallow Grave," I said to Moore.

He blinked a few times. "You *what*?"

"He was also in town to apprehend Milo Ferguson. So we agreed to a temporary partnership in order to obtain a common goal. In that time, Gunner had my back without question."

Moore opened his mouth to protest.

"Sir, please—I'd be dead if it weren't for Gunner. He put his life on the line and expected nothing in return."

"You failed to include any of this in your report," Moore retorted.

I nodded and had to consciously force myself to maintain eye contact with him instead of looking to the floor in shame. "Purposefully so."

"This is unbelievable." Moore scratched his beard one-handed before shoving by and marching to the bedroom door. He stopped, turned, and took one step back in. "And so, what is this?" He motioned to us with both hands.

"Gunner is my guest," I answered.

"Are you mad? He's a *wanted man*."

"I'm not defending his past actions, only speaking on behalf of those I witnessed myself." I didn't actually know how to vocalize to Moore the true nature of Gunner's visit. This part of myself had been hidden for so long, denied for so long, *afraid* for so long, that it was as if I simply didn't possess the necessary vocabulary. So I reached into my coat pocket, retrieved Moore's goggles, and took a few steps forward. "I can't accept these."

Moore stared at the gift, looked over my shoulder at Gunner, and scoffed. He closed the distance, snatched the goggles from my hand, and walked down the hall. "Don't bother coming to the office tomorrow," he said, opening the front door.

My heart sank to my gut. I'd damn well known how this situation would end, but I certainly hadn't expected it to be due, at least in part, to jealousy. "Sir—" I called, hurrying after Moore.

But he slammed the door shut in my face.

I put my left hand on the door and felt Moore's magic recede with every step until he'd reached the ground floor and there was nothing but empty air left between us. I looked at the floor, and after a moment, I held both hands palm down and made a gentle sweeping motion upward. The stagnant water followed my conductor-like movements and created a glimmering sphere of magical water. It hovered at head level as I made a quick motion at a parlor window and a gust of wind threw up the pane. I touched the water and jerked my hand toward the open window, and it shot out into the dark and snowy night. I flicked my wrist and the pane was lowered with another carefully orchestrated gust.

I turned to the bedroom. Gunner had been leaning against the doorframe, looking comfortable sans suit coat, his arms crossed, with his eyebrows slightly raised as he watched my manner of cleanup. He pushed off, strode across the parlor, and said, "Come sit, Gillian." Gunner unbuckled his shoulder holster, took a seat on the settee—an ugly thing upholstered in an argyle pattern of greens and whites—then set the pistol at his side. He looked at me expectantly.

I sighed heavily, removed my coats and hat, hung them on the rack beside the water closet, and joined Gunner. I'd made to push the Waterbury out of the way, but Gunner took my wrist. "I'm only moving it."

He shook his head and patted his lap with his free hand.

"Excuse me?"

"Sit," he instructed again, tugging me closer.

"I'm not a child."

"I'm quite aware of that."

"Then why do you want me on your lap?"

Gunner smiled a very small smile, but it nonetheless warmed the icy lump freezing my gut. "I could explain, or you could learn firsthand."

I really didn't know what to say to that, so I awkwardly lowered myself to Gunner's lap. He slipped one arm around my back to rest on my hip, the other on my thigh, then tugged me closer. I startled and put a hand around Gunner's neck to correct my balance.

"I've got you," he murmured. His hand on my thigh stroked up and down. "Thank you for what you did."

I snorted and pinched the bridge of my nose. "*Thank you.* For what? For putting a target on your back? For telling my director we're fucking?"

"For never reporting me," Gunner replied calmly. "You kept your word."

I lowered my hand and looked at Gunner. "What am I going to do?" I asked, voice hitching at the end.

He didn't answer, merely kept stroking my leg.

I shook my head, cleared my throat, and asked instead, "How did you know?"

"Know what?"

One hand still around Gunner's neck, I hesitantly placed my other on his chest. The fabric of his shirt felt like nothing against my palm, but the heat of his skin underneath—I felt that. "Moore's tendencies. Even I wasn't aware."

Gunner arched an eyebrow.

"Right. Of course. Survival instinct."

Gunner wrapped his big hand around mine, squeezed, then threaded his fingers between my own. "The look on his face—it was a private hurt, not professional."

"And?"

"And then he touched you. Casters are meant to avoid one another, are they not?"

"Well, yes."

Gunner inclined his head in the smallest nod. "There you go. Although, I will admit, I was surprised to learn he was so brazen as to present you with a gift."

My face flushed, and I was suddenly hyperaware of Gunner's goggles still around my neck. "So was I."

He twisted his hold to bring my hand to his lips, but fell short of kissing my skin. Gunner's eyes narrowed a fraction, and he gently pried my hand open to study the latticework of scars along my palm and fingers. "Milo." It wasn't a question.

"I can't feel anything," I blurted out. I wasn't certain if I'd not divulged this to anyone else because of a fragile ego, fear that if I acknowledged the physical setback, it'd become a fixed part of myself, or simply because lying was second nature, but as far as Gunner was concerned, I wanted to be honest about at least one thing.

He shifted on the settee, tugged my other hand from his

neck, and held them both in his own. "What do you mean?"

"I can feel your weight and warmth," I explained with a touch of reluctance. "But not… your skin."

Gunner pressed his thumbs into the palms of my hands. "Is the damage permanent?"

I shook my head and whispered, "I don't know. Maybe."

Gunner moved his thumbs upward, slipped them under the cuffs of my shirt, and rubbed the underbelly of my wrists.

My breath caught on an intake. "I can feel that." Christ, it was so intense, I swear I could count each and every ridge of Gunner's fingerprints.

Gunner raised my hand again and pressed his warm lips to the delicate skin of my inner wrist. The rasp of stubble on his chin sent a shudder through my entire body that he could probably feel. He'd hardly pulled back before I grabbed his face and crushed our mouths together.

Every minute of every day, I had thought of this—of speaking with Gunner again, touching him again, kissing him again—and now it was happening. When we were together, it felt as if we were pulling an ancient magic from the very fabric of Earth and casting a spell foreign to even the most learned scholars and architects. There was a real and tangible magic between me and Gunner. I didn't know how it was possible, but there was no other way to explain this sensation—like I had a billion volts of electricity running through my veins. Like a shooting star had nothing on me. It was incredible.

"I've missed you," I whispered against Gunner's mouth.

Gunner slipped a hand around the back of my head, his fingers threading through my carefully set and oiled hair. "You make a man do wild things, Gillian."

I kissed him again. "Like what?"

"Like travel two days cross-country into a lion's den to put a gun to the head of the state director for the FBMS because you're the one bit of bounty I'm unwilling to share."

"Bounty?" I repeated, attempting to sound indignant and failing miserably at it.

Gunner flashed his handsome, lopsided smile. "I stole you first."

He drew me into another kiss, the tip of his tongue tracing the seam of my mouth before I opened to it. His tongue dipped inside, pressed against mine, and somehow the tang of Black Jack made it more erotic. I fumbled blindly with the buttons of Gunner's waistcoat until he broke the kiss and leaned back to allow easier access. I could feel him watching me, every stutter of my fingers, every flutter of my heart beating frantically in my throat.

I looked up and met Gunner's concentrated gaze—his blue eyes nearly black, the pupils were blown so wide. He liked this: my assertiveness and the show of physical prowess. I was still, admittedly, quite naïve in terms of finding my way around the bedroom with a partner. Gunner was the only man I'd been with, and just the one time too. So while I seemed to enjoy… well, *everything* he did because it was all new and all so good, I had to imagine Gunner's tastes for pleasure had become more fine-tuned through experience. And the way he was staring at me….

I grabbed his tie and yanked hard. Gunner's breath caught as he was pulled up against me. His eyes grew and both hands grabbed around my waist.

"Is this okay?" I asked.

"*Jesus Christ.*"

Due to my own tendency to curse, often in such a brazen manner that the only folks who didn't blink twice were air sailors or drunkards, I wasn't insulted by Gunner's blasphemy. It was more that I was surprised by it. Contrary to sensationalist newspapers, Gunner really was, for all intents and purposes, a gentleman.

He lunged forward on the settee, took me with him as he stood, then settled me on my feet. Gunner grabbed my arm and spun me on his way to the bedroom. The room was still dark, still cold from the window having been open and the steam heat from the parlor not yet reaching this far into the apartment. Gunner bumped into the bureau as he turned to kiss me again. His hands were everywhere—a brief fondle through my trousers, encircling my waist once more in a manner that felt so boldly intimate, deftly unbuttoning my waistcoat and pushing it from my shoulders.

A sense of relief was bubbling over inside me. I had hoped, after October, the experience of having finally been with a man would be enough to sate me for the long haul. But instead, it had only made the yearning stronger. More relentless. A necessity that overpowered my body, mind, soul. And to be with Gunner again—to have him again—it was a thrill.

A *happiness*.

Determined to not behave as cluelessly as before, I immediately unbuttoned my collar and cuffs when Gunner broke the kiss. I tossed them to the floor, yanked my tie free, and unbuttoned my trousers. I felt less mechanical this time and, if only because I was no longer thinking with just my head, more seductive. But I suspected the dark was a great source of my empowerment.

My hand fumbled and snapped the brace over my shoulder when Gunner laid bare his own chest. His braces hung at his sides, and his trousers were slung dangerously low on his slender hips. The hard planes of his chest, the fine black hair traveling south from his navel, his perfectly sculpted arms….

Gunner slid his hands under my braces and pushed them from my shoulders. "You look like you need assistance," he stated.

"Smelling salts."

"Come again?"

"Seeing you like this. I need smelling salts." I pressed my palm to his flat abdomen to stress my point.

Gunner got down on his knees before unbuttoning my shoes. He looked up at me while tugging my trousers and drawers down and helping me step out of them. "Like how?"

"You're teasing me."

"A bit, yes." Gunner ran his hands up my bare thighs, leaned close, and bit the skin. "Do you want me to stop?"

I swallowed but still felt as if I were choking. "N-no. Never."

Gunner put his mouth on my prick and swallowed its length with what seemed like shocking ease. I cried out and knocked into the bureau with a start. Gunner managed to keep his hands on my hips, preventing me from landing on my backside. I grabbed the back of his head, but couldn't figure out if I was trying to push him away or press Gunner forward.

"C-Con—" I bit my tongue short of saying Gunner's name. He didn't need to know how often I thought it, whispered it, when I was alone in the dark with nothing but my hand and memories.

Gunner pulled off with a wet, obscene *pop*. He stared up at me, face stoic, eyes alight. "Say it."

I could have asked.

Told him to clarify.

But I knew.

"Constantine."

Gunner got to his feet, his movement fluid like a cat, the rumble in his chest like its purr. He towered over me, cupped my face in his big hands, then leaned down to whisper against my mouth, "Again."

I swallowed. "Constantine."

He kissed me, and I could feel his smile—taste it, even. Gunner maneuvered me to the edge of the bed, and once I'd sat, he stepped back and finished unbuttoning his own shoes and shucking off his trousers. He took my shirt, as I'd just removed it, threw it somewhere into the dark, and used his long, wiry build to push me down. And then it was like a pinwheel—a whirligig—a kinetic art display of skin and hair and teeth and tongue that even those impressionist fellows in Paris wouldn't be able to accurately portray on their canvases.

I dug my fingers into Gunner's back. He growled, thrust against me, and bit my neck in response. The pressure, the moist heat, the exposure—it was a chaos my body reacted to without permission, without thought. I yelped and bucked my hips against Gunner's. Gunner let up on my neck, kissed the sting, then took my jaw into one hand. He was so gentle, so intimate, when he held my face.

"Have you been with anyone? Since Arizona," he added for clarification.

Thankful for the dark, now more than ever, that hid the flush I felt ignite on my cheeks, I said, "No. That is—I've been busy."

"Busy."

"I'm a federal agent."

"Yes, you are."

"There's always crime."

"Always." He didn't smile, not exactly, but those blue eyes caught the bit of light spilling in from the hall and they shone like buffed and polished gems. Gunner sat up on his knees and asked, "What would you like?"

I followed his motion onto my elbows, took in the definition of his chest and the black hair I itched to run my fingers through, the muscles of his thighs, and erect prick that was, astonishingly, my doing. My mouth was dry, and I felt I had to peel my tongue off my palate just to speak.

"There's—" I cleared my throat. "There's Vaseline in the nightstand." I tilted my head just a little to the left in indication. "I bought it the other day."

Gunner leaned over me, opened the drawer, and removed a tin. He sat back, popped the top off, and dipped a few fingers in. He set the tin aside while rubbing his fingertips together, smearing the Vaseline. Gunner moved closer, nudged my legs open, kissed me, and pressed a slick finger to my backside.

I jumped, broke the kiss, and smacked Gunner's nose with my chin. "Oh God. I'm so sorry."

"It's fine."

"Are you okay?"

"Perhaps we should try something else."

"What? I just—*no*. I want this."

But Gunner had narrowed his eyes, and those tiny wrinkles in the corners spoke volumes. "I don't think you're ready."

"I'm twenty-nine-years old," I protested.

"Age is irrelevant."

I clenched my jaw and ground my teeth so hard, it hurt. I could feel tears pricking my eyes—the sort associated with frustration, anger, humiliation. "I'm not incompetent, Gunner."

"I never said you were." He leaned over me, took my jaw, and held tight when I tried to wriggle free. "If you're so nervous you jump at a finger, it won't be good. For either of us."

"What use am I, then?" I snapped. Gravity got the best of one tear, and it followed the contour of my cheekbone before dripping into my ear. "Please. Just do it."

Gunner's expression was like someone had broken the glass surface of water by skipping a stone across it. He tightened his hold on my jaw and gave a little shake. It didn't hurt, but it certainly wasn't tender anymore. "Don't insult yourself. And don't insult me."

I didn't know what to say. Even if I had, I was afraid to speak and hear my voice crack. If I had thought, only moments ago, this night couldn't be much worse, I'd certainly managed to find the last intact seam in my life to unravel.

Elemental bullets on my streets.

A new gangster looking to take me out.

An enraged boss likely cleaning out my desk that very moment.

And now this.

Gunner released his hold, grabbed the Vaseline tin, and stuck his fingers in again. "Not all men enjoy the sensation," he said, quite simply. "Others need time to work up to it." He stroked my flagging length with a greasy hand, and my eyes about rolled out of my head.

I was stiff and breathless by the time Gunner let up. I opened my eyes and watched as he reached behind himself. "Wh-what are you doing?"

With his free hand, Gunner guided mine to his prick and released a held sigh as I touched him. "I'm rarely allowed an opportunity to indulge," he said, voice thick and low and so unbelievably attractive. "The men I sleep with—"

"Passing ships," I corrected.

Gunner smiled lightly. "That's right. They've got a certain image of me. A certain expectation."

I felt myself blush at those words. Hadn't I thought the very same of Gunner? In Arizona, when I'd belatedly realized his tendencies were a mirror of my own, I had mused on the notion that no person would dare whisper terrible things about Gunner. Because he was so dangerous. So masculine. So... *not me.*

But then... what did that even mean? Because I was

not the ideal physique of a man, had I assumed something about myself too? Convinced myself that, should I ever have the opportunity to sleep with a man, I could only experience one thing? That I would be expected to assume such a role? And why did I relate such an act of intimacy as something I deserved, not because I should be so lucky, but because I was less?

Gunner wasn't less.

He was everything and more.

"You enjoy it?" I asked.

Gunner lifted up, leaned over, and kissed my mouth. "Want to try?" he asked by way of answer.

I gulped for air and managed a curt nod.

That smile was back on his face. Gunner told me to stay on my back while he put a knee on either side of my body. I was more than happy for him to remain in control of the situation, because even with this change, I still had no practical experience, only animal instinct.

"What if I—" I gasped as Gunner bore down, and that tight heat about pushed me to the brink then and there. "—h-hurt you?"

"You won't," he whispered.

I dug my heels into the mattress and grabbed Gunner's hips hard enough that he hissed. "Sorry," I said, managing not to choke on my own tongue.

"It's okay, dear." Gunner sat and began to rock. The muscles in his long, lithe body uncoiled and flexed, and he was so elegant, so fluid, so remarkable. He pried my hands from his hips and dragged them up his taut stomach, making certain my wrists rubbed against his body. "Touch me."

"Christ Almighty," I swore through clenched teeth. I reached for his pecs and dug my fingers into skin and hair as Gunner kept pace. "So good. So good. So—*fuck*." Gunner did something with his muscles—clenching them around my length so that my vision tunneled, my belly tightened, my balls drew up. "Oh God." I brought my hands down, dragged my fingernails along his flanks, and watched him suck in a sharp breath. I started to move my hands around Gunner's backside—it had been automatic—but I came up short upon realizing what I was doing.

Gunner leaned forward, brought his mouth to mine, and kissed me before saying, breathless, "It's okay, Gillian."

I don't know how that one comment seemed to overcome my inexperience and inhibitions. Perhaps it was the certainty with which Gunner spoke, or the way my name sounded on his lips in the midst of sex. Or maybe it was nothing more than my entire adult life being denied this experience—this opportunity to be dominant with someone who seemed to fully believe I could be—and with someone who appeared to enjoy when I let this part of me out.

I swallowed as I grabbed his firm globes of muscle in both hands. Gunner's breath was hot and heavy against the side of my neck. He began to kiss and bite and suck the skin just below where my collar usually rested. My breath caught, voice cracked, and I thrust my hips up.

The sound Gunner made, I thought I'd hurt him. But he reared back and stroked his prick hard and fast. "Again."

"Are you—"

"*Gillian*," he demanded, and his voice had an edge of desperation.

"Sorry." I raised my hips—once, twice, and on the third shove, I felt every muscle in my body go rigid, my toes curl, and then I was spending with a force like a thunderstorm raged inside me. I heard Gunner's breathing hitch, then a warm jet landed on my stomach. I opened my eyes—when had I closed them?—and stared at his face.

His forehead was damp with sweat, strands of raven-black hair clung to it. Gunner's lips were parted as he breathed heavily. He leaned over me once more, kissing my mouth, my cheek, my jaw, my ear. "How was it?" he murmured.

"Incredible."

Gunner pulled back enough to meet my eyes. The corner of his mouth tugged upward, like an invisible puppeteer was controlling his smile.

"*You're* incredible," I reiterated.

Gunner eased himself off my lap and stood from the bed. He said, while walking to the door, "Yank on my tie again and I'll let you brand my backside."

I sat up to watch him vanish down the hall, and a moment later, heard the door to the water closet open. I'd experienced a tidal wave of passion so intense that the lower portion of my body was borderline numb, but what Gunner had just said—confirmation that he liked the distribution of power between us, and that he was clearly relieved in knowing he wouldn't have to lead every time—it made my prick twitch. Doing that with him was… well, *incredible* had been a hell of an understatement.

I drew my knees up to rest my elbows on them. I sat there, ignoring the tackiness on my stomach and dampness of the mattress, while staring out the window to my right. Perhaps New Year's Eve had turned around, if only a bit.

"Everything all right?"

I startled at Gunner's silent return. "Yes. Fine."

He held out a washcloth.

"Thank you." I wiped my stomach and prick clean. Gunner lay down beside me, naked as the day he'd been born and none too modest either. I looked at him, watched his jaw work, and picked up the sweet and herbal notes of his licorice gum a second later.

"Virginia Brights," he stated, crossing his arms behind

his head.

"Pardon?"

Gunner tilted his head toward me. "I used to smoke."

I raised both eyebrows. "Cigarettes?"

"Hm-hm." Gunner held one hand up, motioning with his thumb and index finger. "I liked the trading cards. Parasol Drill was my favorite collection." He glanced at me a second time and clarified with "Women holding parasols."

"Oh."

"Black Jack is the lesser of vices," Gunner concluded before he reached and stroked my bare thigh. "Although I still have the desire to smoke after sex, even now."

I fiddled with the wet cloth but didn't break eye contact. "It's always listed on your wanted posters—known to have a fondness for Black Jack."

"It is," he agreed, his voice dropping low. It occurred to me then that perhaps that former habit was the source of Gunner's huskiness when he spoke.

"I'd always wondered why."

"Now you know." Gunner shifted onto his side, propped his head up with one hand, and pulled me down to kiss chastely. "My apologies. It's nothing of interest."

"I think it is."

He arched one brow.

"If you've not noticed, you're a bit of an enigma to people."

"Am I?"

"I feel rather like a corvid around you—collecting details like they're shiny pebbles or pretty buttons."

"And what have you hoarded so far?"

"You're wicked."

Gunner smiled suddenly, and it was always a bit of a

shock to see the change on his face—the impassive marble to something like a work of art in the blink of an eye.

"Charming," I continued. "Kind. Brave. Can discern Crown perfumes by a passing scent, once had a fondness for trading cards—"

"The parasol women were very beautiful," he insisted.

"You haven't heard my favorite detail learned."

"What's that?"

"Constantine."

Gunner reached up and stroked the closely cropped hair on the side of my head. "And what about you, Gillian Hamilton?"

"What about me?"

"Tell me something I haven't ascertained yet."

"You've already picked up the highlights."

"No. I know your age, your history with the Bureau, your perfume and hair oil. I know your shoe preferences and how you sound in bed."

I flushed. "I'm not sure that's a detail others would fight you for."

Gunner was still stroking my head. "I know you're far more powerful than what the Bureau believes."

I opened my mouth to protest, but Gunner lowered his hand back to my thigh.

"But I haven't figured out why."

"Why what?"

"Why you keep it a secret." Gunner was staring at me again in that manner in which he stripped a person down to their bones. "They assign levels to their magic agents, do they not?"

I nodded curtly.

"And what have they given you? Four? Five?"

Before I could speak, the PDD on the bureau across from the bed began to emit a series of tones—Director Loren Moore.

VI

December 31, 1881

"This is madness."

"Yet there is method in it."

The field office was only a handful of blocks from The Buchanan—a ten-minute walk at a leisurely pace. When I'd answered the PDD, Moore curtly requested my presence, paused a fraction of a second, then said I was to bring *that man* along, as he might be able to provide us with a unique perspective on the Fishback situation. Moore ended the call before I could utter a response.

Gunner and I had dressed, and while I made certain in the mirror that I looked entirely like myself, I couldn't shake the notion that what we'd done—what *I'd* done—was smeared across my forehead in a woman's rouge lip salve. Would something about the way I walked or talked denote a change in me? Would Moore be able to take one look at me and piece the clues together?

"A method in walking *you*, of all men, into a Magic and

Steam field office?" I retorted.

Gunner glanced down at me, and a plume of air escaped his lips as he answered, "Shakespeare. *Hamlet*, act two."

"Right." *Of course*. "I only meant, this isn't wise."

"Moore won't arrest me."

I looked up. "He has the right. The obligation, even."

"The problem with viewing the world in absolutes," Gunner began, "is that sooner or later, you find yourself in a situation where the mind and heart disagree. Of course Moore has an obligation to arrest me. But in doing so, he'd be required to arrest you too." Gunner stopped at the end of the sidewalk. "Which he won't."

"You sound awfully certain."

"He won't."

I snorted.

"He'd sooner not acknowledge the situation. For now, at least." Gunner inclined his head for me to follow as he crossed the street. "Tell me about this Fishback fellow."

I let out a heavy breath and crossed the cobblestone street, snow crunching loudly underfoot. "Frank Fishback," I stated. "Murderer-for-hire."

"Target?"

"Beat coppers—the honest sort. Downtown gangsters have been hiring him for the last two years, until he recently changed vocations."

Gunner had no comment, so I continued.

"He picked up a job as a middle-man for a new gangster."

"Tick Tock. Was that what the mechanical intruder said?"

I nodded. "Correct. And as far as intelligence goes, we have very little. What was gleaned from Fishback earlier this evening was that Tick Tock is moving unknown quantities of elemental ammunition—fire, specifically—packages that came in from the West, which Fishback picked up and delivered to 'a mechanical man.'"

"The mechanical man being one and the same?" Gunner asked.

"We'll never know."

"Why's that?"

"Fishback is dead."

Gunner grabbed my coat sleeve and pulled me to a stop. "You implied he was in custody."

"That's why Moore came to The Buchanan. Roughly the same time Mechanical Man was falling off my balcony, Fishback was murdered while under lock and key."

Gunner removed his hand from my arm. He took a breath. "Gillian—"

"*Hamilton.*"

We both turned toward the third voice and watched a shadow detach from the wall of the looming FBMS field office. A red ember briefly illuminated Moore's face as he lit the tobacco in his pipe.

"Sir," I called back. The distance between us, while no less than half a dozen feet, felt akin to jumping straight down Dead Man's Canyon without any magic to govern the landing.

Splat.

Somewhere overhead, a window opened and drunken delight and laughter spilled out into the night. A gust of wind escaped the narrow alley between the office and neighboring business, kicking up the freshly fallen snow and screaming like a banshee lamenting the death of an O'Neill or O'Connor. A touring automobile plodded along the street, the holiday bells attached to the grille ringing obnoxiously with every bump in the road.

Chiiing, chiiing, chiiing.

The cloud of cherry smoke from Moore's pipe held suspended around his head, and only when he removed the bit from his mouth did it dissipate like fog on a spring morning. "Come with me." He disappeared into the alley.

"Sir," I tried once more, running forward. I skidded to a stop in the entranceway as Moore stepped into a pool of orange light cast from a security lamp over the rarely used side door. "What—that is—your intention—"

Moore slid a large skeleton key into the lock, and I heard the tumblers click into place. He looked sideways at me as he opened the door. "Are you a federal agent, Hamilton?"

"I am."

"And did you receive an order from your director?"

"I did."

"Then move your backside," Moore concluded before disappearing inside.

I spared Gunner a quick glance before stepping into the alley. I heard his steps mirror my own—heels snapping the thin skin of ice on the uneven walkway. I moved into the dim hallway of the office, and Gunner pulled the door shut as he took up the rear. The side entrance led onto a series of congested, maze-like corridors hardly wider than the shoulders of one man. The halls acted as a method for skirting the lobby and booking rooms and not being seen by the general population, as well as providing agents with a secondary entrance and escape route, in the event our building was ever overtaken by an opposing force. The overhead piping clanked quietly with steam, and the glass globes of light were turned down so low, it was easier finding my way by simply following the lingering trail of Moore's tobacco.

At an intersection—right leading to the bullpens and private offices upstairs, and left down to the basement of the building—we took the left. The temperature dipped as the three of us walked single file down the stairs and into a large workspace, sparsely furnished, with unfinished brick walls. A bruiser, the fellow's name momentarily lost to me, stood at the head of two tables with his arms crossed and a deep scowl on his face. On the right were the remains of Mechanical Man carefully laid out, on the left, the charred body of, I believed, Frank Fishback.

It wasn't the sight of dead bodies that caused a cold and tacky sweat to break out across my chest—not exactly. I'd experienced plenty of death in my twenty-nine years and had hardened to it. It was more the way the bodies had been presented. Two slabs of meat atop a doctor's operating tables, broken and left behind for disposal.

Bleeding and screaming and choking and gagging on a miasma of fetid death.

I shook myself, hoping it appeared to be nothing but a reaction to the chill in the air. There was no time for the past, and certainly not in my current company. I took a deep breath and entered the basement room. That same dying magic snapped in the air around both bodies—crackles of disturbed energy at odds with the raw current flowing through the room. The unsettled magic was visible without a conscious need to shift my perception, and it reacted like a startled animal as Moore walked across the room—the way the energy spiked and distorted at the presence of a caster, it was like a cat arching its back and hissing. I watched Moore, but there was still no indication that he sensed the manufactured magic on the level I did.

I tugged my gloves off, stuck them into my coat pockets, and with my arm at my side so as to go unnoticed, I positioned my palm out toward the magic. Then I grabbed the jagged tendrils, made a fist around the energy, and gave it a tug. The heat of a fire spell immediately burrowed into the palm of my hand, like a beetle digging into flesh. The tangled web of broken magic in the atmosphere carried me upstairs—the jail cell where Fishback had been taken out—farther, past The

Buchanan, then it got lost on its way back to the Five Points.

I winced, let go of the magic, and dug my thumb into my palm to try to alleviate that disgusting burrowing sensation. I unbuttoned my coats as Moore dismissed the bruiser from the room, and I watched the gentleman pass Gunner on his way out the door. I shrugged the winter attire off, hung it on a nearby rack, and added my bowler as well. I turned while adjusting my cufflinks to see that Moore and Gunner were staring at each other from opposite ends of the room, the tension palpable despite the distance. Without some quick intervention, there was likely to be four dead bodies in this room instead of two.

"*So,*" I prompted suddenly, my voice far too loud.

Gunner didn't tear his gaze from Moore as he pushed the door shut, turned the lock, then leaned back against it. He crossed his arms, and the butt of his Waterbury was visible in its holster. Gunner planted the heel of his shoe against the door, and with the rakish angle he wore his bowler, he looked every bit the dangerous outlaw. But his attitude wasn't cockiness or smug assurance—it was simply well-placed confidence. Gunner had a coolness about himself that even being in New York City, behind a locked door with my director, in a building full of federal agents, couldn't be shaken.

It should be worth mentioning that Moore, while not appearing visibly distraught—because he was, in his own right, quite the formidable force as well—was not making an effort to meet Gunner's fearlessness. Moore hadn't been introduced to the Gunner I had while in Arizona—a silent and stoic man who minded his manners and had an odd propensity for meretriciously aligning items. He certainly didn't know the Gunner I had from thirty minutes ago—a man who I knew as Constantine, naked in bed, stroking my thigh.

Moore only knew Gunner the Deadly.

And Gunner the Deadly had a reputation worth respecting.

I walked around the far side of Fishback's table and created a sort of triangle with Moore standing near the head of Mechanical Man and Gunner at the door. I put my hands on the table's edge and stared at Fishback's charred body—his mouth agape and hands twisted into blackened claws, screaming in agony even in death. The poor bastard.

"What happened?" I asked.

"A commotion was heard from the cells at a quarter after seven," Moore stated.

I carefully peeled back the burned folds of Fishback's suit coat. "Then what?"

"Special Agents Bligh and Plunket rushed in. Fishback was on fire. Screaming. Dying. No intruder—just a broken window."

I tugged at what remained of his shirt collar, but it snapped off in my hand. I set it on the tabletop. "Someone got in via a fourth-floor window?"

"That's what I said, Hamilton."

I glanced up. "Yes, sir. I only meant… there's no fire escape on the east side of the building. How did they get up there?"

Moore slowly and purposefully directed his attention toward Gunner. "I thought Mr. Gunner might have some insight on that."

"My expertise lies in raiding airships, Director," Gunner said coolly.

"Any criminal worth a dime knows how to make an escape."

"I suppose I'd have to be caught first."

"I need forceps," I interrupted.

They both looked at me.

I pointed at Fishback. "I see a few wound tracks. If those

fire bullets are anything like their aether counterparts, then there should be a bullet to extract. It might be of value to study."

Moore stuck his pipe between his teeth. He turned around and began opening and closing a number of cabinets mounted to the wall. They held a variety of odds and ends the field office had accumulated over the years: handyman tools, oversized evidence that couldn't be properly stored on the second floor with the rest of the open and cold cases—at one point Moore pulled out a box of what appeared, from a distance, to be broken inkwells and handcuffs. He puzzled over the contents a moment, shook his head, and shoved the box back onto a shelf. Moore finally unearthed what he seemed to have in mind from my initial request—a black physician's bag.

He walked to Fishback's table, and standing on the opposite side, set the case down and opened the latch. Moore dug around, puffing on his pipe before saying, "Our first medical kit when the office opened." He produced a rusted pair of forceps and looked at me. "Hand-me-downs from the war."

I accepted the handle of the tool, mindful of how Moore held the tip of the forceps instead of flirting his fingertips close to my own. Like how he used to. I said with forced nonchalance, "I don't think Fishback will notice." I leaned over Fishback, tugged open the blackened flesh of his throat with my thumb, and held my breath as I dug into the hole. For a moment, the only sound in the room was the squish of human innards.

"I suppose," Moore started, "if Mechanical Man ran to your residence immediately after shooting Fishback and utilized the Fourth Avenue fire escape—"

"No."

"My patience is understandably limited tonight,

Hamilton. This is going to be the one time I ask you ignore my earlier request and pull those punches."

"He wouldn't have had the time," I corrected.

"*Why.*"

I looked toward the door. "Gunner, when did we arrive at The Buchanan?"

Gunner removed his pocket watch and studied the face. "Couldn't have been more than a minute or two after Fishback swallowed that bullet," he said, looking up and then nodding his chin at the crispy flesh and blood I was digging through.

"Perhaps you're incorrect," Moore said to Gunner.

"Doubtful."

"Ah-ha." I yanked a flattened, bloodied bullet from the back of Fishback's throat. I offered it to Moore when he pulled a handkerchief from a pocket and held his covered palm out. "There was an atmospheric disturbance at the same time we reached The Buchanan," I explained.

Moore took his pipe from his mouth and pointed it at Mechanical Man. "Fire?"

"Fire, yes, but not from him. The spell terminated here, at the office."

In my haste to interrupt the mounting squabble between two adult men, knowing firsthand how absolutely infuriating Gunner could be with his matter-of-factness, I had failed to filter the magic explanation through my series of lies. Survival was dependent upon downplaying my skills, and finally, for the first time in a decade, a sliver of truth had gotten out.

Moore was staring at me, bullet still in one hand, pipe still in the other. He'd picked up on that one word: terminate. He asked, his voice low and tone cautious, "And where did the spell *originate*?"

I opened my mouth to speak, but I might as well have been catching flies.

"We saw fire, is what Hamilton means," Gunner said, his voice filtering in like the smoke it sounded like. "On the horizon. Then your fellow here ends up kindling at the same time—so it must have terminated here," he explained.

"But a spell being cast in one location, with the results seen in a completely different—"

"It's manufactured," I hastily said over Moore. "It clearly doesn't behave like aether-infused bullets, so we have nothing practical to compare the situation to." I quickly motioned to Moore's bullet with my forceps. "That bullet is a much larger caliber—it couldn't have been Mechanical Man who killed Fishback. Most definitely someone else."

I returned to digging bullets out of Fishback after that, finding half a dozen more and confirming the weapon he'd been shot with was, despite being quite unbelievable, likely a Gatling gun. But other than that passing comment, my mind was elsewhere entirely. Gunner had suggested—no, *told me*—twice now that he knew I wasn't being honest about my magic. I had declined to entertain the conversation both times, but I had an anxiety of sorts, not understanding what evidence he had in order to draw his conclusion. It wasn't merely because he'd witnessed me create aether bullets in Arizona. Yes, infusing ammunition with aether took a skilled and practiced caster, but I was not the only man with this ability.

It was something else.

Something that Gunner had zeroed in on almost immediately but that Moore had overlooked for a decade.

And Gunner knew it scared the hell out of me.

So he'd lied. He hadn't felt the manufactured fire spell when we'd been at The Buchanan. He hadn't seen the tendrils of magic. Hadn't experienced the broken, chaotic web left in the wake of the magic used to kill Fishback and whose origin centered somewhere south of us—somewhere in the Five

Points. He'd not been privy to any of it, but somehow he just *knew* that Moore hadn't known any of those details either, and therein lay the danger.

So he'd *lied*.

I moved to Mechanical Man after finishing my dissection of Fishback, making certain to not look Moore in the eye as I put Gunner's old goggles on. I snapped one hand, cast an aether spell, then moved my hands apart, stretching the magic as if it were bread dough. When the blinding-white energy resembled a crude cleaver, I brought the raw magic down on the body's arm, severing the gun from the elbow. Aether was one of the most complex magics to exist, a combination of all the elements in an undiluted form that could be life-affirming or totally devastating, depending on how the caster wielded the force. And in this instance….

I let the spell dissipate afterward, tugged the goggles down, then picked up the weapon with both hands. I had to swallow the bile making its way up my throat before I managed to say, "Gunner, do you recall the pistol Ferguson had?"

"I do."

I turned toward him and held the bulky pistol up in invitation.

Gunner unhurriedly pushed off the door, approached the table, then took the weapon from my hands. He spun the cylinder, checked the chambers, then cocked the weapon. "Could have done without the bits of flesh and bone, Hamilton," Gunner stated, referring to Mechanical Man's arm protruding from the metal band where the weapon had been fused to his body.

"The gun is reinforced with silver underneath the iron," I remarked, struggling for a casual tone and not that of a man ready to upchuck at the sight of protruding bones. "You know how aether reacts."

He made a sound in the back of his throat before saying, "Same weapon as Ferguson's. More or less."

"More or less?" I echoed, taking it back.

"Ferguson used a modified Waterbury. Same with this one," Gunner explained. "Handcrafted, though, probably with what was readily available." He tapped the bottom barrel. "In this case, the fourth barrel welded here is from a Jordan. Entirely different caliber. Explains why he had to fire twice."

"Tick Tock is moving more than just ammunition," I said in a rush of excitement as I turned to Moore.

He was already nodding. "Custom weapons."

"And reinforced with natural elements to temper the magic enough for noncasters to utilize." I weighed the pistol in both hands. That wriggling sensation I'd picked up when Mechanical Man was freshly dead was gone now. Whoever murdered Fishback, we'd have to catch the criminal alive so I could inspect their weapon properly. Whatever that impression had been, I'd now confirmed it completely dissipated after death, and as far as I was concerned, it was a vital clue as to how this manufactured magic was a success.

"We finally have a starting point," Moore continued. "We need to speak to our informants—ask about any stockpiling locations within the last month or two."

"Please don't say—"

"I want you to find Addison."

I sighed heavily and set the pistol on the table. "Sir, with all due respect, the last meeting I had with Addison ended in a bar brawl and I had to pay for three broken chairs."

"You were reimbursed."

"It's not about the chairs."

Moore smiled and stroked his manicured beard. "I'd like you to come upstairs with me and examine the window."

"Understood."

"But then I want you to pull Addison out of whatever theater or saloon or back alley he's in. This is our first break since October, and I need something to show for our efforts once D.C. learns of this mess with Fishback."

"Yes, sir," I answered. I spun on my heel and then immediately backpedaled to keep from walking straight into Gunner, who was still standing at the table, hands in his trouser pockets, with one eyebrow cocked. "Shit. Gunner—"

"Is it necessary to play this game of hide-and-seek now?" he asked, tone unperturbed.

"As a matter of fact, yes," Moore answered.

"I was speaking to Hamilton," Gunner replied. His voice remained cool and unchanged, but there was a certain sharpness about his person. It was clear to me that Gunner *did not* like Moore, but that this attitude toward my director had nothing to do with their chosen… erm… professions and everything to do with me instead.

I turned to Moore again, took a step back, and forced Gunner to do the same. "If you'll excuse me for a moment, sir. I'd like to speak with Gunner in private."

Moore didn't approve, didn't disapprove, merely puffed on his pipe.

Once I'd put enough distance between the two that they couldn't go at each other like feral toms, I detoured long enough to fetch my coat and hat and put them on as I ushered Gunner out the door. I followed him up the stairs, the stink of soon-to-be bloated bodies left behind in exchange for that very particular scent of radiator heat cranked high. Gunner had clearly paid attention on our initial walkthrough, as he successfully navigated his way to the side door without any prompting from me.

He stopped half a dozen feet from the exit, though, turned, and put a hand above my head on the wall. He used his build to press me back against the wall, and I removed my bowler before it could be knocked off. Gunner was never intentionally intimidating when he took this posture with me—if anything, his long, lithe body just shy of touching my own, having to stare up at his stoic features, brought back memories of Arizona that made my heart race.

But I didn't need to live in the past.

Gunner was right here, right now.

"I have to work."

Gunner didn't reply.

"I've been tracking this lead for two months."

Still no response.

"Please say something so I know whether you're angry."

"I'm not angry," he said, voice low.

"I'm so sorry—"

Gunner brought his other hand to my face, tilted my chin, and kissed my mouth before I could protest as to our location.

"—not a single thing about this night—"

He kissed me again.

I was losing an argument we weren't even having. "—nothing has gone right."

Gunner's eyes narrowed a little, but this was his amused face. "None of it?"

I started to sweat under the weight of my winter coat. "Some of it," I corrected, my voice barely a whisper now. I reached my free hand into my pocket, searching for my apartment keys. "Here. Go back to—"

"No."

"Gunner."

"I'll wait outside for you."

"You can't. This is federal business."

"It was federal business in Arizona too."

"That was different. I don't need your assistance here."

Gunner's hand slid off the wall and he straightened his posture. The twinkle in his eyes was gone. "No? I lied for you, Gillian."

"Well, I-I—"

"And I don't lie."

I swallowed hard and let out a breath that was shaky. Hell, on the verge of tears was more accurate. "Then why? Why did you say that?"

Gunner's gaze flicked to the right, assured we were still alone, and then he said, "Because you needed my help."

I felt as if I'd been shot right through the heart with aether—his words reverberating through every organ and bone in my body. When Gunner's methodical deconstruction of my person had uncovered my tendencies, the intense fear of being found out hadn't lingered long because we'd trusted each other with this shared secret. We had… a sort of affection for each other.

A likeness, certainly.

I liked Gunner a great deal.

And even though it wouldn't be forever, for now, tonight, he promised conversation and lovemaking, and I could pretend I wouldn't be absolutely devastated when he moved on. But this *dissection* Gunner performed with his eyes, a mere once-over that gleaned far more than my simple desire to be touched by him, it presented unparalleled danger that I simply didn't have the emotional and mental tools to handle. He could see my lies. Perhaps he hadn't ascertained the why, but he could still see each and every one of them, thriving in the blackness I called my soul.

I passed a hand over my eyes.

"I'm not asking for you to explain."

"You want to know."

"Of course I do." Gunner brushed my hand away and wiped my cheeks with his thumbs. "But I won't take anything you won't willingly part with."

"Thank you," I finally said, staring at my shoes. "For intervening with Moore."

"You're welcome."

"You must think me such a hypocrite."

"Why's that?"

I snorted and raised my head. "I was so cross with you in Arizona."

Gunner looked—if anything—perplexed.

"I called you a criminal."

"I am a criminal."

"I judged your behavior as if I were morally superior."

"Show me a lawman who doesn't."

"I made you share your name with me, and I can't—"

Gunner smiled at that. Quick. There and gone, like usual. "No one *makes* me do anything, remember? Not even you, Gillian. No, don't protest to the contrary. You have my name because I wanted you to. I'm not keeping score. We all have secrets. Even handsome and charming special agents. I don't think you're a hypocrite. But I do think you're struggling with the truth that you've, perhaps, been straddling a gray line for a very long time."

"I can't be a lawman—*a good man*—if I'm not black-and-white."

Gunner cupped my face so gently, so tenderly, it nearly undid me. "I disagree."

I struggled to swallow the upheaval of emotions lodged in my throat.

"Tell me this one thing: do you lie for the pleasure, or for survival?"

I startled and met Gunner's gaze. Of course he'd somehow hyperfocused on the one word that'd become my life's mantra: *survive*. I cleared my throat and said, "For survival."

"Then if it protects you to avoid the truth about how you sensed that magic, I will lie as well." Gunner kissed me again and let go. "Don't guilt yourself for being alive."

I nodded weakly, took a deep breath, and put my bowler on. I wanted—needed—to say something, but Gunner was already at the door. He opened it, was briefly outlined by the dirty orange security lamp, then vanished into the dark of night.

VII

December 31, 1881

Laughter, the drunk and carefree sort, greeted me at the landing of the fourth floor. I crossed an empty hall and entered the half-sized bullpen situated outside the room of cells for our *select* criminals. The desks were empty, save for the four agents—two casters and their bruiser counterparts—congregating around the furniture closest to the open door to the jail. Agent Rachel Plunket was a trouser-wearing, axe-wielding woman, who defied society's expectations of femininity by chopping her glossy black hair to chin-length and pairing the look with, what was considered by *The Delineator*, a too-bright rouge to her lips and cheeks. She hiccupped as she swallowed a laugh, then lightly smacked the chest of her male partner—Henry Bligh, himself.

When the tread of my steps penetrated their celebratory conversation, the group turned and immediately fell quiet.

Bligh, who sat on the edge of a desk, shifted like he made to stand in the presence of a senior agent, but then realized it was only me and he settled in like he would do no such thing.

"Agent Hamilton?" he asked, a touch of surprise in his tone. "What're you…?"

Coat pushed back, I dug my hands into my trouser pockets and walked through the row of desks. I said nothing to the group, kept my eyes straight ahead, and counted each step toward the jail.

—five, six, seven—

"Agent Hubris, you mean," the other caster corrected before the group struggled to stifle their champagne-induced giggles.

I stumbled, paused, but then kept moving toward the jail.

—eight, nine, ten—

I stepped past the group, Bligh raised his fist, drunkenly coughed, and said under his breath, "Sodomite."

I stopped. Turned.

—ten, nine, eight—

I sidled up to the group, my hands still in my pockets. "I'm sorry, I missed that last comment." I never acknowledged the crude, cruel comments Bligh spoke behind my back, but let's just say that the day's events had left me eating vinegar with a fork, and if there was one aspect of this shitstorm I could control… I prayed it could be this moment.

"You heard it," Bligh countered as he rose to his full height and looked down at me.

I removed my hands from my pockets.

The other three agents behind Bligh shifted uncomfortably.

"I heard you were on prisoner watch?" I looked Bligh up and down, glanced at the empty champagne bottles on the desk, then back to his twisted expression. "It's no wonder Fishback ended up dead."

Bligh's face grew red beyond the alcohol's blush, and he made a fist, lightning sparks snapping and colliding around his knuckles. He took a swing at me, too wide, and stumbled as I side-stepped the attack. "You goddamn fairy—"

Lightning illuminated the eastern windows, and a crack of thunder boomed over the city. Bligh regained his footing in time to study the change in weather that was most certainly *not* caused by his paltry skills. I extended my arm, palm out, and cast a spell I hadn't utilized in a long time—gravity. If it was cast with just the right amount of care, a layman would mistake it for a brutal dose of wind magic. Bligh flew backward and slammed into the far wall. The other agents let out a commotion of gasps, calls to stop fighting, warnings that Moore was in the stairwell, but I didn't care.

The stress of the night was bringing sounds to the forefront of my memory. Sounds that I worked so hard to keep under lock and key. The *snap* of my fingers being broken. The brutal *banging* of soldiers at the front door. And the bodies. The *screaming* of young men, crying for their mamas. Limbs blown off, guts hanging out, begging until their very last breaths. Those sounds haunted me. They ate with me, drank with me. They slept with me, and now, they made love with me. Every single goddamn day, they were there, lurking, hoping to catch me in a moment of weakness. And tonight, when I had no stamina left to tamp down the *snap*, the *bang*, the *screams*, Bligh had to rub my last bit of patience as raw as the nerves in my hands.

Gunner had said nothing changes in life until our own attitudes do. And on a conceptual level, I understood this. I agreed with it, even. But he had no idea how deep the depravity went within me. I believed in the law. I believed in my badge. I wanted to be a good man. But there was no atonement grand enough for the life I'd lived. All I could do was lie, survive, and die.

But before I spent eternity smiling at daisy roots, I was going to put Henry Bligh in his place. Damn the consequences. I didn't deserve to feel the happiness that'd been bubbling in my gut earlier for any sort of considerable length, but Christ

Almighty, how much abuse was I expected to endure when I was already a dead man walking?

All I had wanted was a *single evening* with Gunner.

I walked to the wall, still holding my palm out, watching Bligh struggle with all his body mass to wriggle free from the invisible density holding him in place. He looked like a fly squashed with a rolled-up newspaper, and I admit I enjoyed the shock in his expression. I twisted my hand slightly and Bligh rose off his feet, just enough that he gagged from the pressure on his chest.

I drew closer still, so he could hear me whisper, "If you so much as look at me from across a bullpen for the rest of your career, I will make you regret having eyes, Bligh."

He kicked his feet and wheezed.

"Do you understand me?"

He tried to nod. It didn't work.

"Bligh?"

"Y-*yes*!"

I twisted my hand farther and Bligh was raised higher up the wall.

The panic in his eyes was unmistakable now.

"It's Moore," Plunket hissed from the doorway near the stairs, where she and the other two had moved, leaving her partner to defend himself against me.

"Do not ever call me a sodomite again." I lowered my hand enough that Bligh's toes touched the floor.

He coughed, gasped, choked out, "I-I won't."

I dropped my hand, and Bligh fell to the floor like a brick wall had collapsed in on itself.

Moore's distinct tread entered from the hall at my back just then, and a hush fell over the room. "What's going on?"

Still staring at Bligh, who pressed a hand to his chest as

he fought to catch his breath, I said, "Bligh had too much to drink." Then I walked into the jail as Moore told the remaining agents to clear out.

The now-empty cell that'd housed a sniveling Fishback only a few hours ago was scorched black. The leftover remnants of the manufactured magic were popping in and out of my visual field. There was that same digging and burrowing sensation as in the basement, but second by second, minute by minute, it was dissipating. The problem was still that gaping wound I could feel in the magic atmosphere. And this manufactured spell, finally dissolving, was creating a sort of tangible barrier, resting just below the raw magic like a pollutant.

The narrow hall Moore and I had stood in while interrogating Fishback was littered with broken glass from the window on my right. I tugged my trousers up a bit, took a big step over the mess, spun on a heel, and crouched to examine the window fragments at an angle.

I felt Moore's magic as he moved to stand in the threshold.

"Bligh was drinking on the clock," I stated.

"So it would appear."

"His ineptitude amazes me. Fishback looks like the sort of corned beef dinner I'd cook."

"Don't exactly know your way around a kitchen, do you?"

"I prefer restaurants."

"Bligh will be dealt with for his indiscretion," Moore concluded. "What's wrong?"

"I think this window was broken from the inside." I stood. "This isn't the correct trajectory for the break to have come from outside. It looks—staged." I glanced up.

Moore's expression had sharpened like steel, but despite the control on the surface, there was a raging firestorm of magic just under his skin. "I don't like what you're suggesting, Hamilton."

"I'm suggesting nothing, sir. I'm stating the facts as I see them." I pointed at the mess on the floor. "This isn't how broken glass would fall if the window was smashed from the outside. This is like someone collected the pieces off the sill and threw them on the floor." I directed my attention to the open window, but nearly dropped dead from apoplexy when I was staring at Gunner squatted in the frame. "Gunner!"

"Hamilton."

"What the hell are you—how did—?"

"You did want to know if a break-in four stories up was plausible, did you not?" Gunner's gaze cut to Moore. "Your security leaves much to be desired, Director."

Moore crossed his big arms over his chest. "How'd you do it?"

Gunner raised a single eyebrow. He leaned backward, reached for something out of view, and yanked a chain into the open window. "Steam pneumatic grappling hook."

"Do you have a permit for that?" Moore countered. His tone indicated he knew Gunner did not and he was merely proving a point by asking.

Gunner said, "I don't utilize such novelties."

"You fancy yourself an old-school second-story man?"

Gunner's mouth twitched, but then he looked at me while saying, "I followed a set of tracks along this side of the building. I lost the trail after a block—snow covered them. But there was a turned-over trash can with this hook inside."

"So why the broken window?" Moore asked. He stroked his beard. "Insult to injury?"

"If the intruder smashed it before leaving, they'd have undoubtedly stepped on the shards on the sill while climbing back out. But those aren't cracked, nor are they wet from shoe treads," I explained before shrugging. "Perhaps Bligh or Plunket broke it after the fact to dissipate the smoke."

Moore grunted at the suggestion but nodded. "I've not had the opportunity to get the full story from either of them yet, but I'll be certain to get confirmation about the window."

I glanced at Gunner. He was still watching me. Behind him, it'd appeared the inclement weather had finally come to a stop. "The snowfall's let up," I stated, breaking the quiet. "I ought to find Addison while there's still a chance. Before the fireworks, and the entire city is one big party."

At that, Gunner shifted in his crouched position. "A sensible plan." He stood and, still holding the grappling hook's chain, moved to a ledge on the right, just out of view.

"Wait," Moore murmured, putting a hand up to keep me where I stood. He glanced at the open window before asking, "Is this real, Gillian?"

A flush broke out across my body, like pinpricks of starlight under my arms, across my chest, up my neck. Moore had never crossed this boundary with names. Not once in a decade of working together, not earlier tonight when he tried to surprise me with a gift, not even during the fiasco at my apartment. I was Special Agent Hamilton and he was Director Moore—*always*.

"He's a wanted man," Moore said to my silence. "A murderer."

"A vigilante is perhaps more accurate." I hastened to cut Moore off when he opened his mouth to protest. "Sir, what I said before, about not defending his past, that was the truth. But it's also true that I would be dead if not for his intervention in Shallow Grave."

"Transient affections will make you cynical toward true love."

I smiled, a bit bitterly, brokenly. "I'm already quite cynical, and without Gunner's help."

"No. You're pure-hearted and he doesn't deserve you."

"Sir—"

"It can't last. You know that, don't you?"

"Yes."

"When he's gone, and he will be, I'll still be here."

I shook my head, opened my mouth to speak, but the moment was so beyond my comprehension that I felt I couldn't recall a single word in the English language. Falling into a sky of a million paper lanterns that turned out to be jellyfish swimming in a night that the sun forgot to awaken seemed to make more sense than this conversation did.

"Think about it," Moore hastened to add, taking a few steps forward, glass crunching underfoot as he paid it no mind. He reached out, and the tips of his fingers touched my hair as I moved away from him entering my personal space. "I'd move Heaven and Earth to hold you every night." Then, the danger of our magics be damned, Moore leaned down and made as if he were going to kiss me then and there.

Yours,

Constantine G.

I felt like I'd been punched in the solar plexus. I gasped and blinked back the wet in my eyes. The words were finally there: "Loren, stop."

Moore froze, midway to my mouth.

"I can't explain it, just like you won't understand it. Until Gunner moves on... no."

"Gillian—"

"I'm so sorry."

Moore let out a huff of air, like a steam mechanic in need of repair. His shoulders dipped a bit, and then he shifted to one side and pressed his lips lightly against my cheek. The rasp of his beard felt incredible, followed by the minor discomfort of our magics interacting—a nip of electricity, the heat of fire.

An involuntary shudder went through my body.

He pulled back and straightened to his full height. "Be careful—with Addison."

"I can handle Addison."

Moore smiled, but it didn't reach his eyes. "I know you can."

I considered apologizing again, but an instinct I didn't entirely understand told me no, that'd make it worse. So I did the only thing I could think of to salvage our relationship and my career—hoisted myself through the open window and climbed into the cold night.

Gunner stood ready at the ledge with the grappling hook. His eyes met mine. He knew. Whether he'd overheard our conversation, or this was simply another one of Gunner's moments where he deciphered a complex web of actions and emotions from a single muscle twitch in my face, I couldn't be certain. But really, what did it matter?

He knew.

How infatuated I was.

How desperate.

How preemptively heartbroken.

"My dear?"

But then Gunner said things like that—my dear. *His* dear. And I could pretend for a bit longer that whatever this was between us, it was beautiful and forever and there was no need to worry about the day I woke and he was gone.

I smiled. "Sorry about that."

Gunner spared me further embarrassment by not shifting his gaze to the window at my back. He instead held a hand out. "Need a lift?"

I leaned forward, studied the distance to the snow-covered street below, then answered, "I'll race you." And leaped off the ledge.

VIII

December 31, 1881

The Third Avenue El train came to a stop at Grand Street, the doors opened with the hiss and release of steam, and Gunner and I were greeted by the boisterous nightlife of a working class's entertainment district. I'd tried once again to convince Gunner to wait at my apartment, saying that I'd deal with Addison as quickly as possible before returning home, but he'd merely gathered his bearings on the street out front of the field office, pointed east, and asked if we needed to catch the Third or Second Avenue line.

Typical maddening behavior.

Gunner walked across the elevated platform, set his hands on the railing, and peered down at the street below. The train pulled away from Grand, propelled farther downtown toward Canal, and in its wake, the live music from neighboring clubs picked up and competed with one another. A woman was singing on the corner with a group of men catcalling in response, and drunken laughter spilled out of the front doors of saloons.

After a moment of surveying the neighborhood, he stated, "The Bowery has changed since I was last here." When he looked at me, Gunner had a wry smile on his face. "Are you catching flies, Gillian?"

I snapped my mouth shut.

"I've been to New York a time or two," he explained. "But it's lost a great deal of its charm. These two-bit street gangsters and the sorry excuse for a metropolitan police force."

I pulled back the lapels of my coats, unclasped my badge from my waistcoat, and pocketed it. "You said to Moore—at The Buchanan—"

"Yes, the only quality outlaws left in this city tend to be wanted by your office, and Loren Moore has been decent at his job. What are you doing?"

I glanced up. "Oh. I can't wear my badge around Addison." I realized there was a suggestion to that statement, blushed furiously, and quickly added, "I very much wish to keep my underground contacts alive and employed, is what I meant."

"I won't be upset."

"About what?"

Gunner's gaze shifted to something on my left. "These sorts of clubs weren't open when I was still working the East Coast," he said by way of answer.

"I've—only been a time or two. For a drink, mostly."

"Companionship."

I shook my head. "No, nothing like that. You really were my—*you know*. And I've not returned since Arizona."

"I imagine there's better quality beer to be had elsewhere."

"I wanted to be noticed," I mumbled.

Gunner reached into his coat and retrieved his package of Black Jack. Before sticking the gum in his mouth, he said quite simply, "You're impossible to miss."

I smiled at my shoes before raising my head. "Thank you." I motioned for Gunner to follow me to the platform stairs and said, once we reached street-level, "Addison is a performer in the neighborhood. He naturally picks up a great deal of gossip."

"Naturally."

"He'll sell that gossip to me for the right coin or favor."

"Hm-hm."

"And being so close to the Five Points, there's a lot of bluster from the Whyos and their competing gangs."

"Dancer."

"What's that?"

Gunner looked sideways at me. "He's a dancer, then? At one of these clubs?"

I let out a bark of a laugh before I could restrain myself. "Christ Almighty. No, not that sort of performer."

The snow on the sidewalk had been stomped down by evening crowds, creating a thick, sloppy slush that mingled with the mounds of frozen trash and steam piping along the curbs. Shops that were closed for the night pockmarked the neighborhood—their dark window fronts all but vanishing from sight under the shadows cast by the El overhead. In contrast, the blues and reds and greens of steam streetlamps competed with the warm tungsten yellow and orange of open saloons and clubs, washing the area in a grimy, manmade color that didn't exist in nature.

The Bowery had gone from upper-class respectability— the Astor family had invested money in the Bowery Theatre, for God's sake—to its current state just before the Great Rebellion, and had remained as such. Mulberry Bend was only half a dozen blocks away, so it was honestly only a matter of time before the street gangs infiltrated the neighborhood.

The Bowery Boys and Dead Rabbits were long gone, but the Whyos were the city's new gang headache, and those bastards ruled the Lower East Side with an iron fist. If you didn't fall into line, they sent the Fishback sort after you.

And despite my badge making me a target, I wouldn't be bullied into taking it off. Only when I came to the Bowery specifically to sniff out Addison did I remove it. If he were seen talking with a federal agent, he sure as hell wouldn't be working the area anymore, and I'd lose a very important, if irritating, point of contact. The only other time, of course, was when I'd visited the club in my off time. If one of the men traced me back to the Bureau… blackmailed me… had the upper hand on my tendencies….

I slowed as we approached a club at the corner of Bowery and Broome called Pilly's. It was ablaze with steam lamps and rowdy as all hell, with a placard outside the front door illustrating two bare-knuckle boxers. A dandy of a young man stood at the open door, calling out the night's entertainment to gentlemen in passing whose taste perhaps bordered on more, ah, *stereotypical masculinity*.

I sighed heavily when the pretty man glanced our way, smiled as bright as the lights of the club, and called, "Gentlemen! Don't let his lean build fool you—Dangerous O'Dea versus Monster McGrath. Tonight only. It's the fight of the year!"

"A mere few hours before 1882," I noted.

Dandy pinched his face in disapproval before refocusing his energy on Gunner. "You look like you appreciate a true man's man, sir. Five cent entrance."

"A steal," Gunner said flatly.

"Fighters are available for drinks after the show." He leaned forward, held a hand to the side of his mouth, and added in a loud, scandalous whisper, "Perhaps more."

"Who can turn down paying to ice a man's broken hand."

Dandy huffed and put his hands on his hips. "Do you two want to watch the fight or not?"

I reached into my trouser pocket and retrieved a dime. I set it in his outstretched hand and led the way inside. The hall smelled like wet wool, warm beer, and sweat. The combination of scents wasn't exactly pleasant, per se, but it did have a way of scratching at an itch deep behind my breastbone. Because, in truth, Pilly's had been the club I'd warily attended a few times before unfortunately meeting Addison and now visiting for the sole reason of dragging a nugget of intelligence from his smart mouth. I certainly didn't mind the more artsy establishments that existed on the Bowery, with singing and dancing and costumes, but I was rather susceptible to the whims of a half-naked, well-muscled man trying to impress with a pair of fists that'd seen a thing or two in their lifetime.

I glanced up at Gunner. He was taking in the atmosphere with his usual passive expression. The tables were filled with patrons—a majority of them men, but also a few handsome women in trousers and suits with their prettier partners—clearly looking for unique entertainment, just as I had been, my first time attending Pilly's. In the center of the room was a stage, elevated about two feet off the floor, with a beast of a man walking its perimeter, flexing his arms and chest and, in general, looking very pleased with himself and the attention he commanded from the audience.

Then the volume of the crowd swelled without warning—an obnoxious combination of cheers and boos—as a second fellow hoisted himself onto the stage. He wasn't quite as tall as Gunner, but sported the same lithe build—lean muscle, no fat. Where his pale complexion differed was the spattering of freckles, heavy across both shoulders, chest, arms, even his high cheekbones. His fiery red hair shone like a beacon under the lamplight. When he moved, it sometimes looked copper, other times blond. He wore black trousers with braces on his shoulders, but was otherwise bare-chested for the fight.

"Dangerous O'Dea?" Gunner asked, raising his voice enough to be heard over the audience.

"Better known as Addison O'Dea," I replied before pointing to his opponent, who looked as if he could eat Addison for a midday meal. "I suppose we'll have to wait until the Monster is done with him."

Gunner pushed back the folds of his coat in order to tuck his hands into his trouser pockets. "I hope he doesn't kill your fellow."

"Don't call him that."

"Your contact."

"Better."

Gunner lightly nudged my arm with his elbow, and I couldn't help but smile.

A referee stood in between Addison and Monster McGrath, gave them a moment to square off on each other, rile the audience, and then he called for the bare-knuckle match to begin. McGrath took an Irish fighting stance—arms out, fists curled, feet firmly planted on the floor. The man really was a behemoth. I had no doubt that one well-timed punch to the kidneys would leave Addison pissing blood for a week and losing the match. Which was well and fine for McGrath. The trouble was, McGrath needed to catch Addison. And when you're the smaller man, the scrapper up against impossible odds, I knew firsthand that there wasn't any room for gentlemen's rules.

Addison bounced on the balls of his feet, moving back and forth around McGrath as he searched for an opening. He tried for a jab at McGrath's side, but the bigger man's reach landed first on the counter, his fist slicing a deep cut into Addison's lower lip. Addison stumbled back a few steps, hand to his mouth as blood oozed from between his fingers.

Some of the audience cheered, others shouted in protest.

Before the referee had a chance to intervene, to order McGrath take the ring off his finger, Addison lunged. He gave McGrath a few blows to the gut before taking one himself that threw him off his feet. Addison landed hard, rolled to one side as McGrath ran at him, then stuck his leg out. McGrath flailed his arms for purchase before crashing to the stage, his gigantic frame shaking the structure as if he were testing its stability.

More shouting from the audience. More cheering. More bets being placed and more beer being poured.

McGrath got to his feet and let out a furious roar. Gone was the Irish fighting stance of waiting for an opening and making the hit count. He was blind rage and wounded masculinity—a dangerous combination. McGrath ran at Addison, pulled back his arm, ready to let a punch fly, but Addison slipped past his reach, dealt a blow to the left kidney, the right, kneed McGrath in the groin, then clocked him so hard in the jaw that had McGrath's head not been attached to his body, it'd have spun like a child's toy top.

McGrath's eyes rolled back, he staggered, and then he fell and didn't get back up.

The referee called the match as he raised Addison's hand in the air. "You saw it at Pilly's—Dangerous O'Dea has broken Monster McGrath's year-long winning streak!"

Addison was breathing hard, and both the blood on his face and sweat on his chest glistened in the glow of the steam-powered lamps. But despite the commotion all around him, I managed to catch his eye while politely clapping for his win. He nodded his head just once, enough to assure me he understood the reasoning of my presence, then climbed off the stage. Addison shook hands with a few patrons as he made for a side door marked Fighters Only. Other men were less subtle in their compliments, patting his bare chest, squeezing a bicep—one appeared to flat-out proposition him. Addison took that man by the nape, drew their foreheads together, said something that made them both smile, then disappeared through the door.

"What an interesting club," Gunner said at length. He was watching two men on stage help McGrath to his feet.

"You think so?"

"They have certainly simplified the process of meeting men."

"I suppose they have."

"Even cater to a very particular interest."

I cleared my throat. "There's something to be said for a well-built man." I looked up at Gunner again. He was staring at me. "You've been eyed up and down no fewer than half a dozen times since we entered."

He nodded a fraction, like he was already quite aware.

"And the man behind me at the bar intends to bring a beer to you."

Gunner's gaze flicked in that direction but didn't linger. "You're quite observant when the attention isn't focused on you."

Sweat prickled under my arms. I shrugged, trying to appear casual, but I'm sure I looked, if anything, manic. "Perhaps… territorial, is more correct."

That made the corners of Gunner's eyes crinkle. "It's rather too fish-in-a-barrel for me. I enjoy making eye contact with a man across a tavern. Getting that swell in your gut, like the ground has fallen out from under you."

I tried to swallow, but my throat was parched—dry like animal bones bleaching in the desert sun. "Like you've been pinned to the wall."

Gunner took one step closer to me. "And you realize you share a tendency."

"Now you've got to put it into words."

Another step. "When it's right, you don't need words."

Carefully preserved memories of Arizona began to come to life, like viewing still images through a zoetrope. But instead of a galloping horse, it was Gunner leaning over me, pressing me against the door. It was me kissing Gunner behind the saloon on Applejack Row. It was opening the folded receipt from Bartholomew Industries for the first time and realizing the gravity of his trust in me.

I needed to trust Gunner in return. No matter how small the gesture, I felt anything would help to convey how thankful I was for his brief presence in my life again. How happy he'd made me tonight, despite our intimate holiday having been turned upside down like a Gugelhupf cake on its head. And how… I wished that this night would lead to something more. Something official. God, call it what it was—a *courtship*.

I took the final step to close the space between us. My hands shook as I grabbed Gunner by the hips, a brazenly intimate gesture in a public place, the welcoming setting being beside the point, mind you. I had refused his touch on an empty street before and needed to make that right.

Gunner took off his hat, leaned down, and kissed my mouth. He was warm and alive and left a bite of licorice on my lips as he drew back. "What about these one million residents?"

"I'm sorry."

"You needn't apologize for them."

I fiddled with the button holding one of his braces in place. "We're relegated to locked gazes across a room and kisses behind saloons and touches only in a club like this *because* of society." I drew my hand up, thumb stuttering along the buttons of Gunner's waistcoat. "Someone ought to apologize for what they've done, since I see no indication they plan to make amends."

"I see."

"Besides," I added after a moment, trying desperately to

sound casual, "I needed the man at the bar to take his interest elsewhere."

Gunner looked in that direction before saying, "I'm not so certain you've convinced him."

"Really?" I turned, but Gunner took my hand, spun me around, and held my face as he kissed me again. And this was one of those kisses where he pressed his tongue into my mouth—so explicit, we should have been arrested on the spot.

Gunner gently let go of me and, while putting his bowler on, always at an angle, asked, "Where are you supposed to meet O'Dea?"

"Sorry?"

"Addison."

I blinked a few times and remembered myself. "Oh. Right." I glanced toward the Fighters Only room—door still closed—then motioned Gunner to follow me back out to the sidewalk. "Side exit."

Dandy stood at the open door, still hocking, although his angle had changed since the fight's conclusion. "Dangerous O'Dea knocks out Monster McGrath! That's right, you heard it here—sir, care to step aside—five cents, thank you. A scrappy Irish lad breaks the Monster's unbeatable streak just before the stroke of midnight!"

Gunner pulled his silver pocket watch from his waistcoat and consulted the time.

"Sir, care to meet the man who put the Monster on his backside? Freckles, yes, O'Dea—five cents. Thank you, sir."

I moved away from Pilly's entrance and rounded the corner on my left. Addison leaned against the brick wall of the club, the door to his left propped open by an empty brown bottle wedged into the crack. He wore a threadbare winter coat over his bare chest, sucked on the end of a cigarette, and absently massaged under the split in his lip.

"You need stitches," I said.

Addison glanced toward us before pushing off the wall. "*Oy*. What the fuck, Hamilton?"

"Here we go."

"I knocked the last bit of brain the Monster had right out of his skull."

"Hm-hm."

"You see it?"

"Yes."

"You hear that crowd?" he continued, jerking his head back to indicate the door left ajar.

"I do."

"They're wild for me. I'm going on a brannigan and getting properly fucked tonight."

I sighed.

Addison took a final drag from his cigarette before flicking the butt into a pool of slush at my feet. "I want my asshole to hurt more than my fucking face."

"Are you finished?"

"Just because you're more high-strung than the saints of Erin—"

"Blasphemy *and* poetics?"

"Go hifreann leat."

"I don't speak Irish." I put my goggles on, raised a hand, and cast an aether spell, the glow of magic causing Addison to wince. "And neither do you, beyond a few colorful phrases picked up in saloons." I took his chin with my free hand, gave Addison a not-so-gentle yank closer, and pressed the aether against the deep gash that was still bleeding.

Addison grumbled from the corner of his mouth not receiving treatment, "And whose fucking fault is it?"

"I don't want to have another discussion about your

mother, Addison."

"My *máthair*," he said with a hint of a sneer.

I gave his chin another firm shake before pulling my magic away. The tear of his flesh that would have undoubtedly scarred was nothing more than an irritated-looking paper cut now. The spell dissolved in my palm but still managed to rub the nerves the wrong way, and I hissed under my breath as my fingers involuntarily curled. Addison stepped around me in that split-second of preoccupation, and when I turned while tugging my goggles down, he'd broached Gunner's personal space in all the ways that made my blood boil.

"Aren't you a sweet thing," Addison said. "You Hamilton's partner? I thought the saint worked alone."

Gunner's face was as placid as ever. "No professional association."

"What about a private one?"

"Addison," I said sternly.

"Tell me your name," Addison continued without missing a beat.

"John Gaylord."

"Addison O'Dea. Dangerous O'Dea, they call me."

"I heard."

"But did you see?"

"For the love of—Addison," I tried again.

Gunner's mouth twitched. "I did see."

"And are you going to give me a story full of blarney, John? Like Hamilton does? Or you going to tell me you liked what you saw?" He pushed his open coat back, soliciting more than just appreciation from Gunner.

"Goddamn lobcock," I muttered, pinching the bridge of my nose.

"Mind your fuckin' tongue," Addison snapped, but he was

grinning as he took a step away from Gunner. "Hamilton's a small, ornery bastard. Repressed, I say. That's why he wears them high collars." He put a hand to his throat to imitate my dress choice, as if his decision to be half naked outside in December was more reasonable.

"I need everything you've got on Fishback," I said with contrived patience.

"Fat Frank?"

"For a fellow who was likely to disappear in the event that he turned sideways," Gunner said thoughtfully, "you New Yorkers really need to choose your monikers better."

Addison jutted a thumb at Gunner but asked me, "Who the fuck's this guy, throwing his fancy fifty-cent word around?"

"It's irony," I said to Gunner, ignoring Addison.

"I know what it is," he answered. "It's just very heavy-handed."

"You prefer obvious."

"No one can mistake your intentions with a clear and concise alias."

Addison had been looking between us, much like a shuttlecock punted back and forth across a badminton court. "It don't get better than *Dangerous O'Dea*," he proclaimed, trying to worm his way back into the conversation, before he caught sight of Gunner's holstered Waterbury when he reached into his coat for more Black Jack. "Oy. Hamilton wants gossip on Fishback—what he's hustling—and you got the nerve to carry a fuckin' Waterbury in his company?" Addison returned to Gunner and gave him a firm shove to the chest.

I tried to protest, but I hadn't even the chance to formulate a proper word of warning before Gunner had grabbed Addison's coat collar, slammed him against the opposite wall, and put the triple barrels of his pistol under the redhead's chin.

"What the fu—"

"How's Gunner the Deadly for concise?"

Addison's eyes were as big as saucers, and his Adam's apple bobbed as he stuttered, "Y-you're Gunner the Deadly?"

"That's what I said."

"But Gunner the Deadly ain't been seen in a city since '75."

"Is that so?" Gunner asked, voice still that husky-calm.

"*Dangerous* ain't enough for you, eh?" Addison asked, shooting me a quick glance. "I can punch harder… make it deadly—*oy*! It was a fuckin' joke!" he protested when Gunner dug the Waterbury into his throat.

"You have no sense of decorum," Gunner stated. He stepped back, spun the Waterbury, and holstered it in one fluid motion.

Addison huffed loudly as he adjusted the collar of his coat. "I ought to report you to the coppers. Hamilton, hear that? Gunner the Deadly used excessive force against me, an upstandin' citizen of this city."

"I'm not a copper, you can't file a formal complaint against an outlaw, and you are absolutely not an upstanding citizen. Tell me about Frank Fishback before I ask Gunner to shoot you instead."

Addison reached into his coat and retrieved another hand-rolled cigarette. "First, tell me why you're cheating on me," he countered, walking toward me. He shoved the cigarette between his lips and leaned down with a sort of expectancy about his person. "Is it because his picture is in the rogues' gallery?"

"*You're* in the rogues' gallery, Addison," I countered, snapping my fingers and bringing a flickering flame to the paper and tobacco. "Although for not nearly as notorious a reason. Gunner has had… a prior run-in with the situation here in New York. So we've agreed upon a truce while he aids my office."

Addison straightened and sucked in a lungful of smoke. He appeared to contemplate that half-truth for a moment, finally nodded, and said, "Fine. But he still roughed me up some."

"You liked it," Gunner answered a bit absently.

Addison smirked and reached down to cup himself through his trousers. "Aye, that's true." He took another drag before continuing. "Fat Frank was contracting his strong hands to the Whyos."

"Yes, until a few weeks ago."

"And the Whyos are mighty angry."

"Tell me why."

"Frank made them a good penny, you can imagine. All these lads runnin' amok—half of 'em ain't even Whyos. Just sucking the teat of Driscoll's name and his organization, yeah? And the rest—stealin' a drunkard's pocket watch or stabbing a pretty girl? Come on. But Frank made them good money. Money keeps them in power."

"Frank killed honest coppers walking the beat. Let's not forget that."

Addison held up both hands in defense. "I didn't say I liked what he did, Hamilton. Just that he made the Whyos money doing it. So then the bastard ups and leaves sometime in November. Some of the lads who come by Pilly's for fun, when Driscoll ain't watchin', I get them good and drunk and they tell me their troubles."

"And what are those troubles?" I prompted.

Addison raised his head and blew smoke into the cold night air. "A new gangster—goes by Tick Tock."

"Where's he located?"

Addison waved his hand in an arc, the ember of the

cigarette burning bright against the dark. "In the area."

"Five Points?"

"Aye. Somewhere around the Bend, I suspect."

His statement was confirmation that backed up my initial assessment of the fire magic I'd felt just outside The Buchanan—that the origin, although muddied and not exact, was somewhere in the Five Points. The worst of New York City's slums. The most dangerous neighborhood in all of Manhattan and operated by the Whyos.

"This Tick Tock," I began, "did he pay a fee to the Whyos—for setting up shop on their turf?"

"No, don't believe he has," Addison answered.

"What do you know about Black Bart?" Gunner asked suddenly. He made a point of taking his time while drawing out his gum package again and giving Addison another eyeful of his weapon.

"Who's that?" Addison asked.

"A thief," I answered. "Out in the territories. Robs Wells Fargo—airships." I said that last word slowly, as I digested my own statement.

Gunner made a sound under his breath.

"Friend of yours?" I continued.

He opened the package once or twice, then put it away without removing a stick of gum. "I robbed one of Wells Fargo's first airships, back in '73. There was twelve dollars and some legal documents for Montana's territorial governor, Benjamin Potts, in the strongbox."

Addison laughed and scuffed the cobblestone under his feet. "Tough luck."

"The second airship I robbed had a hundred pounds of gold bars destined for Denver." Gunner now had Addison's undivided attention. "By '75 I'd amassed something like ten thousand dollars."

Addison dropped his cigarette and moved toward Gunner. "You're rich?"

"He gives it all away, Addison. Don't try to slip a hand in his pockets," I said around a suppressed sigh.

"Give it away?" Addison echoed. "You fuckin' daft?"

Gunner's eyes narrowed. "My point is, an outlaw can't keep a lucrative territory to themselves for long, and neither can an urban gangster. The difference being that Black Bart has the decency to be a gentleman about it. He keeps to the California routes, never shoots teamsters, and never robs passengers. I don't believe the same can be said in this situation. Tick Tock has moved into the heart of the Whyos' neighborhood, hijacked one of their best men for his own purposes, and already sounds more organized in his money-making methods than these hoodlums."

Addison turned his attention on me again. "True enough. It was a week ago—Patrick Tuffey came 'round Pilly's spittin' mad. He's telling the lads he found Fishback in some shithole tenement, meeting with some kind of mechanical man. Patrick ain't never seen anything like it before—said his entire face was silver, had some kind of gun attached to his shoulder. So Patrick keeps watch, right? Fishback leaves empty-handed, and this abomination comes out with a big case that's been traded off. And then, *fuck Patrick sideways*, guess who's been keepin' watch and meets the mechanical man?"

"Whyos," Gunner answered.

Addison looked surprised but nodded. "Right."

"So some members are double-dealing?" I asked. "Working for Driscoll and Tick Tock?"

"Aye, sure looks to be the case."

"Has Driscoll dealt with them?"

"They ain't been seen since that night. Patrick, he didn't go after them. Figured they'd resurface in a day, pretendin' nothing's amiss. He told Driscoll instead. Says Driscoll nearly shot him for not handlin' the situation then and there."

"That's why Patrick showed up angry," I concluded.

"Aye. I tended to his needs, if you understand me, but he weren't much more pleasant after."

"Addison," I began, digging out my wallet and passing him several folded bills. "I have evidence that this package is likely a combination of illegal ammunition and custom-built weapons from the scraps of Jordans and Waterburys."

"Magic?" he asked, tucking the money into his trouser pocket.

I nodded and said, "I need to know where the parts are coming from, so I can trace Tick Tock's entire enterprise before it grows too large to contain."

Addison puffed his cheeks as he expelled a long breath. "This is dangerous, Hamilton."

"Then this should be right up your alley," Gunner remarked.

Addison reluctantly grinned at that. "It won't be coming from the Whyos. Dig deeper than the surface violence—look to the architects."

"*Who*?" I pressed. "Every year we arrest unregistered architects dabbling in illegal magic. There can't be many left in the city."

A whistle screeched overhead, and the three of us looked to the heavens as the sky erupted in fiery blossoms that could have shamed the summer flowers of Madison Square Park. Strontium red and barium green and sodium yellow illuminated the sky. Hours before the clock struck midnight and already city pyrotechnicians were giving Independence Day something to be jealous of—and over the slums and Bowery, no less.

"I heard a name worth remembering," Addison said

over the boom and crackle. He looked down at me briefly, his face highlighted in a kaleidoscope of colors. "He ain't local, though. Out in San Francisco is what they say. Goes by Weaver. I'd be looking at shipments coming into Pier 17, Hamilton."

Then, an explosion like nothing I'd experienced since cannon fire during the war shook the ground beneath our feet.

IX

December 31, 1881

The fireworks were still erupting overhead, but their celebratory detonations were completely silenced by this unrelated blast. Another shrill whistle cut through the crash—not that of a firework soaring into the sky; this was metallic—a patrolman in distress.

"What the fuck was that?" Addison shouted, his hands over his ears. He looked toward the street corner where several pedestrians were watching something out of our line of sight to the south.

The whistle kept shrieking.

My arms and chest pimpled with painful gooseflesh before a sudden, sickening heat broke out across my entire body. The world was reduced to a low static hum deep in my ears, and my hands cramped and my fingers curled into unintentional fists as an excessive sum of manufactured magic in the atmosphere attacked my already-damaged nerves. My vision tunneled, but I managed to stumble backward and was sick into a pile of rubbish heaped against the brick façade of

Pilly's. My body was sweaty and clammy, and my arm shook as I wiped my mouth on the sleeve of my coat.

"Hamilton?"

Addison's voice was barely audible at first. But one at a time, each sense came back to me, like convalescing after a bout of influenza. The heat dissipated from my skin, my vision cleared, and the roar of fire filled my ears.

"*Hamilton*?" Addison called again, and this time his hand landed heavily on my shoulder.

I shook his touch off, turned, and ordered, "Get back inside."

He hesitated, glanced at Gunner, then nodded and yanked the door open. He kicked the bottle that'd left it ajar as he entered, and the glass skittered across the frozen cobblestones in his wake.

I turned to see that Gunner had already unholstered his Waterbury and had his body angled to the street, but was staring at me. "I'm fine," I said before rushing past him and returning to the corner of Bowery and Broome. Two blocks south on Hester Street, a mushroom cloud of black smoke swelled from what I suspected was a warehouse. The yellow and orange of a raging inferno illuminated the skyline.

"Firework gone astray?" Gunner suggested over the growing commotion.

"Whatever the cause, I think we just found where Tick Tock's been storing his ammunition packages."

I broke into a run before another minute was wasted on talk and no action. I raced down the Bowery, working against the crowds moving away from the fire, shouting for onlookers to clear a path, and identifying myself as law enforcement. The heat of the fire could be felt even on the northern end of Hester—in fact, it pulled me up short, and I heard Gunner come up behind me as I studied a four-story building burning like Hell on Earth. The flames were huge, leaping from broken windows and the rooftop, licking at the El tracks that ran down the Bowery, and putting the system's structural integrity into immediate danger. The crank sirens of fire department water tankers wailed from the east, but even with a dozen leather hoses, those boys were about to learn the hard lesson of how ineffective plain old water was against magic-induced fire.

I raised both hands to cast just as a figure came tumbling out the front door. I hadn't recognized him at first, what with the copious blood and bruises, but I'd been studying rogues' gallery photos for years. Recognition was inevitable.

"Tuffey?" I called over the thunder of destruction.

Patrick Tuffey stumbled toward me. I don't think he knew who I was, knew I was a federal agent. I don't think he cared. He reached his arms toward me and shouted, "What he done to those lads—it's like playin' God. It's all magic in there. I only wanted to bankrupt Tick—" A shot rang out from the warehouse, and then there was a hole in the middle of Tuffey's chest.

"Tuffey!" I lunged forward and grabbed under his arms as his eyes rolled back and he dropped to his knees. "Hang on—what's happened? Is it about the Whyos double-dealing? Tuffey? *Tuffey*. Goddamn it." I eased into a crouch and laid the lifeless body on the ground.

"Gillian," Gunner prompted.

There was something in his voice—nothing overtly obvious of course, and not any one emotion either. But it was a curious combination of something like doubt and wariness in Gunner's tone, and it was different enough from everything I knew about him that I quickly directed my attention to the warehouse as I stood.

Standing just outside the entrance, flames ripping and tearing at the threshold behind him, was a beast of a man. He was easily Gunner's six feet, but built far wider and stockier than my favorite outlaw, with the ten barrels of a Gatling gun resting on his left shoulder. I belatedly realized the glinting orange glow on his face wasn't merely illumination from the fire, but a reflection on a smooth, polished surface.

Silver.

His entire face was made out of silver.

"Special Agent Gillian Hamilton," I announced as he approached. "Federal Bureau of Magic and Steam."

Gatling Man took another heavy step.

"I'm placing you under arrest for the murder of Patrick Tuffey and for transporting with intent to distribute illegal magic firearms and ammunition."

Another step.

"Stop where you are," I demanded.

Gunner cocked his Waterbury.

I held one palm toward the sky, and electricity zapped and crackled in the air around us.

Gatling Man kept lumbering forward. He raised his left arm up, a motion that mimicked having to reach for the rung of a ladder, but instead, the Gatling gun activated with the movement and the barrels swiveled to point directly at us.

"Christ Almighty," I whispered.

Then Gunner and I dodged in opposite directions as the man brought his arm down and the gun opened fire. The heat of fire ammunition scorched the air at chest-level just as I threw myself to the road. The bullet hit the streetlamp to my right, sent it up in immediate flames, and the glass globe burst from the heat, raining shards down over me.

I raised my head and looked toward the cross streets in time to see Gunner roll to one knee, take aim, and fire. The round from the Waterbury hit Gatling Man square in the chest and he stumbled back a step, but unlike before with Mechanical Man, there was no blood. Gunner fired a second round, then ran for the cover of a parked automobile when the gunfire was returned.

I got to my feet and pulled my goggles on. That monstrosity was clearly reinforced with silver underneath his clothing, otherwise two aether rounds would have sent him to his knees. Silver as an element held up inherently well against aether magic, which had been why Milo Ferguson's locomotive was built with it. Silver had a high melting point, which kept the machine intact, but most importantly, it put Gunner at a distinct disadvantage. I'd been able to melt through the silver and iron hull of the locomotive with time and concentrated spell-casting, but this situation was different. Because silver on its own—and looking no thicker than an extra layer of skin—was an *extremely* conductive element. This man was built to withstand the intense heat of the magic ammunition he was volleying at us, but not lightning.

I raised one arm up, hand extended toward the sky. Clouds rolled in over the Lower East Side, and thunder rattled my bones. I tempered the million volts of lightning, because I wanted this bastard alive, and when the crash of energy came down from the storm, I hurled the blinding lightning at Gatling Man. The electricity ballooned around our assailant as it came into contact with his fire ammunition. I pumped a bit more magic into the spell, just enough that it overtook the manufactured elements, cocooned him in a brilliant yellow glow, then threw him right off his feet, skidding along the road. The Gatling gun bumped and banged against the cobblestones, shooting wildly into the sky before his body came to an abrupt stop.

A beat copper ran into the cross streets from the east, still blowing his whistle.

I let the spell go and reached into my coat to hold up the badge I'd removed earlier. "Magic and Steam!"

"The fire department is on the way," he called back, red in the face from both the cold and incessant whistling. "One of the tankers got stuck in the snow."

Steel screeched overhead—the El tracks were now completely enveloped in flames.

I pointed north toward Grand Street and said, "Get to the platform—stop the trains."

"But the fire department—"

"They can see the flames from goddamn Tammany Hall," I retorted. "Go—*now*."

The copper nodded as if his head were bobbing from a string, and raced toward the staircases on Grand. He was blowing his whistle the entire way.

Gunner was shooting again, and I spun in time to watch a gangster, pistol in his outstretched hand pointed at my back, drop the weapon, blood trickle from triple shot in the middle of his forehead, then collapse face-first in the road. More shooting rang out from south of us, and Gunner ducked behind the automobile and returned fire. A second gangster with heavily bandaged hands was stooped beside Gatling Man, helping the abomination to his feet. I recognized him from my earlier jaunt in the neighborhood when I'd been chasing Fishback. That felt like so long ago and not a mere few hours.

"McCarthy!" I raised both hands, palms out, and they began to glow and snap with electricity. "Stop right now, or you won't have any hands left to bandage when I'm done with you."

McCarthy got his shoulder under Gatling Man's arm, whose face was cracked and caked in black soot from the lightning, then looked toward me. "This means war, magic pig."

Thousands of pounds of steel groaned overhead, then the split and wrench of tracks and steam pneumatics came crashing down. The destruction of the El was practically on top of me in the time it took to acknowledge my inevitable fate. There wasn't a chance to slow the moment down and react logically. No. There was only the animalistic drive to survive—a very rabid thing I kept deep inside, tucked away in that blackness I carried, a shroud of shame around my soul. Gunner had taken a candlestick to that darkness, shined a light on everything gross about my person. He had seen, without understanding, some of my worst disgrace. I needed to trust he would be sympathetic when I explained it all, but that violence scared me.

And now—it was awake within me again.

I snapped my left hand in a quick, circular motion, whipping a squall of wind upward while bringing my right up as if to hold a tangible item over my head. The wind and gravity magic wove together, caught the plummeting framework midair, and was held suspended overhead. The cobblestones beneath my feet cracked and broke as the weight of the tracks competed with the gravity spell. I screamed—a sort of incoherent, wordless rage—and sent the debris flying. It landed a dozen feet away in the middle of the road.

I spun toward the warehouse, the wind still thrashing around me like a standstill tornado. McCarthy and Gatling Man were gone. I snapped again, and a heavy blackness rolled over the night sky that could send shadows scurrying for safety. Thunder boomed and rumbled, and then a torrent of rain fell over Hester Street. The wind was still spinning, churning the flames, spiraling them up and up, out of the warehouse and into the clouds. The clash of this manufactured magic—wild and unregulated, without the custom weapons or curious mechanical men to maintain the levels—was like being kicked through a wall by cannon fire.

My hands glowed blue with the water spell. I dipped more aggressively into the stream of raw magic, tearing fistfuls of energy from the atmosphere and pouring my own lifeforce back into it as the rain pelted the cyclone of fire harder—harder—the last of the flames finally pulled from the blackened husk of the warehouse and overtaken by the storm raging in the sky. The scars that crisscrossed my palms pulsated with the beat of my heart while the rest of my body began to tingle as if I'd fallen asleep in a horribly convoluted position.

It's happening again.

I reached a final time for the current of magic around me, gathered those glittering tendrils, wove them together, built them bigger, until I had an aether spell over three feet in diameter. The blinding-white energy washed over the neighborhood, illuminating nooks and cervices that'd maybe not seen light for the last decade, and then I hurled it into the sky. The aether tore through the wind, the rain, the clouds, swallowed the fire, and then everything ceased.

Stillness.

Silence.

And then I passed out.

$$\maltese$$

January 1, 1882

The first time I awoke, it was to a foreign space. Not that I had actually opened my eyes, but everything felt off. The ceiling was too low, the walls too close, the cold air leaching in through the window was on the left instead of right. I asked where I was—at least, that was my intention, but the words felt garbled and slurred in my mouth. I wasn't even certain they were understood, so I tried again.

An ice-cold cloth was pressed to my forehead and cheekbones, and the shock of it made me wonder if I'd come down with a sudden fever. Even this touch was alien. Gentle in the sense of… feminine delicacy. Not the sort of gentle roughness of a man that I'd recently become acquainted with. And the scent. Lavender and citrus, but not Sandringham. Too lemony. Too clean. Too bright a base.

I wasn't at The Buchanan and this wasn't Gunner. But before I could ask again where I was, before I could open my eyes and see who this was, I sank deeper into the bedding and a galaxy of a million stars swallowed me whole.

Like counting knots in the beams overhead.

Good night, Special Agent Hamilton.

"Jesus goddamn Christ."

There was a low chuckle to my right. Warm and husky and familiar. "Mind your manners, Hamilton."

I opened my eyes and struggled to sit up in a bed not my own. My head was pounding, and the pulse behind my left eye felt as if the thing were about to rupture. I rubbed hard enough to create black spots in my vision, then belatedly took in the state of my partial undress. No suit coat, waistcoat, tie—cuffs and collar were gone too. The first few buttons of my shirt had been undone.

I peered to my right to see Gunner in a wooden chair, his posture relaxed despite what looked to be a terribly uncomfortable seat. He'd also ditched his suit coat and had rolled back the sleeves of his shirt to advertise the cords of muscle in his forearms. Beside him stood a woman, perhaps my age. She wore a dress decidedly middle class—a pretty thing of mauve, with a bit of ruffle around the middle and buttons all the way up to her lace collar, but it was, despite its festive color, a practical piece of wardrobe. Her hair was coiled and pinned in place atop her head, bringing focus to her brown eyes and the dusting of freckles across the bridge of her nose.

I hastily pulled the front of my shirt closed, then remembered the bite mark Gunner had left on my neck and plastered a hand over it. "Where am I?"

"Ms. Zelda's Home for Wayward Agents," Gunner answered.

I blinked a few times. "Did you just tell a joke?"

His mouth twitched as he crossed his legs.

Ms. Zelda, I presumed, smiled sweetly. "You overtaxed yourself, Agent Hamilton." She moved to the table beside the bed, where a glass of amber liquid and a bowl of what looked like breakfast cereal sat, then picked up a hand mirror. She offered it and discreetly touched the hair at her own temple.

I took the mirror, raised it, and swore. *"Damn it."* I brushed a fresh streak of steel gray hair back and tried to comb it underneath the brown with my fingers. It didn't work. "Pardon my language, ma'am."

"That's quite okay, sir. This very thing happened a time or two to my brother."

I raised my brows as she took the mirror and set it aside. "Your brother is a caster?"

"Was," she said with another smile, but this one was hollow. "He passed in the war."

I could barely catch my breath at her words, like they'd punched me in the chest and left me gasping with bruised and broken ribs. "I—I'm so sorry."

She inclined her head in that polite way one does about such subjects, then motioned to the table again. "A hearty meal and a bit of brandy will right you."

"Thank you."

Gunner stood and opened the door as Zelda turned to leave. She requested he send for her if anything was needed, to which Gunner agreed, and after she lingered, blushed, and hastily saw herself out, he gently shut and locked the door.

"It's your arms," I stated.

"I know."

"You're going to cause an innocent woman to faint."

"I'll take my chances."

I picked up the bowl of cereal, stirred the contents without enthusiasm, and looked at Gunner again. "Why's that?"

"Because you enjoy looking too." He inclined his head at

the bowl and said while walking across the room, "Eat your breakfast."

"It's morning?" I asked before taking a bite.

Gunner pulled back the curtain at the window and early-morning sunlight seeped into the little room. "You slept through the fireworks."

I grunted.

"And our New Year's kiss."

"This tastes like wallpaper."

"Connoisseur of arsenic and lead, are you?"

I raised my head. "What?"

Gunner approached the bed, leaned down, took my chin, and kissed my mouth. His stubble tugged lightly against my own and sent a pleasant shiver through my body. "For auld lang syne, my dear."

I smiled and leaned up for a second kiss. "Happy New Year." As I pulled back and studied Gunner's face, I noted that exhaustion was visible in the cracks of his porcelain expression. "Have you not slept?"

Gunner straightened his posture, his hand still on my jaw, thumb rubbing my whiskers. "We need to talk about what happened last night."

"Lie down with me?" I asked, but it came out like a whisper.

Gunner nodded, circled the foot of the bed, and brought his abandoned chair to the door. He wedged the back under the knob, knelt to unbutton his shoes, and then took the bowl from my lap and set it on the table. Gunner offered the brandy, which I choked back in one swallow, and then he climbed into the too-small-for-two bed.

We both lay on our side, staring at each other. I reached a hand out, tentatively slid my fingers between Gunner's, and brought his hand to my neck. He caressed for a moment, the gritty roughness of his calluses against the bite causing my prick to stiffen. Then Gunner brought his hand up and fingered the new gray hair at my forehead.

"Mama's side of the family."

I swallowed hard and said, "I lied."

"I know."

"To survive."

Gunner simply stared at me.

"How can anybody be so perceptive?"

"You'd rather I wasn't?"

"I didn't say that," I replied. "I just… don't understand how you can see what no one else ever has."

Gunner threaded his fingers through my hair, his hand eventually settling on the back of my head. "We've both lived lives, Gillian. Mine made me an observer. Whatever you lived, it made you a survivor."

A survivor.

I closed my eyes and pinched the bridge of my nose. "Sounds pathetic."

"Survival is anything but." Gunner's fingers started playing with my hair once more. "I want to understand the magic you used last night. That's all."

I pulled my hand away from my face but didn't look at Gunner.

"I've no qualms with pointing a Waterbury at a tanker and demanding a ride to a decent lodge outside of the Five Points—"

My eyes snapped open. "You didn't."

"I certainly wasn't going to carry you for a dozen blocks."

"Gunner—"

"This wasn't anything like what happened in Arizona, Gillian. You were unresponsive the entire night. What would have happened if you'd been alone—left face-first in the middle of the road on the goddamn Bowery?" Gunner's voice hadn't risen, but his tone had become frighteningly emotional. "Best case, you'd have been robbed. Worst case, fucked and probably killed." Gunner removed his hand from my head, rolled onto his back, and sat up. He swung his legs over the edge, set his feet on the floor, and stood.

I quickly followed his movements, but had to stop with my legs hanging off the side of the mattress as a wave of dizziness overcame me. I studied Gunner's back—the rigid posture and firm line of shoulders. He put his hands on his slender hips and paced to the door. "Are you mad?"

Gunner made a quick about-face in his stocking feet. "I'm worried," he corrected. "When I look at you, Gillian, I see an intensely private man, and I can respect those boundaries. But I also see heartache and shame and despair. And I see you using these long-ago-obtained sentiments to control the life you have now."

"Are you done?"

"No." Gunner returned to the bed, looking down at me. "I see a man who is terrified of himself. Of his magic—"

"I am not," I said while hastily getting to my feet.

"Of his tendencies—

"How dare you?"

"And of his feelings."

"You're goddamn full of it," I said, jabbing a finger into Gunner's chest.

He ignored that and finished with, "I see a man who's so desperate to keep surviving, he just lied to my face three times."

Something inside me blew. Like the gasket on a steam contraption. Suddenly it was spewing scalding-hot vapors, pressure gauges were going haywire, and the escaping steam was hissing like a demon deep in the pits of Hell.

I started laughing as I said, "You want me to say you're right? Fine. You are. About everything."

"Gillian, that's not the point."

"I'm New York State's only registered level five caster," I explained. "Level five because if the federal government found out I can test much higher, I'd disappear. So I lied to the FBMS. And I'm not a physically appealing man," I continued, thumping my chest. "I'm short. I'm small. I'm not handsome. And when a man isn't fucking Adonis," I said, motioning at Gunner as if to make my point all the more clear, "he becomes the butt of some very cruel jokes. So I deny my tendencies. But I just want to be loved *so badly*, Constantine. And every day I feel utterly ashamed of myself for it. I feel so gross for relishing the attention you show me, because my entire life, all I've heard is how terrible sodomites are. So I keep lying about *everything* because I don't know any other way to live."

The room had dimmed as clouds rolled across the morning sky. My face was wet with tears, but before I could raise a hand to wipe my cheeks, Gunner moved forward, wrapped his arms around me, and lifted me off my feet.

He hoisted me up enough that I could wrap my legs around his hips, and then he whispered in my ear, "You're loved, my dear."

XI

January 1, 1882

The lines around Gunner's eyes were more relaxed in sleep, but otherwise, his expression was remarkably unchanged. Still. Unperturbed. Maybe just a touch serene. Which I found incredible, considering what had transpired between us a few hours earlier.

But, I supposed, that was exactly the sort of person Gunner was.

He didn't hold a grudge. He wasn't easily hurt. And he didn't lie. He simply said what he felt was necessary, in that polite yet brutal way he had about himself, and that was it. Gunner had told me exactly how he felt, called me out on lies he considered worth acknowledging, and—

You're loved.

—and then he'd admitted something that I couldn't ever imagine saying with such frankness as Gunner had.

He'd set me on my feet after that, wiped my face dry, and told me he needed to sleep. I'd managed to rest a bit myself, but for at least an hour, I'd been fitfully tossing as I replayed the exchange over and over in my mind. I had no doubt that Gunner had been sincere in his declaration, but what exactly did it mean for us? And had he noticed that I hadn't… really admitted to anything?

At least, not the genesis of my troubles—past, current, and undoubtedly future.

"You're a very loud thinker," Gunner murmured.

I glanced at him. His eyes were still closed. "Sorry."

"What's wrong?"

"You don't already know?"

"Well, I haven't opened my eyes yet."

"You're a bit of a smart aleck."

Gunner smiled a little, and it was devastatingly handsome. He reached out, found my face, and stroked my jawline. "Are you upset?"

"Embarrassed," I corrected.

His eyes snapped open and zeroed in on me. "By what I said?"

"What? *No*. Heaven's no. That was…." I struggled for the correct response as Gunner remained silent and let me slowly hang myself. "Er… nice." *God save me*. "I meant me—my behavior."

Gunner said nothing as he studied me. I had to resist the desire to squirm as he picked me apart. After what was only a few seconds—but could have been a century, as far as I was concerned—he tugged me forward and rolled onto his back, the momentum forcing me to straddle his leg.

"Tell me one thing," he said, unbuttoning the rest of my shirt. "And don't lie to me. Anyone else, but not me." Gunner tugged the shirt free, tossed it aside, then did the same with my undergarment so he could splay his hands against my bare chest. "Understand?"

I didn't trust my voice, so I simply nodded.

Gunner's fingers danced along my ribs, lower still, until he could slip them into the waist of my trousers. "What level do you actually test at?"

"There's no way to be certain. The examination only goes to five."

"But high enough that it was necessary to intentionally botch your results for the FBMS?" Gunner popped the button on my trousers, then drew his hand down to touch me through the heavy fabric.

I gulped and said on the exhale of a shaky breath, "Yes. The Caster Regulation Act—I came forward because I decided it was—God, *ah*—better to keep my enemy close."

Gunner removed his hand from where the attention was appreciated and lightly combed the hair at my temple. "And this?" His other hand settled on my backside, kneaded a bit, and encouraged me to move.

I rubbed myself against Gunner's thigh as I said, "Overtaxed myself, as Ms. Zelda said."

"How?"

"Gunner—"

"How?"

"C-casters have this—we call it a tap. When the tap's open, there's the take of raw magic in exchange for lifeforce energy. When the body reaches a point of physical exhaustion, the tap closes." I was still rubbing myself against him, watching as Gunner hastily unbuttoned his own waistcoat and shirt. "It works like a muscle. It can be trained to handle more—some casters manage to go up one new level."

"But?" Gunner asked as he laid bare his hard and hairy chest.

I reached forward to dig my fingers into his skin, rubbed the inside of my wrists against the black hair, and shuddered.

"My tap never closes. Wh-when I surpass the threshold, it leaves physical indicators."

"It's different from the aether spell you performed in Arizona."

I nodded and said, "Aether is just a pain in the ass. Reverse spells make the world distorted for a while, is all." I drew closer, enough that I could lean over Gunner and bite his neck. He gasped loudly, and it sent a thrill straight to my balls.

"Harder," Gunner growled, and he arched his back when I obliged. "What about architects?"

I let up on his neck—I'd left a deep purple mark that was unbearably exciting—and asked, "What about them?"

"Can they surpass level five?"

"They do," I confirmed. I sat up, yanked Gunner's braces from his shoulders, unbuttoned his trousers, and tugged them low enough to expose his hardened prick. "Gravity spells were constructed by an architect who surpassed the threshold of wind magic." I kissed Gunner and dipped my tongue into his mouth the way he did with me. "I can only cast what architects have woven into the atmosphere."

Gunner made quick work of my trousers and drawers. He shoved them to my thighs, spat into his hand, and reached down to stroke us together. "And what casters can perform gravity spells?"

"Liars," I answered around a gasp. I had no inhibitions left in me and humped desperately against Gunner. "Now you tell me."

"What's that?"

"When we met—how did you know? That I was stronger than suggested?"

"I've worked a time or two with the magic community," he said breathlessly. "You were dispatched without a partner.

You were proficient in aether. Your—*Jesus, Gillian*—wind spell was strong enough to carry a full-grown man." Gunner sucked hard on one finger before reaching around and pressing it against my hole.

I jumped but he stilled me.

"Just a bit—there, is that okay?"

It was an… odd sensation. Not bad, per se, but strange. I struggled to wrap my brain around the concept of something considerably thicker than a finger being at all comfortable, let alone pleasurable, despite some of my crudest fantasies. I tried to imagine enjoying receiving such attention, like the throes of passion Gunner had been in the night before, and the daydream was coming up short when finally faced with the reality. But then Gunner pressed deeper, angled his touch, and a sweat broke out across my entire body. It was like pinpricks of light—hundreds—*thousands*—consuming me from the inside out. Gunner brought me down into a kiss to silence my cries, and then I was coming and so was he and it was perfect.

Gunner rested his hand firmly on one bare cheek, stroking in an almost possessive manner. After he caught his breath, he asked, "Do you feel gross?"

"No."

"I don't expect you to think differently of yourself overnight."

"I know."

"Only that you try."

I sat back on my knees and tugged my trousers into place. "We should go. Addison said Tick Tock is holed up somewhere around Mulberry Bend, and after his warehouse was blown up, who's to say what his next move might be? I want to visit the docks as well—poke around a bit and see if we can narrow down the origin of these packages. Perhaps glean some intelligence on that Weaver fellow too, if Lady Luck is smiling upon us today."

Gunner didn't say a word as he wiped his stomach clean with the corner of the starched bedsheet. He got to his feet, pulled his trousers on, and opened the window wide. A cold rush of January air helped to quickly alleviate the smell of sex from the rented room.

I finished tucking my shirt in, tugged my braces over my shoulders, put my suit coat on, and collected my belongings from the bureau top—all carefully aligned by Gunner. I paused on the purple-tinted goggles, fingered the worn brass, worried a minute dent along the bridge. "Constantine?" When I looked up, Gunner was staring at me from across the room, silently buttoning his waistcoat. "You were serious about what you said earlier."

"Of course."

"So what does it mean for… us?"

"What do you want it to mean?"

I was gripping the goggles now. "I think it would be difficult for me to see you with others at this point." Gunner began walking toward me while putting his suit coat on, and I hastened to add, "But I would understand. I should like to find happiness with you, but I'm not nearly as comfortable with it all as you are. I *am* trying, but it might take me… some time. We're also liable to be apart more than we'd be together. And let's not forget you work to actively undermine all of the laws I represent."

Gunner didn't agree or disagree as he reached into the inner pocket of his suit. I expected Black Jack and continued silence before I'd eventually come full circle, tell him to forget I'd said anything, and we'd leave it at that. But instead, Gunner held up the receipt from Bartholomew Industries that I carried on my person like a religious talisman.

I touched my own breast before reaching inside the empty pocket. "How did—?"

"It slipped from your pocket as I was undressing you last

night." He eyed the folded note. "It's rather worn out."

"Paper doesn't have much of a life expectancy."

"Why did you keep it?"

I felt myself flush and struggled for nonchalance. "You—you said you were mine."

Gunner smiled. He tugged back the lapel of my coat, tucked the receipt carefully into my pocket, then patted my chest. "That's right."

XII

January 1, 1882

We left Ms. Zelda's boardinghouse around ten o'clock that morning and made a brief trip uptown to The Buchanan. Between the smell of smoke on my clothing and sex on my person, I was feeling particularly grubby, never mind that I was in desperate need of a shave and had also lost my hat amid the chaos from the night before.

After our detour, we walked east toward the Second Avenue El. Gunner was, of course, gorgeous in another head-to-toe black wardrobe, save for the glint of his silver watch chain. His face was smooth—I had, erm, made certain of that before stepping out the front door of my apartment—and despite his preferred perfume being near a decade out of style, I couldn't imagine anything more fitting than the spicy woodsy Sandringham he wore.

"Scally caps suit you," Gunner had said, prompted by nothing other than the fact that I'd lost my second nice bowler since being in his company and had been forced to unearth a tweed flat cap from my closet before we'd left.

I'd absently touched the brim and answered, "Makes me look like a boy."

"I think you look very handsome."

I admit, as we walked across the avenues bustling with the upper class enjoying their day off and the lower class working as if New Year's Day was like any other, I'd admired my reflection a few times in the windows of business fronts.

Fulton Fish Market sat one block north of Pier 17. And while the market served a mostly wholesale clientele these days, the oyster vendors were still parked on the curbs with their carts and stoves, serving to passerby and employee alike. Gunner and I stood huddled around one on the corner of Front and Fulton, cold air whipping off the East River at our backs.

Gunner reached across the makeshift countertop, picked up a glass bottle, and drizzled vinegar atop his freshly shucked raw oysters. "Patrick Tuffey," he prompted, before knocking back an oyster.

"One of Driscoll's inner circle," I answered.

"O'Dea said that Tuffey witnessed a trade-off between Fishback, now deceased, and a mechanical man that fits the description of the one that hightailed it last night." Gunner picked up another shell and asked, "How reliable is O'Dea?"

I sprinkled some salt on my own oysters while saying, "His reports are often hearsay, but he doesn't fabricate or embellish those details. He's a trusted, if obnoxious, informant." I swallowed the oyster, cool and slick and a little briny, then picked up another. "His story pairs with what happened last night. Tuffey said, before his chest was blown apart, he only wanted to bankrupt Tick Tock. Sounds to me like he figured out which warehouse was being used for storage of their shipments and set it ablaze."

"Unbeknownst to him, it was a powder keg."

"Literally." I slurped down the second oyster. "The gangster who aided Gatling Man's escape, that's a fellow by the name of McCarthy. He's a Whyo, but judging by his appearance on the scene, I'd say he's another of the double-dealing sort. He told me, *this means war*."

Gunner stared at the oyster vendor for a moment, a man who was doing his very best to not appear interested in our conversation. "Gatling Man took out Fishback."

"Never mind the bullet caliber matching, we've already established the timeline makes it impossible to have been Mechanical Man."

"What if there are more of these magical, semimechanical humans about the city?" Gunner drizzled more vinegar on another oyster. "More than two, that is."

I considered this comment, a mirror of Moore's concern, while helping myself to more shellfish. "I think, if I were the betting sort, I'd be going home with heavy pockets. Remember what Addison said about the lookouts Tuffey saw at the handoff—never being heard from again?"

Gunner nodded.

"Tuffey also said something about playing God." I waited until the vendor turned his back to stoke his coal fire and collect some oysters frying in a pan of oil before leaning close to Gunner and whispering, "Sure as hell sounds as if someone is building an army of some sort."

"Out of low-tier, double-dealing Whyos."

"Right."

Gunner finished his last oyster and said, "It's rather brilliant. This gang, despite their brutal disorganization, seems too powerful and widespread to be easily replaced by a new name. Am I correct in that assumption?"

"You are."

"Then what better way to rid the streets of competition than to take it down from the inside out? A wound Driscoll doesn't even know is festering yet." Gunner reached into his pocket and set several coins—too many—on the countertop.

"Thank you, sir," the vendor said. "Happy New Year."

"It was only twelve cents for the two of us," I said as I put on one glove and led the way toward the piers.

"Courtesy of Wells Fargo."

"I shouldn't allow you to pay for meals with *procured* funds."

"By all means, stop me, Agent Hamilton."

I rolled my eyes and managed to restrain a smile.

With the advent of steam technology by the end of 1865, Vanderbilt had been one of the first businessmen to embrace the concept of air travel for the masses with the construction of Grand Central—his pièce de résistance. The world followed in his footsteps after the first airships successfully landed and passengers disembarked through the palace he'd built. From Wells Fargo replacing their stagecoaches with zeppelins in '73, to the import and export companies along the East River petitioning the city to remodel the piers to accept goods by air instead of water in '75, the world had turned to the skies and never looked back to the ground in remorse.

The original structure of Pier 17 was still utilized, but merely as a boardwalk to reach the ramps and pneumatic lifts to the airship landings overhead. It wasn't at full capacity today, what with the holiday, but zeppelins were still coming and going at a constant rate—the pier in ever-shifting shadows as massive steam-filled canvases blotted out the sun. Workmen stacked crates all along the pier, foremen signed off on cargo receipts for captains, and overhead was the constant bickering and barking of airship crewmen.

"What makes you think O'Dea's California architect is involved?" Gunner asked, following at my side, hands in his winter coat pockets so as to keep the Waterbury concealed. "He'd only heard the name, not that the name was directly tied to Tick Tock."

"Fishback told Moore and me that the packages came from out West—specifically California or Arizona."

"That connection is tenuous at best."

I stopped to study a stack of wooden crates taller than myself, checked the leaflet on one to confirm its provenance, then kept walking. "There are two hundred and thirty-five registered casters in the country. The FBMS estimates at least an additional one hundred are alive and well, but not yet registered."

Keeping my arms to my sides, I turned my bare left hand out and followed the ebb and flow of magic. Even here, at the southernmost point of Manhattan, I could still feel the rip in the atmosphere above Hester Street. I could feel the hurt of the energy, like an animal licking its wounds. And I could feel that invisible, tangible barrier between me and the raw power become just a bit more dense as the manufactured spells were slowly but surely being woven into the planet's magical atmosphere.

"There's about a third the number of architects in the country—"

"One hundred and eleven," Gunner supplied. "Give or take."

"Er—yes. Seventy-five of whom are registered, and eighteen have been arrested since '65 for illegal magic."

"You believe one of the unaccounted for eighteen is the architect working with Tick Tock?" Gunner concluded.

"Correct. Of course, for an enterprise such as his, this would require an architect of noted strength, which reduces the count even further. The average skill level of scholars, architects, and casters in this country is two point five."

Gunner stopped walking and looked down. "What sort of

level would be required?"

I met Gunner's gaze and offered a noncommittal shrug.

He seemed to understand that.

"*So*," I continued, "if Addison has intelligence on an architect located on the other side of the country, it's likely the news traveled for good reason."

My fingers twitched as I came into contact with the remnants of days-old magic. I turned away from Gunner, shifted my focus, and followed the weak, glittering trail toward a shipment coming off a dinky airship sputtering and wheezing steam from its aft-end.

"Excuse me," I said, approaching a foreman counting the crates as they were piled onto the pier. "What's this shipment?"

He paused his count, finger still pointing at the nearest container, and looked down at me. He was built like the side of a barn—tall and wide and red in the face. "Who's fuckin' askin'?"

I pulled back my coat lapels to show my badge. "Special Agent Gillian Hamilton with the Federal Bureau of Magic and Steam." To the left, a dock worker pushing a full box cart down the ramp from the airship slowed to watch our interaction. I returned my attention to the foreman and repeated, "What's the shipment?"

"It ain't nothing you magic coppers ought to be concerned with," the foreman answered.

"Special Agent," I corrected. "And if that's the case, you should have no issue showing me the provenance."

The foreman raised his clipboard out of my reach. "I know my rights."

"Don't make this difficult," I answered.

"I'll do as I damn well—*hey!*"

Gunner had, unnoticed by us both, approached from the

right and snatched the clipboard from overhead. He handed it to me while keeping his gaze trained on the foreman. "I believe Agent Hamilton requested you not be difficult."

I accepted the clipboard, gave the documents a cursory once-over, then asked, "Pinkerton's Ladies Wear?"

"Aye, you arrogant son of a—"

I glanced up when the foreman abruptly cut himself short. Gunner hadn't done anything so blatant as unholster his Waterbury and wave it around for the foreman, workers, and God to see, but he had set his hands on his hips so the open lapels pulled back enough to show he was armed.

"From California?" I prompted.

The foreman shrugged. "That's what the paperwork says."

I gestured with the clipboard, saying, "Luxury items such as these are typically imported from Paris."

"You'd know all about ladies' gloves, would you?"

I narrowed my eyes and passed the clipboard back with a bit of a shove. "Was this the only shipment of Pinkerton's in the last week?"

The foreman spared Gunner a glance before agreeing. "Aye."

"Let's take a look, then."

"You ain't got the right to be pilfering—"

Without breaking eye contact, I raised my left hand and snapped my wrist up. A wind spell tore the nails out of the nearest wooden crate, sending the top flying and skittering along the pier a dozen feet away.

Clipboard in hand, the foreman raised both arms up like he was done arguing.

I reached inside and sifted through a number of poor quality sets of gloves—haphazard stitching, fur likely that of vermin—and then my fingers settled on metal. I removed a pistol that was similar in structure to a Waterbury, but the barrels were too long, like it'd been built from other parts. And instead of a handle, the gun's end was fitted with gears and snaps and locks—a limb attachment.

Gunner took the weapon, checked the chambers, then said, "Modified Jordan rifle."

I dug through the crate again, pocketed one of the cheaply constructed gloves for evidence, and tossed aside the rest of the accessories, which were clearly a front and nothing more, before unearthing a box of ammunition. The magic inside the bullets had waned during its travel cross-country, but the manufactured fire was still potent enough to make my skin itch. I suspected once it was activated by a gun, much like Gunner's aether bullets, combined with the curious mechanical men, this ammunition would regain its full strength.

Perhaps this answered the ongoing query as to why I sensed the spell originating in one location, despite the detonation occurring in a completely different place. This manufactured magic settled into its storage, like honey sinking in water. It left a sort of dense signature, so when the mechanical men collected ammunition from Hester Street to use on myself and Fishback, the manufactured fire followed the trail of its own signature back to where the boxes had been left for a prolonged period.

Interesting.

Looking at the foreman, I said, "You'd better start talking."

A clatter on the ramp distracted me, and I turned in time to see the workman with the full box cart had let go of the load. It rolled, fell, and toppled into the East River, and he took off in a full sprint toward the Fish Market. Gunner grabbed the palm-sized box of ammunition from my hold and threw it. He hit the man squarely in the back of the head, and the worker stumbled before planting face-first.

"That's who you want," he stated.

In the end, I took both men into custody.

I'd hoped the foreman would admit to some level of guilt after insulting me at the pier, but Gunner had been right—he was only a clueless bastard. The workman, on the other hand—Joseph, he said his name was, although Judas would have suited him just as well—was frantic to roll over after his initial underestimation of my person.

"You nackle-ass cocksuck—"

I sidestepped a punch, shoved my palm into Joseph's chin, and threw him to the floor of the booking room at the field office. I put a knee into his back, dug in enough to make him grunt, and asked, "What were you about to say?"

Joseph turned his head to spit some blood from his mouth before saying, "N-nothing."

"Are you certain? Something about me being a nackle-ass cocksucker?" I pressed harder with my knee.

Joseph made a sound of pain this time. "No. I swear."

I lifted off his back, slipped my hands into my trouser pockets, and stared at him as he rolled onto his backside and sat up. "Tell me about Pinkerton's Ladies Wear—no, don't move. You sit your ass right there on the floor. How long have they been a front for the distribution of illegal magic weaponry and ammunition?"

"Two months, maybe."

I looked over my shoulder to the open doorway. Just outside the room on the left, Gunner leaned one shoulder against the threshold, silent and dangerous. On the right, Moore stood with his big arms crossed over his chest. The two of them were like the moon and sun, night and day. My director nodded once for me to continue.

I looked at Joseph again. "How many shipments in that time?"

He shrugged. "I can't say."

I took a step toward him, my hands still in my pockets. Joseph scuttled backward like a crab. "Were you handing off specific crates to Frank Fishback?"

"Aye."

"Then you very well *can* say how many shipments came through Pier 17."

Joseph swallowed hard and peered around me at his only exit, blocked by a deadeye marksman and fiery caster.

"You look at me," I directed. "Not them."

"M-maybe ten," he answered. "About one a week."

"And Fishback would come by when?"

"Early. Before sunrise. Pinkerton's was usually the first shipment of the day."

"Why so late today, then?"

Joseph shook his head. "Airship trouble. That hunk of junk broke down over Jersey for most of the morning." He wiped at the bit of blood trickling from the side of his mouth. "Ain't seen Fishback all day, though."

"You wouldn't. He's dead."

Joseph's eyes grew as big as saucer plates. "You lot murdered him?"

"Would you like a repeat of my knee digging into your spine?"

"No, sir."

"Agent."

Joseph nodded and whispered, "Agent," under his breath.

"Fishback was murdered by the same man paying him, and you, I presume, to get those packages into Manhattan.

Who's the contact in California?"

"I got no idea."

"Who would know? What about the captain of the junker airship?"

"It's a different captain every time, sir—Agent Hamilton."

"Then who is *your* contact?" I tried.

Joseph hesitated.

I rolled my shoulders, removed a hand, and pointed at him as lightning crackled and snapped around my fingers. "Joseph—"

"*Wait*! Wait, I'll tell you! Good Christ, don't kill me."

"Less pissing and more explaining."

"The department head of Grace Gallery."

I furrowed my brow, lowered my hand, and asked with a touch of wariness, "At the Iron Palace?"

Joseph nodded several times. "You're familiar with ladies' consumption? No, I ain't mean nothing by that, sir—Hamilton—*Agent Hamilton*! Oh my God, I fuckin' pissed myself!"

"I did warn you," I answered. "How is this individual connected?"

"I don't know."

"The floor manager of a women's boutique having a relation to illegal magic is *absolutely* something you know."

Joseph was outright sniveling now. I was fairly accustomed to such dramatic reactions to my being. After all, it wasn't that long ago that magic was still outlawed and considered an immediate threat to society. But this man had *soiled* himself in my presence. I turned to the open doorway a second time and offered both Gunner and Moore a sort of *What can I do?* expression and hand gesture.

Moore expelled a breath and then said, loud enough to be

heard, "Mr. Greene?"

"Y-yes, sir?" Joseph whimpered.

"Please answer Agent Hamilton. Of the three of us, he's the one you need to befriend."

Joseph's panicked expression met mine once more, and he sobbed, "I-I used to work at the Iron Palace as a cash boy. Got a job at the piers when I was older, a proper man's job, you understand? The manager sends me a telegram one day, out of the blue. Says he's got a job offer for me. Ain't nothin' I gotta do but allow a fellow named Fishback to come by and collect a few crates from Pinkerton's. What he don't take, the rest goes to Grace Gallery."

"Nothing else?" I reiterated. "Because if you're lying to me, Joseph—"

"No, no, I ain't. I swear, *really*."

I was quiet for a beat before asking, "And what of Tick Tock?"

"Just a name I heard. Never met the man."

I stared at Joseph a long moment, collected my flat cap off the table, then slipped between Gunner and Moore on my way out. I heard Moore shut and lock the door in my wake before I turned to walk backward, saying, "This entire situation is becoming absurd."

"Hamilton—" Moore started.

"Have you noticed that not one individual has ever met Tick Tock?" I asked.

"I had gathered," Moore answered.

"So far, in a plan to overthrow the Whyos, we have determined the involvement of a murderer-for-hire, a pier workman, a department store manager, and an undetermined number of mechanical men and double-dealing street gangsters. I mean, what is this, some sort of... six degrees of separation?"

"Six degrees of what?" Moore echoed.

"I suspect," Gunner said, bringing up the rear, "Hamilton means to imply that despite the number of unique vocations involved in this underground plot, these individuals are no more than, for example, six social connections away from whoever Tick Tock *is*."

"Thank you," I said to Gunner.

Gunner touched his index finger to the brim of his bowler in response.

Moore stopped abruptly in the hall. Voices and footfalls carried from the stairwell at my back. In order to leave through the side exit, we'd have to walk Gunner past any number of special agents coming downstairs, who would see him as nothing more than a wanted outlaw. And with the momentary cease-fire between him and Moore, it would also prove to be a sticky situation for our director to explain. Moore opened another door and jerked his head in invitation.

I backtracked, stepped inside, and was silent until Gunner and Moore had entered and shut the door. "I want to go to the Iron Palace and find this boutique manager."

Moore held a hand up. "We need to move on this quickly—"

"Exactly." I took a step forward.

"But not stupidly, Hamilton," he said, coming to meet me at the midpoint of the room. "Have you slept? You look tired."

"I'm fine."

"That wasn't my question."

"I slept, sir."

Moore's brown eyes narrowed suddenly, and he touched his own temple. "Do you—do you dye your hair?"

"Sorry?"

"I don't recall so much gray in front."

I struggled for a believable explanation as I touched the newest loss of color. Then I remembered, as a young boy, my mother reveling in every word of *The Lady's Guide to Perfect Gentility* as if it were holy scripture and using one of the home recipes to darken her hair to a more fashionable shade of the time. "Yes," I blurted out. "A bottle of wine and a quick visit to the druggist will do the trick."

Moore gave me a dubious expression.

"I'm only twenty-nine," I said, by way of excuse.

The corner of Moore's mouth lifted in a tentative smile. "You look nicer with the gray."

From where he stood at the door, Gunner chuckled. He had a lazy drawl to his laugh when he was low-key amused.

Moore puffed his chest out a little as he turned around. "Something you find funny?"

"Your boldfaced attempt to take what's not yours, Director," Gunner said evenly. He paused, smiled widely, and added, "Despite the unequivocal *no* you received last night."

"You are a criminal," Moore retorted. "A thief and a murderer."

Gunner didn't seem particularly perturbed by this accusation. He merely shrugged one shoulder.

I made a quick dash to stand between them before a fuse was lit, and said to Moore, "The window, sir."

Moore's face, distorted by unbridled anger, twisted like a corkscrew into something softer and more socially acceptable. "The window?" he echoed.

"Upstairs," I clarified.

He expelled a held breath. Nodded. "Agent Bligh confirmed he broke it upon entering the room in order to dissipate the smoke."

"Why not simply open it?" Gunner asked.

"Bligh was about two bottles into his New Year

festivities," I explained.

"You don't like him."

I turned to stare at Gunner. "I didn't say that."

"You didn't have to."

"Stop it." I returned my attention to Moore again. "Is he working today?"

Moore stroked his beard. "After failing to protect Fishback, he certainly wasn't getting the day off to nurse his hangover. He's retched twice."

"I want to speak with him."

"I don't think that's wise."

"I want to question him about last night," I reiterated. "Now that he's sober. Clues about the break-in."

Moore was still stroking his handsome beard. "You seem convinced it was this—what'd you say—Gatling Man from last night."

I had, of course, informed my director of what transpired last night on Hester Street, just before interrogating Joseph Greene. But I had, also of course, skirted the finer details as to how the fire had been put out and instead heaped praise on the fire department. Those brutes wouldn't hesitate to accept the lie as gospel if it meant a commendation from the FBMS, simply because it would piss off the metropolitan police.

Nothing but childish blood feuds in this city, I swear.

"It was, I'm quite certain," I replied. "But McCarthy helped him escape, so he's not here to question. And even if McCarthy or Gatling Man or Tick Tock are still lying low around Mulberry Bend, that's a lot of ground to cover."

"Dangerous ground," Moore murmured in agreement.

"And I'd rather glean as much as I can about the situation before storming the neighborhood. Therefore, I'd like to speak with Bligh about what he remembers in a more sober state of mind."

"Very well."

"Then it's to the Iron Palace," I finished before joining Gunner at the door.

"Let me assign a bruiser—"

"Do you expect the satin handbags to open fire?"

"Hamilton."

"Gunner will be with me, sir." I opened the door.

"That does not, in any way, ease my concerns," Moore answered.

"Come now, Director," Gunner said in that easy, almost monotone manner of speech. "I might be a criminal, but I'm the best this country's ever seen."

XIII

January 1, 1882

Once we'd left the office, Gunner vanished into the midday crowds on Twenty-Third Street. Having remembered my Personal Discussion Device on our way out of The Buchanan, I rang Henry Bligh and requested he join me out front in five minutes. He took seven, which could have been as much about his ego as it was the effects of his overindulgence. I was studying the disembodied hand of Lady Liberty across the street at Madison Square Park, the gilded copper of the flaming torch gleaming in the noonday sun, when the door opened behind me.

"Agent Hamilton," Bligh said brusquely.

I turned on my heel as Bligh came down the front steps. He stopped on the last tread and forced me to look up. "I'd like to ask you about Frank Fishback."

His bleary blue eyes narrowed and a cloud of air puffed around his mouth on his exhale. "I gave my report to Director Moore last night."

"Yes, I am aware. But now *I'm* asking you. Is that a problem?"

Bligh shifted from foot to foot, looked away, and ground out, "No, sir."

"I'm sure that hurt."

Bligh's gaze shot back to me, and if looks could kill….

"What did you hear that made you open the door to the jail?"

Bligh crossed his arms, and I could so easily imagine his aristocratic features on the face of a child, cheeks stained red as he threw a tantrum until his parents lavished on him whatever his heart desired. Bligh himself had indicated on his registration documentation that his caster abilities hadn't manifested until he was seventeen, quite late in comparison to the national average of thirteen years old, or myself at the tender age of five. He'd had a normal childhood, whatever that meant. When Bligh had realized he had an ability to utilize the raw stream, magic was already legal. And his parents, with money so old, they were able to sway the public ever so gently on the benefits of the magic community, worked diligently to find Bligh a position with the Bureau and then convinced high society it was an elite opportunity instead of what it was most of the time—thankless and dangerous work.

"Bligh."

"I heard the window."

"Breaking?"

"I—yes."

"You told Director Moore you broke the glass."

Bligh blanched a bit. "I did. I mean—I heard the window rattle in its frame. It sounded as if something were breaking. By the time I opened the door, the cell was on fire and the hall was full of smoke. I broke the window."

"It wasn't left open?" I clarified.

"Why the fuck would I break the window if it was already open?"

"You were drunk," I stated.

Color came back to Bligh's cheeks—embarrassment and anger. "Are we done?"

"Not quite. What did you see once you entered the hall?"

"What do you mean? Fishback was on fire."

"And?"

"And that's it."

"Where was Agent Plunket?" I asked next.

"How the hell should I—?"

"Section Four, Article Two of the Bureau's hand guide specifically states that agents in the field must be made informed of their partner's whereabouts at all times, which extends to both office hours and—"

"She was in the toilet," Bligh protested over me. "Jesus Christ, Hamilton."

"Don't skirt details with me because of undue modesty."

Bligh shook his head at that and let out a sort of aggressive laugh. "I suppose you really don't know anything about women."

I was reminded of the countless editions of *The Delineator* I'd purchased and read over the years—the women's publication my secret to successful communication with the opposite gender. Feeling heat rise to my cheeks despite the cold day, I said, "Yes, and you're a damn wizard simply because you're engaged? Plunket is a special agent. The fact that she is a woman is not relevant—"

"Your fairy tendencies are showing."

I bristled. "My human decency is showing, Agent Bligh. If I see you treating your partner as lesser, in words, in writing, in person—in any goddamn capacity, do you understand me?—I will make it my personal mission to see you stripped of your badge and tossed to the curb."

"Well, we all know you'll do anything to keep others from getting promoted, so I can't say I'm surprised."

"Not all casters can obtain level five certification. That does not mean I'm sabotaging you. Your skills are maxed out."

Bligh pushed closer into my space, and I was forced to take a step back, lest my magic unintentionally hurt him. "Hogwash."

"Hardly. I oversaw your training. You're a level two. *Period.* And you're upset I'm a senior agent? I've been at the Bureau for a decade, putting in the work every day. You've been here three years. Earn your keep."

"Earn it?" Bligh laughed mockingly. "By doing what, cradling Moore's sac? That's probably your favorite assignment. You're an ugly little sodomite. It's what everyone thinks."

"Do you not remember what I said to you last night?"

"Do *you* not realize how easy it'd be for me to ruin you?"

I clenched my fists so tight that my fingernails were digging crescents into my scarred palms. "I can't imagine you admitting that I whipped your ass would be something you could stomach. And I don't think Moore will be terribly receptive to one of his agents blackmailing another for kudos toward his next review."

The smile that crossed Bligh's face just then was different from the cruel and mocking grins of the last three years. This one was ice-cold. Dare I say, malevolent. "You're a fucking slum rat, Hamilton. I can always pick out the ones who act above their station, trying to prove they aren't trash. But they are. I bet you scurried out of the shit and piss of the Lower East Side. Moore might be desperate to keep a level five lightning caster on his roster, so much so that he's willing to ignore any complaints filed against you for your filthy tendencies, but you forget, I'm not like you."

"We're special agents. We're all held to the same set of reg—"

"That's where you're wrong, you dumb fuck. Not when you're from Fifth Avenue. All it'd take would be a whisper to my mother-in-law during a dinner party. She's got the biggest mouth for gossip in this whole damn city. You'd be right back in the gutter you crawled out of."

"Don't you dare pretend you know a thing about me," I said.

"I don't have to pretend. I can smell your destitution, you toad."

I'd had to learn some important life lessons at a very young age: no one is going to come to your defense, weakness is certain death, the small are underestimated. These cautions were true as a child, but perhaps held even more weight in adulthood. Because right here, right now, on a busy street in Midtown, not one person had spared me a second glance as Bligh bullied his way into my personal space. If I hesitated, cried, screamed, Bligh would have all the confirmation he needed, and *God only knew* he'd spare no expense to get me off the corporate ladder so that he could bask in his preconceived success. So I did what I hadn't done in a very, very long time. I relied on physical prowess and took Bligh by surprise when I socked him right in the face.

He stumbled back, tripped on the stair, and crashed to the icy steps while holding his nose. Blood seeped from between his fingers.

I winced and shook my hand. My knuckles were red, not so much from the strike, but the interactions of our lightning magics. "That's twice now I've put you on your ass," I said, squaring my shoulders. "I'm not impressed by your riches or your lineage. Your character is what matters. And clearly, Henry Bligh, you have none."

Bligh removed his hand and gingerly touched his nose. The tip was scorched black. "You're a son of a whore."

"Unfortunately, I knew my father."

Bligh got to his feet while wiping his face. "Your days are numbered." He flicked his hand and splattered blood across the front of my coat. "I'll see to that personally." With that, he turned, walked up the stairs, and vanished inside.

The Iron Palace was exactly that—a six-story behemoth taking up an entire city block on Broadway and Tenth. Its front featured cast-iron ornamentation and support columns, it had a glass skylight, endless expanses of windows on every floor in order to maximize the usage of natural light, and *nineteen* department stores inside. The Palace employed something like 2,000 people, from the managers to cashiers, bookkeepers to ushers, to the army of seamstresses that made the consumption of fashion so easy nowadays. And while I'd never had reason to step inside before today, based on the crowds coming and going from the main doors, it was a marvel of business and marketing savviness that should have made the rest of Ladies' Mile envious.

Whether Gunner had watched the scene between Bligh and me from a safe distance, or the freckling of blood on my nice coat told the story, or even if my disposition alone was enough warning, we passed the trek without conversation. To say that I had never liked Henry Bligh was an understatement. Upon his hiring three years ago, he'd been assigned to work with Rachel Plunket, but was to complete additional studies under myself for his first year in an effort to hone and strengthen his lightning casting.

It hadn't been successful.

Bligh was an egotistical and arrogant motherfucker. He hadn't liked showing me respect as his senior from the start, which I suspected stemmed from his upbringing of sucking on a golden spoon, but when he got it in his mind that I was… not like most men… all hell had truly broken loose. And perhaps what had been most upsetting was that he seemed to truly believe there was a secret to reaching level five casting skills that I simply refused to share with him.

I'd written an official report to Moore six months into Bligh's training, indicating that he had reached his maximum potential at level two and it would simply be best to assign cases reflective of his and Plunket's current abilities rather than to waste federal revenue chasing the unobtainable.

Bligh hadn't liked that.

Whatever professionality had been hanging by a thread between us snapped afterward.

While his insults and name-calling had been relentless and painful, I had always felt that as long as I kept my head down and didn't get caught up in flippant emotions for another man, everything would be okay. In the last three years, Bligh had never actually filed a report against me because he had no evidence. He had never gone to Moore, or D.C. for that matter, to complain about working with a sodomite. He'd shared his theory with others of course, and those who hadn't liked my presence before were thrilled with his jokes, but my career had always remained intact. And now, with Moore's truth known to me, and the pseudo-understanding currently existing between us, Moore would certainly make any complaint against me disappear.

Except this time, Bligh hadn't threatened to go to Moore. He'd threatened to hit up society. And New York society loved only one thing more than money: other people's scandals. If Bligh parsed the story exactly right, he could gain immediate sympathy from Mrs. Olin, who would undoubtedly move mountains to save her daughter's upcoming marriage and acceptance into an Old Money family. There'd be public pressure on the FBMS to toss my sorry hide onto the street for having wronged poor Henry Bligh. After that, humiliation would chase me out of New York entirely.

I heard the *snap* of my fingers being broken, stuck on a repeating static loop like a PDD in need of recalibrating.

Snap.

Snap.

Snap.

I stopped in front of the doors to the Iron Palace, removed my flat cap, and fanned my heated face. I had to swallow several times before the bile threatening to come up my throat settled uncomfortably in my gut.

Gunner moved away from the door an usher had opened for him. He returned to my side and asked, "Are you not well?"

"I just need a moment."

"The oysters."

"Sorry?"

"One of the oysters must have been rancid."

A weak smile flirted across my face. "You know the oysters were fine."

Gunner raised an eyebrow.

"But thank you for pretending you don't notice everything."

"I wouldn't be if that blood was yours," Gunner answered with a minute nod at the rust-colored stains.

I said nothing of that, put my cap back on, and walked through the front door with Gunner at my side. "Something about Bligh's story is bothering me," I said as we entered the open layout of the ground floor—a massive expanse with shoppers moving every which way, dozens of finely dressed women sitting in parlor chairs, enjoying sodas, and all of it lit from the overhead windows and rooftop, the glass tinted in the faintest shades of color to produce a living kaleidoscope that shifted in intensity as the sun moved throughout the day.

"And what's that?" Gunner asked, raising his voice to be heard over the commotion of hundreds of echoing conversations. He stared ahead at the lads mixing drinks at the fountains.

"What intruder would spend precious escape time closing the window behind them?"

Gunner cast a sideways look at me.

"Gatling Man scales the building—unseen, mind you—slips into the jail through the only other ingress, blows Fishback to hell and gone, but spends the time, while the room is on fire, to finagle the window shut from the *outside*?"

Gunner grunted. He was staring at the fountains again.

"Don't you think that's—you're not listening to me."

"Do you think they have ginger soda?"

"Er, I have no idea." I finally looked in the same direction. "Did you… want one?"

"O'Dea wasn't wrong—I'm not often in a city, especially one that has a soda fountain. I like ginger."

"I'm sure that pairs excellently with licorice gum," I said with a sigh. I motioned Gunner to follow, and we strode through the throngs of patrons and approached the counter. I raised a hand to get one of the boys' attention. "Do you have ginger syrup?"

The lad winced and shook his head. "Sorry, sir. Our shipment didn't arrive, on account of the holiday."

I looked up at Gunner and read actual disappointment in his expression. It was so… *endearing*. Had we not been standing among thousands of passersby, I'd have stroked his arm. Maybe kissed him. "What do you have?" I asked, hoping some flavor, as equally unappealing as ginger, would be available for Gunner's curious palate.

"Pineapple, lemon, raspberry—"

Gunner's look did not resemble one of enthusiasm over the fruity offerings.

"—cream, and sarsaparilla."

Gunner's eyes shot toward the boy. "You have sarsaparilla?"

"One sarsaparilla, one raspberry," I told the boy, sliding a few coins across the counter. He returned a moment later with two tall glasses of carbonated water, laden with a sugary aroma.

Gunner took a sip, smiled, then took a longer one.

"Good?" I asked.

"Thank you," he said by way of answering. "So, Gatling Man closing the window from the outside." Gunner looked at me. "I'm always listening."

I laughed lightly. "Noted."

"It hardly makes sense. It'd be one thing if there were multiple entrances, and by closing the window, it becomes more difficult to track him after the fact. But that isn't the case—there's only one ingress, as you've stated."

I sipped my sweet raspberry drink before adding, "The broken window is still bothering me."

"You said Bligh was drunk."

"He was. But when you break a window, the glass falls *out*."

"Are you going to say it?" Gunner asked. "Or do you want me to?"

"It's not a possibility I can entertain."

"*I* can."

"The Bureau—"

"Isn't foolproof, Hamilton. Men like you are the exception, not the rule."

I finally looked at Gunner. His expression was smooth.

Placid. Like that first fine layer of ice forming atop a body of water in winter. "Men like me."

He reached out, brushed back my coat lapels, and tapped the badge pinned to my waistcoat. "Men who believe in this—who are humbled by the authority given to them." Gunner finished his sarsaparilla soda and then said, "Bligh broke the window to set a scene."

"You can't say that," I protested.

"I most certainly can. I don't work for the FBMS."

"And it's a damn good thing," I answered, "because accusing a federal agent of taking a kickback…. It doesn't even make sense. Henry Bligh doesn't need financial incentive. His father is Frederick Bligh, for God's sake."

"Ah. The banker," Gunner said with the faintest note of interest.

"That's him. Bligh Trust and Savings. He has offices all over the country."

"I should rob one."

"What? *No.*"

"Just because a man isn't interested in a little extra coin," Gunner said thoughtfully, tapping the bar top with the tips of his strong blunt fingers, "doesn't mean he can't still be bought. Why do you not like him?"

"This isn't the proper venue to discuss it."

The corner of Gunner's mouth twitched upward. "I find your propriety both charming and excruciatingly tedious."

"*My* propriety?" I shot back, but I couldn't help the mocking laugh that escaped. "What about you?"

"What about me?"

"The gentleman thief says his pleases and thank-yous, pays his bills, minds his tongue—"

"That's manners."

"Manners. Is that not what I have?"

"Did you want to have this discussion?"

I laughed a bit louder, turned my back to the counter, and leaned against it. "Oh, now we must. Go on. Tell me that I don't say please and thank you."

"You do."

"Or that I don't pay my bills."

"You do."

"That I don't mind my tongue."

Gunner narrowed his eyes a bit. "You curse like you were raised aboard an airship."

My eyebrows raised. "I suppose so, yes. Two out of three, though."

"Two out of three, with attitude."

"Pardon?"

"You have an attitude, Hamilton. No, don't get upset. Your natural temperament is what I like about you. It's quite different from your manufactured decorum."

"Not wanting to speak ill of a colleague in public is not manufactured decorum."

"I disagree."

"We can't all simply say what's on our mind whenever we please."

"Why not?"

"It's not polite."

"And that's why manners are important. Mind where you sprinkle that salt of yours and no one will realize you've insulted them in broad daylight," Gunner concluded.

"You're mad."

"I'm a gentleman," he corrected. "Go ahead and try. Why do you not like Henry Bligh?"

I huffed, shook my head, but after a moment of consideration, said, "He boasts a sense of entitlement that is inappropriate for a federal agent."

"And?"

"He doesn't show proper respect toward his seniors in the business."

"Hm-hm."

"And—and he's a crass, cruel, self-centered man-child," I finished.

Gunner waved his hand absently. "Decent, until that last one."

"Too much salt."

"A bit." He took a step back from the counter and indicated I follow with a nod. "May I tell you what I've gleaned of Henry Bligh?"

"I don't think you have to glean all that hard," I replied as we began walking out of the soda parlor and toward a massive display of brass and glass that housed a full directory of shops and their locations within the Palace.

"Henry Bligh is Old Money—that's common knowledge. His grandfather and great-grandfather made their fortune in water trade before Frederick reinvested their wealth into the banking industry and began robbing good folks through unreasonable interest rates." Gunner stopped in front of the directory and studied the map. "Henry Bligh struggles with working at the FBMS because there is no pedestal for him to stand on."

I crossed my arms and read the shop descriptions underneath the layout. "Spot-on."

"When you said he doesn't respect his seniors, you were being specific—in that this behavior is directed at you."

"How did—?"

"Because Moore would not stand for a fool to

metaphorically slap him in the face. And," Gunner continued without pause, "because that comment triggered some very frustrated emotions in you, I can only deduce that since Bligh has been working at the FBMS, he has made some statements to you, perhaps to others, about specific insecurities we will not revisit. And, because you are a complicated man, Hamilton, you felt you had to take this abuse. For survival purposes."

I stared at Gunner's profile as he came to his conclusion. "I don't know how you do that."

He shrugged.

I directed my attention to the shop names again and tapped number nine on the list, and Gunner matched it to a department on the third floor. "Bligh's elemental default is lightning. That's what got his foot in the door." I headed toward one of the lifts, its brass and copper gleaming in the afternoon light. "The Bureau was hoping to elevate his level with some training and oversight from myself."

"It wasn't successful."

"Bligh blames me for his own shortcomings, I suppose." A lift agent pulled back the cage door, requested the floor, and then shut the gate after we stepped inside. "Why are we still discussing him?" I asked as the steam pneumatics underneath the unit activated and we shot upward, voices and faces on each floor passing in a blur.

Gunner didn't speak until we'd exited the lift, he'd gathered his bearings, and we'd started down the long hall on the left. "I wanted to ascertain whether Bligh could be bought—that he didn't simply break the window because he was drunk." Gunner stopped outside the open doors of Grace Gallery and turned to me. "To confirm for myself what you've already been suspecting since last night."

I removed my flat cap and ran a hand through my hair a few times. I could smell the Macassar oil on my fingertips as

I returned the hat to my head. "Career-motivated."

"A rivalry with you."

"But letting Fishback die when he was on guard duty—how on Earth would that help him?"

"I'm not certain," Gunner admitted. "But his death foiled your only angle of investigation."

"Correct."

"Hear me out, Hamilton. Perhaps Fishback's death was necessary. Bligh might know a player or two involved in Tick Tock's plan, perhaps more. And while Fishback's death would initially reflect poorly upon him, it would also hinder your work, thus giving Bligh the time needed to essentially 'solve' this case before you. It would make for a hell of a headline."

I shifted from foot to foot. "And already when he's talk of the town due to his upcoming wedding. It'd be a promotion, for sure."

"It's also blackmail."

XIV

January 1, 1882

Grace Gallery had a very particular presence about it. Like a sliver of Europe had been transplanted into the reckless frontier of America—a piece of material paradise for upper-class women, short of having to purchase an international airship ticket to window shop in Paris or London. Glass shone, crystal gleamed, both catching sunlight and speckling the floors and walls with prisms, and brass was polished within an inch of its life. The department store also had a very strong, flowery scent. Violet. Cut with a subtle hint of sandalwood—but not nearly enough.

I rubbed my nose and did my best to not give off the appearance of a man choking.

Ladies, both those barely into adulthood as well as others pulling young children along, perused the aisles and displays of accessories. From handbags to gloves and hats to an absolutely terrifying contraption being advertised as the Lotta bustle: "Now with springs! 8 springs—45c, 9 springs—50c."

I was momentarily distracted by the cage that seemed

more apropos for catching lobsters than it did for a woman to wear, and hadn't noticed the middle-aged man on the floor until he was already making a beeline for us. He was taller than myself—then again, weren't most men?—his salt-and-pepper hair perfectly parted down the middle, with a rather thin mustache curled and waxed on the ends. His face was long, his nose pointed, and his eyes so dark, they were practically black.

He stopped before us, sniffed loudly, clasped his hands behind his back, then asked in a nasally voice, "Are we gift-shopping, gentlemen?"

"Pardon?"

The manager sniffed again. "For a darling, or the missus?"

The question was quite straightforward—was I courting or married? This, in theory, would change the accessories the manager would push me to purchase. But it took a moment for me to collect my voice, because the inquiry—darling or missus—was another stark reminder that *The Etiquette of Courtship and Matrimony* would never apply to me. There would be no conducting myself around parents, ring shopping, proposing....

I realized I was rubbing my left ring finger as if trying to cover up the fact that it was naked and exposed. Which, of course, was equally as ridiculous, because even if I *had* been attracted to women—married to one—I wouldn't be expected to wear a wedding band like her. And I always felt like that was a downfall of our society. Men should be happy to express their love and commitment as much as women. It was a simple piece of jewelry, after all, and could be perfectly masculine with the right style.

If I had lived in a world where I could court a man without concern, openly kiss or touch a man outside the clubs on the Bowery or the privacy of my home, a world where I didn't feel disgust or fear because of my tendencies, I'd have very happily worn a ring for him. That is, if in this other existence, a man *wanted* to marry me.

"Darling," I said in a rush. "And you'd be?"

"Carl Higgins," he answered, puffing his chest out and raising his chin to display like a peacock. "Floor manager of Grace Gallery."

"Gillian Hamilton," I said, offering a hand.

Higgins sniffed again and gave me a limp fish to shake before returning his hand behind his back. "Might I suggest for your darling—"

"Gloves," I told him. "Pinkerton's. That's what she wants."

Higgins's gaze darted to Gunner, who'd still not said anything, then nodded. "Pinkerton's, of course. We keep a small inventory." He motioned for me to follow.

Gunner trailed behind, keeping a few feet of distance.

Higgins slipped behind a glass case and motioned to three sets of gloves inside. Suede and kid with decorative stitching, as well as silk with beads and buttons. They were a far cry from the shoddy craftsmanship I'd pawed through at Pier 17.

"And this is your most up-to-date line?" I asked.

"Everything at Grace Gallery is of current fashion trends, sir. We pride ourselves on carrying the very best luxury accessories."

"Why Pinkerton's, then?"

Higgins sniffed, louder this time. "What do you mean?"

"High fashion tends to be imported from Paris, is it not? Why do you carry California-made products?"

Higgins's cheeks grew rosy, and he raised his head back enough that he had to quite literally look down his nose at me. "They're a sort of... starter brand, if you will. Decent enough to be carried by Grace Gallery, but affordable for young, single women. That is, until a husband can purchase something of higher quality. Which is why I'm going to recommend to you our Clark & Game line, sir. If you've any intentions of making a proper wife of your darling—"

"I should think that if I were, in fact, courting a woman, any decision to wed would be entirely her own." I reached into the inner pocket of my winter coat. "And a word of advice: advertising accessories based on nothing more than a woman's marital status is demeaning. I'd be upset if I were allowed only certain tie and collar choices, after all." While Higgins was sniffing and huffing and puffing, I set the glove I'd taken from the shipment onto the countertop.

Higgins grew quiet as he stared at the vermin pelt before his dark eyes cut to me. His expression had rearranged itself into something cold. Dangerous.

I pushed my lapels back, showed my badge, and said in a low voice, so as not to draw attention from the surrounding shoppers, "Special Agent Hamilton, Federal Bureau of Magic and Steam. I already know about Fishback and your former cash boy, Joseph Greene, so spare me the lies."

Higgins slowly set his hands along the edge of the case. "What do you want?"

"Who's Tick Tock?"

"I haven't the faintest."

"Why'd he reach out to you?"

"I can't imagine."

"Who's the architect in California sending all these goods?"

"Architect?"

"Mr. Higgins, I will give you exactly one more opportunity to impart the truth, or I'll be forced to continue this conversation at my office."

Higgins smiled as if he'd been waiting for that very threat, and said, "I'm afraid that's where you're wrong." His index finger tapped where it'd been resting on the frame, and then steam hissed as the paneling of the case dropped forward and half a dozen gun barrels were revealed to be aimed at my gut.

I felt no aether bullets or other sort of manufactured magic. This was just good old-fashioned gang work. I slowly raised my hands, not high enough to draw attention to myself, but so Higgins understood I took the threat seriously.

"Your next move better be real smart, Agent."

I had no move calculated, no action to implement. There were too many innocent patrons in the department store, no easily accessible cover—and who the hell knew how many other of these displays were rigged to open fire—and most importantly, I didn't know where Gunner was. Behind me, sure, but how far? Enough to see the threat, or did he still believe us merely chatting?

"*Well*?" Higgins spat.

I glanced at him. "We're just talking, Mr. Higgins."

"I've got my orders. Stop this line of investigation right now, or I'll fill you with so many holes, your partner won't have enough fingers to stop them up."

"All right—"

And then glass shattered to my left. We both turned toward the commotion as someone plowed through the floor-to-ceiling window, swinging from a steam pneumatic grappling hook. The stranger let go of the handle, heavy boots slamming down on the wooden floor, before he straightened from a crouch.

Tommy McCarthy. Still big, stilly bulky, once again wearing his mechanical fighting gloves, but as he stood, his throat and jaw shone in the sunlight like a star falling to Earth. *Bronze.* After escaping from the warehouse with Gatling Man last night, McCarthy looked to have undergone the same monstrous procedure we'd seen on the others— sacrificing his routine life to Tick Tock's cause—disfiguring and modifying his body in impossible ways in order to utilize illegal weaponry and magic. McCarthy zeroed in on me and flashed a wicked grin, his teeth all jagged bronze canines.

Bronze was a curious choice, though. Whoever had been altering these gangsters had understood, at least at a cursory level, how magic interacted with elements found in nature. This person had reinforced Mechanical and Gatling man with iron and silver—two extremely high melting points that could withstand the brutality of manufactured fire magic. But bronze? Bronze had a low point in comparison. And McCarthy didn't appear to have a gun on his person either, so no illegal bullets?

"I told you this meant war," McCarthy said, the words fractured, like he spoke through a mouthful of broken glass. He raised his glove, a pressure gauge whistled, and then his fist shot across the room, propelled via an internal steam pneumatic on a retractable coil.

I was so taken aback by the reality that McCarthy's hands had been *surgically removed* in favor of these modified gloves that I registered the attack too late, took the blow to the gut, and flew across the showroom before crashing into a table of evening purses. I gasped for air as I hit the floor and took a quick physical account of the immediate aches and pains. I didn't think I'd cracked a rib, but the sudden rush of adrenaline was already drowning out the hurts, making it difficult to assess. I pushed up onto my elbows as store patrons screamed around me, some rushing for the exit, others cowering behind the nearest displays and support columns.

McCarthy retracted the glove and pointed one of the big fingers at me. "I told him this was between *you* and *me*, you little magic pig. Go ahead and try to electrocute me now."

Bronze... a low threshold for heat, but it held up well to electricity. I hissed as I shifted onto my knees. "You told *who*? Tick Tock?"

"You think Tick Tock could do all this alone? He's good, but he ain't *that* good," McCarthy countered, spreading his arms wide in gesture. "He does what Driscoll ain't smart enough to—hire out."

"You're a low-tier, double-dealing street thug. You aren't privy to any of the details you want me to believe."

McCarthy smiled that wicked, shining, broken smile again. "I met him, you arrogant pig."

"*Who*?" I pressed a hand to my side as I lurched to my feet.

"Sawbones, they call him." McCarthy held his fists out in front of himself and laughed. "Get it?"

"Shut up!" Higgins shouted, his voice pitching high. He brandished a pistol, cocked the hammer, and pointed it at McCarthy's head. "Shut your metal mouth, you wooden spoon!"

An unaccounted for shot whizzed across the room, so quick and so sudden that the manufactured aether being activated by the Waterbury barely reached me before Higgins was hit in the shoulder and went down screaming.

"I've been shot! Oh, *God*. I'm bleeding!" he cried from the floor behind the glove display.

I looked to the left—there stood Gunner, arm extended and barrels of the Waterbury smoking. Gunner never missed his target, so he must have intentionally wounded Higgins—a lesser threat to handle afterward.

McCarthy spun and let loose his pneumatic fist again. It shot across the showroom, barely missing Gunner as he spun and fell backward to avoid the assault. The mechanical fist plowed through a case of fine jewelry, littering the floor with glass shards, diamonds, and wayward pearls, all glittering like dew in Central Park on an early spring morning. Gunner sat up, sans bowler, and shook broken glass from his hair. One palm pressed into the glass-ridden floor, and his other hand cocked the Waterbury, aimed, and shot as McCarthy retracted the fist. The round of aether bullets hit the fist just as it locked into McCarthy's mechanical wrist, causing it to ricochet and punch the gangster in his own face.

"*Fuck*!" McCarthy bellowed.

Gunner jumped to his feet, ran across the store, and barreled into McCarthy with his shoulder against the man's chest. They went flying and sprawling across the floor, McCarthy's bronze reinforcements screeching and gouging the polished wood as they skidded to a stop.

The few remaining patrons took the opportunity to rush for the exit. A young woman remained behind, though, the skin of her face and neck red and blotchy, her eyes wet with unfallen tears as she struggled to right her heavy skirts and stand from where she'd been hiding. The wail of a baby beside her immediately marked them as a target, and I ran toward them, the suddenness of my movement sending a sharp pain throughout my entire right side. I swallowed a gasp upon reaching her, bent to collect her sobbing boy, not even old enough to be out of his infant dress, and with my other hand, took her arm and led her stumbling to the open doors.

"*Go*," I said sternly, pushing the babe into her arms. "Hold on to him and leave the building, understand?"

"Y-yes, sir," she said, biting her lip. "Thank you."

I waited long enough to see her run for the lifts, despite the restrictions of her fashion choices, and then I returned to Grace Gallery. Gunner was atop McCarthy, the Waterbury pointed at McCarthy's forehead while the gangster struggled with one functional hand to prevent himself from being on the receiving end of a third eye.

"—put a hole in your face for every hair on his head you've disturbed," Gunner was saying, his voice low, husky, and frightening in its sincerity.

"Gunner, wait," I protested. "I need him alive."

The look Gunner shot me—possessive fury—it did something strange to my already-tender gut.

"Please," I insisted.

The internal deliberation was evident on his face, and I had to remind myself that this was *Gunner the Deadly*. Gunner killed men and did not feel regret afterward. Albeit, they were bad men, but he still killed them. But then Gunner rearranged his features into that cool, gentle expression I knew much better than the one of a man incensed, and he climbed to his feet. When McCarthy started to move, Gunner turned and stomped down on his mechanical hand with the heel of his shoe, causing sparks and steam to spew from the joints, and McCarthy howled.

"Don't. Move," Gunner said.

I tugged my trousers up before crouching beside McCarthy. "How'd you know where to find me?"

McCarthy winced as Gunner ground down harder on his mechanical hand, and his upper arm and shoulder spasmed wildly. "Tick Tock has eyes all over the city, pig." He spit at my feet.

Gunner pointed his Waterbury at McCarthy and cocked the hammer.

"Gunner." I held up a hand. "He's having me watched?" When McCarthy didn't answer, I searched the outer pockets of his winter coat and removed a PDD. "Do you speak with Tick Tock directly?"

McCarthy's facial muscles, just above the bronze plating, twitched in an almost convulsive manner.

"McCarthy," I snapped. "Answer me. What's his code?"

Something was wrong.

"Tell me about Sawbones," I demanded. "He did this to you—how? Is he Tick Tock's partner?"

McCarthy's breathing was becoming audibly labored at that point. He swallowed like he had something lodged in his throat, cut his tongue on the razor edges of his new teeth, and his mouth filled with blood.

I dropped the PDD to the floor, pushed Gunner's foot off McCarthy's mechanical hand, and held on to the broken contraption. Magic leached from the bronze, that same wriggling sensation I'd picked up on Mechanical Man in death, but more potent, more alive. It had a structure similar to aether, but not the elemental qualities. Almost… the lack thereof. This was as if casting aether through a looking glass. There was something obscene and other-worldly about it.

A magic with no name.

McCarthy began choking and gasping, his entire body spasming in a maddening way before his back arched him right off the floor. His mechanical hands, one broken from Gunner's shot, flexed manically, and his bronze teeth gnashed violently as he struggled for air.

Gunner grabbed my arm, pulled me to my feet, and drew me against himself.

I'll admit that, for a moment, I lost my sense of place and put a hand on Gunner's chest, gripping at the material of his waistcoat as McCarthy's entire body suddenly fell limp. The store was quiet. "The goddamn hell just happened?" I whispered.

Gunner holstered his Waterbury, placed his hand over my own, then pried my fingers free, leaving a blood smear on my skin. He moved to stand on either side of McCarthy's right leg, crouched, and hastily pawed through the pockets of his waistcoat and trousers before producing a small glass bottle. He slowly stood, studying the label.

"You're bleeding."

Gunner grunted.

"What'd you find?" I asked.

"Chocolate-coated strychnine tablets." Gunner glanced at me and tossed the bottle.

I caught it in both hands, saying, "Isn't this… used as a therapeutic? Paralysis, irritable nervous systems, that sort?"

"In high doses, it's a brutal and immediate poison."

"How immediate?"

"Minutes."

I looked at the label. "He would have taken them just before breaking through the window."

Gunner made a sound of agreement.

"But why?" I asked, looking up. "If his intention was to kill me?"

Gunner's gaze met mine. There was a brittleness about his expression—there and gone, like always, but I saw it. For one second, the blue of his eyes cracked and a blackness seeped to the surface. It wasn't a lie—because Gunner didn't lie—but a secret. Something I hadn't stumbled across, ascertained on my own, so he'd had no reason to explain it. And whatever it was… it hurt him.

"Gunner—"

"My dear," he interrupted. "Tick Tock and this Sawbones fellow want you dead, and they are not above getting rid of any and all evidence that might lead back to them after the fact."

I started to speak again, but was distracted by a muffled curse, the *chink* of glass rolling across the floor, and I remembered Higgins. I swiped the PDD from beside McCarthy's still body, pocketed it and the tablets, then ran across the mess of Grace Gallery's showroom. I moved around the side of the glove display and pointed an index finger at Higgins. Sparks of electricity snapped and popped from my fingertip. "Drop it."

His face white and suit covered in blood, Higgins shakily

released a bottle he'd been holding to his lips, the dark liquid spilling across the polished floor.

I retrieved the bottle as Gunner joined me. "Warner's Elixir," I read.

"Just a health syrup," Higgins protested.

Gunner removed his pistol.

Higgins started up that high-pitched sniffle-sob again.

I dipped my pinky into the bottle, collected a bit of the remaining syrup, and brought it to the tip of my tongue. There was a spark of rejuvenation mixed into the gag-inducing medicine. "This is laced with aether."

"Planning to heal and run?" Gunner asked Higgins.

"Grace Gallery is not a certified pharmacy," I said, waving the bottle at him. "And even if you had an authorized counter, all medications with aether as an active ingredient are illegal."

"I do believe he's well aware of that, Hamilton," Gunner said, a touch of humor finally returning to his tone.

I huffed but said, "Carl Higgins, I'm placing you under arrest for violation of jurisdiction codes S. 212: The transportation of illegal magic, S. 212.5: Intent to sell said illegal magic, S. 300: Threat of bodily harm to an identified federal agent, and—fuck—I don't even remember the code for medicinal products, but you're under arrest for that too, you piece of shit."

XV

January 1, 1882

"The prisoner transport just dropped off Mr. Higgins and the body of Tommy McCarthy," Moore confirmed, his tenor voice a bit tinny over my own PDD. "You're not here, though. Where are you?"

"Dr. Rose Lillingston's office."

"Dr. Lillingston?" Moore's tone immediately changed. "Are you hurt?"

"I'm as well as can be expected," I answered into the handheld transducer. I stood in front of a radiator in the small and cozy study on the first floor, empty save for myself, experimentally stretching this way and that until my muscles twinged in discomfort.

"Pulling your punches again, are you?"

"You did tell me last night you didn't have the patience for my bald-faced honesty."

"Yes, well, I think I'm in a better frame of mind for it today." There was a hint of displeasure in Moore's voice, but only a hint.

"Bruised rib, perhaps. Gunner sliced his hand. He's getting a few stitches."

Moore grunted.

"I was thinking," I continued, deflecting Moore's animalistic grumble. "This Sawbones fellow—if he's actually a doctor, as the name implies, he could have easily been the one to supply McCarthy with the strychnine tablets."

"It's a reasonable assumption," Moore admitted at length, and I could imagine him stroking his beard as he thought aloud. "But why murder the abomination you spent all night building?"

"Gunner said Tick Tock, and by association, Sawbones, are trying to take me out—the point agent on this investigation—at all costs. He suggested that they might also be attempting to cover their tracks in the process. McCarthy knew I was a lightning caster, and he went out of his way to see himself fitted with bronze, not silver, in order to pick a fight with me. Sawbones could have told McCarthy these tablets were anything in order for him to ingest enough to cause asphyxiation. None of them could have anticipated that Gunner would be with me. Perhaps Sawbones was banking on McCarthy making quick work of me, followed by the inevitability of his own mortality—thus, no loose ends to reach him or Tick Tock."

"This is becoming messy."

"Through no fault of the Bureau, sir."

"We've rounded up half a dozen suspects, and in less than twenty-four hours, half of *them* are dead." Moore blew out a breath that distorted over our communication devices and the hiss of static hurt my ears. "D.C. has been so far up my ass for answers this afternoon that I haven't been able to sit properly."

"Investigations take time."

"Not when we can successfully link Milo Ferguson to utilizing a prototype weapon on a federal agent. The same weapon that is now cropping up en masse across the biggest metropolis in the United States." Moore swore under his breath and then grew quiet.

The radiator kicked on, sputtering and hissing steam, fogging the window overlooking the street. I reached out, touched the glass, and an ice spell unfurled from my fingertips, covering the window in an opaque glaze. I moved the transducer away from my mouth, leaned forward, and blew warm air on the pane. Then, with my fingertip, I wrote something very childish:

C + S

"Still there, Hamilton?"

I blinked rapidly, raised the transducer, and answered, "Yes, sir." I wiped the love note from the glass.

"What are you thinking?"

The doctor laughed suddenly, her voice rising in volume as she opened the door at my back. I turned around to watch Gunner put on his bowler while thanking her, and then he looked at me. Dr. Lillingston, a longtime medical practitioner for the Bureau, was indicating to Gunner's bandaged hand while speaking, but he hadn't stopped staring at me from across the study.

My heart pounded against my breastbone. "I'm thinking...."

C + S

And then Gunner smiled at me.

"I need more time," I said, the words choked up in my throat.

"Time is an indefinite resource, Hamilton."

"Sorry—what?"

"Time," he repeated. "Nothing I can do about it—have as

much as you want. Although, I will suggest you not dillydally, because once D.C. has finished turning my asshole inside out, they'll be coming for you."

"I have to go." I cleared my throat and added, "Interview Mr. Higgins, please. I've a few avenues left to explore."

It was late afternoon when we returned to The Buchanan, but winter made the days terribly short, and dusk was already settling upon New York. I tossed my coats, hat, and both mine and McCarthy's PDD to the settee, and moved to one of the parlor windows. I drew up the sash, put my hands on the sill, and breathed in cold air that smelled of unfallen snow.

C + S

What had gotten into me? Everything, perhaps. Gunner, ready to kill a man in cold blood to defend me, and the terrifying reality that my marksman was still a mortal man who bled like the rest of us. But also the unabashed affections, the lovemaking, the suggestion that Gunner would somehow, someway, give me whatever I asked for—*a real courtship*—if only I would vocalize that need. If only I learned to trust myself, forgive myself, love myself. If only I had the courage to say to Moore, to Bligh, to society: this is who I am.

Who I am.

I took in a shuddering breath and blinked away hot tears.

But it didn't matter the lies I told and why I did. It would never change that who I was—was a monster.

"Gillian?" Gunner's voice was low from where he stood a few steps behind me.

"Please give me a moment," I managed to say with a reasonably leveled tone.

Gunner said nothing more, and after breathing in enough cold air to leave me light-headed, I registered the clink of glasses and slosh of liquid. I passed a hand over my face and turned so I was sitting on the sill to watch him. Gunner had made himself comfortable—no suit coat, sleeves rolled back—and was mixing two drinks from the small liquor collection I had on the mantel.

"Bitters?" he asked at length.

I crossed my arms and said, "Behind the absinthe."

Gunner nodded and finished the concoction. He picked up two glasses, returned to the window, and offered one to me. "Gin cocktail. Sans lemon peel."

I thanked him and took a sip. "It's good."

Gunner combed his fingers through my hair. "Your disquiet worries me."

I shook my head, staring at my shoes. "These anxieties aren't anything new."

"But something has set them in motion."

I counted the buttons on each shoe before whispering, "Sometimes I can't breathe. I—I hear sounds from memories, and they repeat over and over and it makes me sick." I took another sip of the cocktail and realized my hand was shaking. "It's gotten worse since meeting you. And now it sounds like I'm blaming you."

"Are you?" There was no malice in Gunner's question. Just straight and to the point, as always.

I shook my head. "Of course not. It's only… when you look at me, when you see what I've lied about…. It's as if I managed to convince myself, for years, those lies were truths. And now the house of cards has come down, I'm looking at the wasteland my life really is, and I don't know what to do."

Gunner set his glass on the sill, pulled me to stand, then took my glass and set it beside his own. He closed the window, brought me close, then settled his hands on my hips—those two warm weights grounding me in the here and now. I leaned into him, wrapped my arms around Gunner's neck, and pressed my face against his chest.

"I want to tell you," I said.

"Are you ready to?"

"No…."

"Then I won't push it further. Let it go, Gillian."

Gillian….

Gunner drew a hand up, eased one of mine from his neck, and held my hand in his own. He began to sway from foot to foot, in tune to no music, and asked, "Are you familiar with Soldier's Heart? They say it's an invisible illness. Many soldiers who survived the war began to exhibit peculiar symptoms of distress, despite being physically sound."

"Like what?" I whispered.

"A fatigue of sorts. Some described the war on loop in their brain—never shutting off. They feel as if they were reliving it over and over. Others expressed being unable to sleep or an accelerated heartrate even when standing still. I know you were only a boy during the war, not a soldier—"

My knees locked and I dug my other hand into his nape.

Gunner stopped speaking abruptly, leaned back, and tilted my chin up so our eyes met.

I viciously shook my head. "*I can't.*"

Gunner wiped under my eyes with his thumbs and kissed my forehead. "Okay," he said simply.

I pushed him away without warning and walked across the parlor while clearing my throat. "Forget about this moment."

"You know I can't do that."

"Then *pretend*," I snapped, turning to face Gunner.

His eyes narrowed as if he'd been slapped.

I growled under my breath, scrubbed my face with both

hands, then said, "How did you know about the strychnine tablets?"

"Strychnine isn't a secret."

"It's method of poisoning," I corrected. "How'd you know?"

"Strychnine is used as a muscle stimulant," Gunner answered. "It's also used to kill rats. Are you angry with me?"

"No," I retorted, although from my tone, God himself would call me a liar. "But you have a practical understanding of it. I know. I saw it on your face. Don't lie to me."

Gunner didn't move, didn't breathe—he was so still, in fact, he might have been a victim of Medusa. Then, without warning, he squared his shoulders, rolled down his sleeves, and said, "A man I loved died from an overdose of strychnine." Gunner collected his coat he'd left beside mine on the settee, pulled his arms through, then said to me, "I never lie."

"Where are you going?" I asked, turning as he passed me and headed for the door.

"To take a walk."

"Constantine—"

He looked at me as he said, "Whatever you've lived through—*survived*—Gillian Hamilton, I am sorry. Sorry that you endured immeasurable pain and heartache at such a young age, and without trust in our current systems, were forced to carry that sense of abandonment into adulthood. I *am* sorry. But you said you remembered everything I told you in Arizona? Remember this: we aren't so different." He stepped into the hall and pulled the door shut behind him.

The steam-powered lights of my apartment weren't bright enough to work by. I'd collected the bulbs from the water closet and bedroom, piled them onto my cleared-off writing desk in the parlor, and touched each of the foot contacts until my magic fueled the filaments and filled the apartment with a low hum. I fetched the toolkit from the bottom drawer, unrolled it across the tabletop, then walked across the parlor while tugging the purple-tinted goggles over my eyes. I fetched my gin from the windowsill, McCarthy's PDD from the settee, and settled down to conduct a little engineering of my own.

I knocked back half of the cocktail, attached an ocular loupe to one of the lenses, and began to unscrew the tiny mechanics of the handheld transducer. Unfortunately, McCarthy either hadn't owned it for long or didn't use it often, such as my own tendency, because the brass punch buttons still shone and suggested no wear on the most commonly used numbers.

A man I loved died from an overdose of strychnine.

Had that man loved Gunner back? Had he ever lain awake in bed, until that moment late night becomes early morning, thinking about Gunner? Had he ever kissed Gunner and equated it to touching Heaven? Had he realized what a *good man* Gunner was? That he deserved honesty and integrity, and this cat-and-mouse game with his heart and his freedom was further proof of what a despicable human I was—

The nerves in my hand spasmed and I fumbled with the tool. I cursed under my breath, flexed my fingers for a moment, then finished taking the cover off the transducer. Tightly coiled wires were attached to plugs activated by the push buttons. I pushed the second ocular loupe down for a greater magnification, switched tools, and started testing the wires for repeated usage.

Brutal and immediate poison.

How did I compare to that man? Was he taller? Stronger? More kind than me? More handsome than me? Was he afraid like me, holding back from meeting Gunner even halfway, begging for more time because I wasn't ready to lose him (and that would most assuredly happen when I told him the truth), or did that man… did he just love Gunner and damn everything and everyone else?

5… 5… 3…. Two more digits and I'd have the code most initiated from McCarthy's PDD.

I tinkered with the next coupling of wires and plugs.

What side of the law had that other man been on?

Gunner's, probably.

At least, I was fairly certain Gunner hadn't made it a habit of fucking coppers prior to me.

"Danny," I muttered.

Wait—what?

I dropped the tool and leaned back in my chair. "Danny?"

I glanced at the cocktail, picked up the glass, and sniffed. Gin, yes, but Gunner had added absinthe as well. No surprise, what with the subtle licorice flavor associated with the Green Fairy. But I should have told him not to use absinthe—it got me drunk quicker than most liquors. Maybe it even caused mild hallucinations, because I had not a clue where—then, quite simply, I recalled the last thing Milo Ferguson had said to Gunner, while we were aboard his airship in Shallow Grave: *I'm going to make you suffer. The same way that Danny did.*

Pushing the chair back, legs stuttering loudly against the wood floor, I stood, fetched my coat from the settee, and began to pull it on in order to go find Gunner. Sure, he didn't lie, but he also wasn't the talkative sort. If I didn't ask, point-blank, he rarely offered further explanation on any given subject. So I'd go find him and I'd ask: who's Danny? Is he the man you loved? And then I'd tell Gunner—I'd tell him I was sorry for earlier.

But I didn't make it to the door.

I didn't even leave the settee.

If I asked, Gunner would tell me. But *why* was I asking? Why did it even *matter*? I was behaving like an insecure fool. Jealous of a man who'd held Gunner's affections before we'd even met, for Christ's sake. And now that man—be it Danny or someone else—was dead. He was dead, and Gunner, for at least the time being, was mine. As long as I didn't make a mockery of Gunner's trust and emotions—and yes, I did still need to apologize—time would be in my favor for a minute more.

I immediately shrugged out of the coat and returned it to the cushion beside my own PDD. It *was* a touch disconcerting however, that Milo Ferguson was part of the conversation. I could be wrong about Danny, of course. He might very well have been someone else, and the reference to suffering, although applicable to a painful death by poison, could have been nothing more than my panicked brain trying to turn over parts of a mystery where my sleuthing was not appreciated. But perhaps I could receive confirmation via a safer route— one that wouldn't jeopardize the complexities between Gunner and myself. I was a federal agent, after all. And one with considerable security clearances. What the hell was the Bureau even doing with funding and contacts if I couldn't manage some basic information about a likely dead felon? It'd appease my curiosity, assure me that Gunner wasn't in any sort of danger himself, and then—done. Matter dropped.

I picked up my PDD, set the receiver over my ears, punched in a code for the Bureau's rogues' gallery department, and identified myself when I was answered by the agent on duty. "I need a file pulled, if there is one—suspect went by Danny—cross-check with any Daniels on record. Last name unknown, occupation unknown, now deceased."

The static voice on the other end asked in a slow, disbelieving tone, "You want me to find a file for a now-dead rogue, based on absolutely nothing but a first name?"

"I don't believe I stuttered." I wasn't sure if that knee-jerk response was my natural salt, as Gunner called it, or the absinthe.

"Do you have a last known location?"

"No. Prioritize the West Coast, but the entire country is fair game."

A prolonged sigh was followed by, "It might take a bit of time."

"It's not an emergency." I thanked the agent, disconnected, and tossed the PDD back on the settee. "Happy?" I asked myself. "Christ Almighty…." I returned to the writing desk, parked my backside, and resumed solving a mystery that *was* entirely my business.

55387.

McCarthy's most pinged recipient was 55387.

It took longer than I'd anticipated to crack the final digit. McCarthy seemed to have had a tendency to mispunch the code and so I'd waffled between 7 and 4 for some time, but when I'd finally made the call with 4, I received an obnoxious, high-pitched tone in the receivers that indicated the code routed nowhere. I removed the ocular loupes, set them on the table, then tugged the goggles down to rest around my neck. I downed the rest of the cocktail and studied the recently taken-apart, now put back together, device.

This code might very well lead to Tick Tock himself, as McCarthy had suggested, and hearing his voice was going to be our biggest lead yet. If he answered, I could request Convey & Dispatch, the country's leading purveyor of PDD support, to triangulate the code's location. I'd avoid running blind into the dangers of Mulberry Bend, and arrest this bastard gangster threatening not just humanity as a whole, but specifically the magic community. Because without expedited control of these illegal weapons and bullets, we were in trouble. I'd seen firsthand the devastation that uncontrolled magic could do, but worse, my very existence had only been legal for seventeen years. Seventeen years ago, my ability to control the elements, a skill I never wished to possess, was seen as something to fear, to *attack*. And if Tick Tock wasn't stopped… well, society hadn't made enough strides forward to not slip back into that old dread. Of this, I was certain.

I heard the *snap*, *snap*, *snap* of my fingers being broken and a cold sweat came over me. I told myself this was not the time, took a few deep breaths, then punched in 55387.

"McCarthy?" Tick Tock answered brusquely.

It took a heartbeat for the voice to register.

And then a fury I hadn't known in years welled up inside me, my blood like that of the Seventh Circle of Hell: *The river of boiling blood in which are steeped, All who struck down their fellow men.*

"Henry Bligh."

XVI

January 1, 1882

Gunner returned to the apartment amid a self-induced whirlwind.

"This is Special Agent Gillian Hamilton with the Federal Bureau of Magic and Steam, and I've been trying to request— no authorization? What do you mean? *I'm* the senior agent on this case. Oh, to hell with that, sir!" I all but hollered into my PDD at the poor bastard at Convey & Dispatch. I had one arm through my winter coat sleeve, the other hanging like a broken wing as I paced the parlor floor. "This is a matter of citywide security. I need that code's last pinged location traced *now*." I clenched my jaw as the representative insisted there was nothing he could do without the request coming directly from Moore, as it was simply too intrusive into the client's privacy.

I swore again, louder, tore the PDD from my ears, and threw it at the wall. I turned while yanking my other sleeve on to see Gunner standing in the open doorway. "Constantine."

His eyebrows rose in response.

I rushed toward him, grabbed ahold of his tie, gave it a firm tug, and like I'd flicked a switch inside him, Gunner melted against my body and kissed me hard. "I'm sorry," I whispered against his mouth.

"For?"

He damn well knew. But he deserved to hear the words. "For my accusation—that you would lie. And it's not my business, this other man. It's not my business who you've slept with before me, or… or loved before me."

The corner of Gunner's mouth hooked up. "Gillian," he said, and never had hearing him say my name in that husky voice felt so good. "If you ask me, I'll tell you. But I'd prefer you didn't. Not right now. It's a loss I'm still working through."

I quickly nodded and swallowed the knot of jealousy I couldn't manage to let go of, despite the absurdity of it. If he wasn't going to pressure *me*, I had to respect Gunner's boundaries about this particular subject in return. "I understand."

Gunner gently pried my hand from his tie, his smile growing as he did. He leaned back to check the hallway, as we had, I realized, shared that moment in the open doorway. Looking at me once again, Gunner smoothed his blunt fingertips against the grays on the side of my head. "What has you so upset?"

No authorization.

55387.

Henry Bligh.

"It's Bligh," I said in a rush. I pushed Gunner into the hall, shut the apartment door, and ran for the stairs. "Bligh is Tick Tock."

"*What?*" Gunner's tone was total disbelief as he followed close behind.

I should have liked to see that very human expression ripple across his typically flat features, but I was already rushing down the stairs and didn't dare stop. "I tinkered with McCarthy's PDD, figured out the code he pinged most often. When I rang it, Bligh answered, and he knew McCarthy—was expecting him!" I jumped the last two steps, skidded around the corner, and kept going down the final set of stairs. "He hung up on me and wouldn't answer when I tried again. I've asked the communication support in the city to triangulate Bligh's location, but they won't release the address to anyone but Moore."

"Why haven't you called Moore?" Gunner returned, his feet hitting the landing behind me, and the two of us rushed out the front door, past Dawson and into the cold night.

"I did. Several times!" I called, heart pounding and blood pumping as I ran down the block. "He's not answering. I can't fucking imagine where he'd be—he was supposed to be interviewing Higgins."

It was five blocks from The Buchanan to the field office—four streets and one avenue. Even with the stitch in my side from the blow by McCarthy, we reached the alleyway with the unassuming side entrance in just over a minute. The city had been a blur of steam-powered color—reds and greens burning like the eyes of a colossus—black and uneven cobblestone roads like broken teeth in its gaping maw, and all the while, the monster didn't catch me—couldn't catch me—because I was fueled by the mounting panic that something was *very wrong*.

Moore always wore his PDD around his neck. I'd have believed he slept with it, for Christ's sake. His agents knew, no matter where he was, what he was doing, or the hour of day, Moore would answer. And not to push a sense of egotism, but I was *not* the man Moore would choose to ignore. Even if he was angry, livid, beside himself with me, with Gunner, with the concept of *us*, Moore would not choose this moment, *this case*, to enact some petty sort of revenge by leaving my calls pinging into the ether.

And if Moore couldn't answer….

I skidded to a stop in the alley, found my keys, and unlocked the door. While I hadn't explained my sense of urgency to Gunner, he followed on my heels without question as I ran along the winding corridors and started up the stairs to the offices. He had to have understood that the state director not answering calls from a senior agent was troublesome. The two of them might not have liked each other, and that was putting it cordially, but I do believed Gunner held Moore in esteem. In fact, if Moore wasn't so good at his job and Gunner could come and go from New York as he pleased, I didn't think the reluctant respect between them would exist.

But most importantly, Moore was my colleague, my boss, and the closest thing I'd ever had to a friend. I cared deeply for him, even if it was not in the manner Moore wished.

Rachel Plunket, Bligh's bruiser partner, was coming down the stairs with a stack of files in both hands. She looked at me, blushed a furious shade of crimson, and tried to avert her gaze while slinking by.

"Plunket." I sidestepped and cut her off. "Where's your partner?"

She huffed a little, but the attitude toward me had always seemed… forced, as if it were a performance for Bligh's sake. Plunket looked at me, the paperwork, me, Gunner, me again, then shot Gunner a second once-over. A crease settled between her brows, like he was a familiar face she just *couldn't quite place* at the given moment.

"Plunket," I said again, more firmly. "Where is Agent Bligh?"

Plunket redirected her attention and then shook her head. "Still with Moore, I suppose. We've been regulated to paper-pushing duties after last night and—"

I held up a hand to stop her. "What do you mean, still with Moore?"

"Moore called him into a meeting, maybe fifteen minutes ago."

"Without you." It was not a question.

Plunket colored again, and it made her strong features pop. "Um, I don't believe the impromptu oversight review had anything to do with our partnership."

"That's a very polite way of admitting your partner stepped in it," Gunner said to her.

I moved around Plunket and continued up the stairs.

"Hamilton," she called after me. "What's going on?"

"If you see Bligh, you detain him," I answered over my shoulder. "That's an order."

Gunner kept on me until we reached the fourth-floor landing, where I hastily led the way down the hall toward Moore's private office, luckily in the opposite direction of an open-floor bullpen of scholar agents. His door was closed. I knocked and called loud enough to be heard through the heavy wood, "Sir? It's Agent Hamilton. I need to speak with you at once."

No response.

"It's an emergency," I continued, grabbing the knob and trying it, only to find it locked. I looked at Gunner. "He never locks the door."

Gunner put a hand on my chest, gently pushed me aside, then raised his foot and slammed his heel into the door. The wood audibly cracked but seemed to hold, so Gunner smashed it again. On the second try, the entire lock plate snapped, the door crashed against the inner wall, and broken bits of wood flew every which way.

The sounds of alarm from the bullpen were immediate, but I didn't wait around to explain myself. I rushed inside and took in the particulars of the office—flashes of detail that registered like a piano student's first attempt at staccato.

Curtain drawn across the window.

Tumbler overturned on the desktop.

Amber liquid and a shattered decanter.

An arm on the floor, just visible behind the desk.

"Moore!" I moved around the furniture, shoved his chair aside, and got down on my knees. Moore was unresponsive and bleeding from the side of his head. I grabbed his waistcoat in both hands, smoke and sparks already materializing between us, and shook him hard. "Moore. Please… *Loren*, wake up."

A stampede thundered down the hallway and then voices were filling the doorway, agents from the bullpen demanding I identify myself at once.

I sat up so they could see me over the desktop. "Fetch Dr. Lillingston at once." The half dozen of them hesitated a second too long, and I snapped, "*Now*!" As they scrambled from the office, Gunner hooked his hands under my arms and hoisted me out of the way. I flailed wildly against him, saying, "Stop it—*stop*—let me cast aether."

"Calm down," Gunner ordered. He shoved me against the window and took up the space beside Moore. He pressed his fingers to Moore's neck, and his eyes narrowed.

"No pulse?"

"I don't think so."

I put a hand to my chest as if my own heart were about to give out. "Aether won't work without a goddamn *pulse* from the recipient."

Gunner yanked off his bowler, threw it across the room, leaned over Moore, pinched his nose, and blew a deep breath into his mouth.

"Gunner," I protested. "What're you—expired air won't

do him any good."

But Gunner ignored me. He blew a second lungful of air, a third, and after the fourth, Moore coughed and inhaled on a ragged breath. Gunner sat back and looked at me. "Come cast your aether."

I moved forward without conscious thought, staring at Gunner with what I suspected was a wild and disbelieving expression, but then I was on my knees beside Moore's head, his temple still bleeding, and I righted my focus to the matter at hand. I put my goggles on, cast aether in one hand, and pressed the bright magic to the wound. Even though I wasn't physically touching Moore this time, my magic bridged the inches between us, and I could feel his heat warming the underbelly of my wrist. A bit of smoke coiled in the air between us, and Moore grunted in discomfort.

"No, don't move. Don't open your eyes," I told him.

I poured more magic into the aether spell, already feeling the exhaustive side effects of such a complex magic being used in its most potent method possible—healing. Destruction with aether was an incredible force, but it was always easier to break the world than it was to mend it. As I'd done to Addison's face, I stopped the bleeding and sutured the skin some, but the major complaints of any wound would still need to be addressed by medicine, not magic. Aether couldn't repair broken bones, torn muscle, or God forbid, raise the dead. The caster simply didn't have the energy required for that level of healing—even a caster such as me.

Cautiously, I curled my fingers into a fist, cutting off the aether's energy stream and managing to keep my nerves from having a caustic reaction again. I slowly unfurled my hand, tugged the goggles down, and dared to lightly press my fingers against the semihealed wound. Moore winced as electricity jumped from me and nipped his skin.

"Sorry," I said. "I'm trying—"

"Gillian?" Moore asked, his usual smooth tenor rough around the edges.

"Yes."

He cracked a smile and asked, his eyes still closed, "Are we alone?"

"Gunner is with me."

"Ah…." A pause, and then he said anyway, "When I imagined having my head in your lap, it wasn't quite like this."

"Your head in my lap would result in spontaneous combustion and electrocution, Loren."

"What a way to go out."

I laughed a little, removed my hand from the still-red skin, and said, "I was scared for a moment."

Moore hummed under his breath.

"What happened, sir?"

Moore opened his eyes and stared at me, looming upside down over his face. "Bligh had interrupted my interview… with Higgins. Yes. He was adamant about joining me."

"Did you allow it?"

"I forbade it. He was infuriated."

"Bligh is never happy," I pointed out.

Moore was frowning. "Not like this. I must have sent him into the hall—I heard him answer a PDD call… wasn't his Bureau-issued device."

"I called him," I explained. "I took apart McCarthy's and traced the most pinged code. Bligh answered it, expecting McCarthy."

"That's right." Moore closed his eyes and massaged his temples. "I remember thinking, does Bligh know Carl Higgins? Why, when this has never been his case, is he so insistent to be part of *this* interview? And when I heard

McCarthy's name…." He weakly snapped his fingers.

I glanced at Gunner and said, "Triangulating Bligh's location is a waste now. He was *here*."

"Call him again. He doesn't have much of a lead on us."

"I said he was a self-centered man-child, not stupid. He won't pick up." I looked to Moore once again. "How'd you end up in your office?"

"It's a blur. I wanted to speak with Bligh—about what I'd overheard him say. I think… I must have poured a drink. I left the decanter on the desk." He looked at me again. "One of my agents is a gangster."

"It would appear as such, sir."

"I needed a drink," Moore muttered. "That's the last thing I recall."

Gunner rose to his feet and moved around us, broken glass crunching underfoot. "Bligh entered your office, grabbed the bottle, and smashed it over your head. He locked the door as he left and intended for you to bleed out."

"Speculation," Moore replied.

"Hardly. You're covered in blood, whiskey, and glass."

Moore's expression grew quizzical as he looked down at himself. "Almost done in by my Dublin, twelve years."

"Agent Hamilton," a woman called from the doorway, slightly out of breath. "Dr. Lillingston has arrived. She's on her way upstairs now."

"Thank you," I answered. And to Moore I said, "I have to find Bligh."

"Dead or alive, Hamilton. And given the recent turn of events…."

"Understood, sir."

XVII

January 1, 1882

"What's the plan?" Gunner asked, following me down the hall that led away from Moore's office. The stairs came up on our right, and the half-sized bullpen that overlooked the cells where Fishback had met his end was on the left. Just beyond either was the doorway that led to the open floor of scholar agents, several of whom were now hovering in the archway, watching me.

Watching Gunner.

It only took one of them to connect the dots: blue eyes, black hair, lean build, six feet.

"I'm going to kill Henry Bligh," I answered, my tone mere window dressing for the blackness raging inside me.

I didn't need a view to confirm a storm was rolling in across midtown—I could *feel* it. Undoubtedly, the wary scholars at the end of the hall could sense it as well. Perhaps my magic, a whirlwind of violence building by the minute that I felt no desire to temper, was all that kept them from proclaiming Gunner's arrest in my presence. I had been an enigma to them before, but now I was dangerous and they knew it.

Gunner grabbed my arm, pulled me to a stop, and spun me to look up at him. If he was at all troubled by the agents surrounding us—him—he in no way showed it. "We still don't know where Tick Tock—Bligh—holes up. That family isn't hurting for country estates. Why would he willingly use Mulberry Bend as a refuge?"

"He's been successfully maintaining two distinct lives— for months, at minimum," I answered. "He's built Tick Tock up, by name alone, as a new terror to this city. If a face is put to it now, he'll lose that ever-present threat of death he holds over the other gangsters. He's not some sort of high collar criminal. If Bligh is found out, his esteemed position with the Bureau, as well as his family inheritance, will be gone. No, he'd absolutely keep away from Millionaire's Row or any other location that could be linked back to his name."

"There's still far too many possibilities around the Bend," Gunner countered. "Warehouses, tenements, storefronts. These are not the sort of citizens who welcome a badge into their neighborhood, my dear."

I smiled at that—one of self-mockery, but a smile nonetheless. "I thrive where I'm not wanted."

"Gray looks good on you."

"My director gave me explicit orders."

"I know."

"This isn't vigilantism."

The corners of Gunner's eyes crinkled. "I know. What do you need from me?"

I gave the room over my shoulder a glance, then said, "I'm going to speak with Higgins. I think the connection between him and Bligh is a critical one—he might know the specifics of Tick Tock's hideout on the Bend." I looked at

Gunner again. "Be ready outside."

"It's a shame," he replied, his tone casual, if not *this side* of bored, "airships being prohibited south of Grand Central."

"What're you planning?"

Gunner merely smiled in response. He turned to go down the stairs, but I took his coat sleeve, pulled him toward me, and kissed him. I kissed him and made certain that everyone watching couldn't mistake it for anything but what it was.

Love.

"If I'm going to war with gangsters and untold illegal magic, I don't want to have any regrets," I whispered after pulling away.

"You've made a scene," Gunner said, just as quiet, although he hadn't broken eye contact with me.

"This is who I am. I'm sick to death of being afraid. All these lies, survival or not, they've built a life that has no room for you—and that's not worth it to me. If I cannot be both an agent and happy, *to hell with them.*"

Gunner smiled once again, so warmly that it could have thawed the winter night entirely and brought about an early spring. "I do believe this breath will matter tomorrow, Gillian Hamilton."

I exhaled a choked-up laugh. "I'll be downstairs in a moment." I watched him descend the stairs before turning to the group with their mouths agape. "I want five agents on Director Moore's office at once. And if the doctor decides to move him out-of-building, I want a dozen more at his side. A combination of caster and bruiser partners—Agent Boggs, please see to assignments at once."

Boggs, a middle-aged scholar who'd been with the Bureau for a number of years, albeit at a desk, seemed to waffle between taking a direct order from a senior agent and pointing out the obvious—a sodomite was among them. "*Ah....*"

"Was I not clear?" I countered.

"No—I mean, yes, sir. Of course." And with that, Boggs turned and began barking orders, calling agents out by name, and taking control of Moore's immediate safety.

I stormed into the half bullpen and called over my shoulder, "And someone arrest Agent Plunket! I have no idea what team she's playing for…." Despite a boarded-up window and scorched cell on the other side of the two stone-cold sober agents standing guard at the jail door, this was still one of the most secure rooms in the building for housing suspects in the interim. "Out," I ordered.

The team looked at each other, the bruiser declining to speak while the caster said, "Director Moore ordered—"

"Agent Henry Bligh just tried to kill Director Moore," I interjected. "I'm in charge. *Out*."

Thunder rumbled from outside the windows, and flashes of lightning were visible at the edges of the curtains. Magic-induced static shot through the air, raising the hairs on my arms. But even as my emotions threw the raw elements into chaos, I could feel the energy bumping against the tangible threshold the illegal magic had been creating and building with every fire bullet shot.

Luckily, the two agents scurried from the room without further argument.

I held a hand out and threw the jail room door open with a well-timed blast of wind magic. As I entered the narrow hallway, Higgins made an audible squeak.

"Don't you come any closer," he exclaimed, pressing himself against the far wall of the cell. "I'll scream. I swear it."

The air rustled around me as I approached. "I hope you do."

Higgins's face blanched, his eyes bugging out, and I swore his waxed mustache drooped. Standing behind bars, sans suit coat, shirt caked and hardened with dried blood, his arm in a sling… he looked pathetic. "Wh-what do you want?" he all but whimpered.

"Tell me about the aether syrup."

Higgins sniffed. Then sniffed again. "The—syrup?"

"Is there an echo?" I asked.

"It's a sugar concoction," he protested. "With a dash of liquid aether. It works wonders for the complications of women—uterine and ovarian pain, for example—"

"You're not a doctor," I shouted. "'It works wonders….' *Christ Almighty*. Next you'll tell me it's a miracle drug like laudanum."

"Aether isn't addictive."

"No, it only has a curious side effect of sudden death if cast incorrectly. Did you, even once, consider the possibility that you were transporting and selling a magic-induced medicine cast by someone without the essential training? Or hell, someone with wicked intentions?"

Higgins's mustache quivered as he sniffed and sobbed.

"I want a list of customers."

"A list?" he repeated, and when the air kicked up around me, Higgins held out his good arm in protest. "I only mean, I can't possibly! Half of the ladies in society come to me on the regular. There's a demand and I've got the means in which to fill it."

"Explain."

"A little warehouse downtown for bottling and labeling. Warner's Elixir is my side business."

"How has this gone completely undetected by the Bureau?"

Higgins tried to shrug both shoulders and then hissed in pain. "My enterprise is small, sir. Nothing on the scale of what Tick Tock was doing. And women—women are cunning. They know how to keep a good thing secret. Aqua Tofana killed some 600 unwanted husbands in Italy before the Queen of Poison was finally found out."

No doubt Gunner would have understood that reference more than I did.

I shook my head. "You must have a principal customer. The one who is referring others to you?"

"Oh… uh… yes."

"And she must have a name," I ground out.

Higgins swallowed hard and said, "Martha Olin. You're familiar? Her daughter, Emma, is about to marry into Old Money."

I pushed Higgins out the front door of the field office, holding on to his cuffed hands from behind as we walked down the steps. The sky was alight with bolts of lightning, the city echoing with the symphonic booms of thunder, and a wind had kicked up the top layer of snow, swirling it around us like miniature whirlwinds.

I was saying, "You're going to direct me to this warehouse of—*what on Earth*?"

Parked in front of the FBMS was a pristine white touring automobile. The front body was an open-style with no hood, so as to flaunt the expensive brass and chrome steam engine and radiator. The exhaust pipes on either side spit hot steam into the night air, and pressure gauges whistled in time with the wind. The front grille had been completely dismantled and replaced with a unique Gatling gun that was fired from a crank on the driver's dash once the roadster hit a certain speed.

I knew this because the Bureau had confiscated the custom automobile several months ago, citing half a dozen illegal uses of steam power. The inclusion of a nonmagic weapon had caused the metropolitan police and FBMS to fight over who had the jurisdiction to see the case to its conclusion, and so the evidence had been parked on the west side of the field office under lock and key since, hell, September, I believed.

Gunner stepped around the front of the auto and said, while putting his goggles on, "You didn't expect to walk to Mulberry Bend, did you?"

"How did you get this from evidence?" Then I held up my free hand and shook my head. "No, never mind. I don't want to know."

"*You*," Higgins said suddenly, jutting his chin toward Gunner. "The Waterbury—that *atrocious* wardrobe—you're Gunner the Deadly, aren't you?"

The corner of Gunner's mouth tugged upward, and I felt I knew his smiles well enough by now to know that particular look wasn't amusement so much as a warning of danger.

I jerked Higgins's handcuffs. "Don't give him an excuse to shoot you again."

"The Bureau is doing business with an outlaw," Higgins continued, now struggling in my hold. "I'm reporting this. You hear me?"

"I'll be happy to look into it for you."

"Not *you*!" Higgins exclaimed. "You're crooked. A double-dealing, two-timing—"

Gunner unholstered his Waterbury and took aim at Higgins's face. "Stop."

Higgins immediately fell silent, his mouth still hanging open.

"Where's your warehouse?" I asked after a breath passed between the three of us.

Higgins sniffed a few times. "Bayard and Mulberry."

"Nice neighborhood," Gunner remarked dryly as he put

his Waterbury away.

"That's where Tick Tock is," I said.

Higgins startled and tried to turn and look at me. "*What?*"

"Are you certain?" Gunner asked.

"Mr. Higgins's best customer of his famous Warner's Elixir is none other than Bligh's mother-in-law, Martha Olin," I explained. "Knowing she had access to some quality magic, Bligh could have easily been put into contact with Higgins. All of the social connections immediately fall into place."

"I've never spoken to Mr. Bligh," Higgins interrupted.

"No," Gunner said to Higgins, turning his head slightly to study the other man. "But you spoke to Tick Tock—who you've never met in person, I'm sure."

Higgins didn't have a retaliation to that comment.

"Bligh—*Tick Tock*—knew you had an illegal caster out West for the aether syrup, so he simply utilized your already-established contact, right?" I asked Higgins.

"Yes, but Tick Tock needed an architect too, to build the manufactured spells. Luther, my caster, found the architect in California."

"Luther," I repeated. "Luther Jones?"

Higgins nodded.

"The Bureau's been wanting him for years—thank you for the intel."

"Who was the architect?" Gunner asked Higgins.

"I don't know, honest. Luther only corresponded with me twice—once that he'd find someone so we could take on Tick Tock's business, then again to confirm he'd found an architect he could work with."

"Was the architect's name Weaver?" Gunner pressed.

I shot him a look, but all of Gunner's attention was on Higgins.

"Yes," Higgins murmured. "I don't believe it's his real name, but *you* would know— criminals and their aliases."

"You're a damn criminal too, Carl Higgins," I said firmly, giving his handcuffs another shake.

"How long ago was this?" Gunner continued.

"Gunner—" I started, but he held a hand up and cut my protest short.

Higgins awkwardly looked over his shoulder at me, then back to Gunner. "I don't—that is—just last February? Yes, that sounds right. Tick Tock reached out to me, I inquired with Luther, and he'd found Weaver within the month. There were some prototypes that didn't make the cut a few months ago…."

"Milo Ferguson," Gunner replied. "You gave them to Tinkerer to test."

An automobile rounded the corner of Twenty-Third Street, the hiss of its steam and bump of wheels on cobblestone barely audible over the storm.

"*I* didn't!" Higgins cried. "It wasn't my idea at all. And Tick Tock was—I thought he was going to kill me. He was livid that some of the ammunition had been leaked because fools at the FBMS found out about it."

I shook Higgins for a third time.

"Ow! My shoulder, little you bastard."

The other auto, a black touring with brass fixtures so buffed and polished that the housing of the headlights and exhaust pipes built around the shape of the engine hood practically glowed in the dark, slowed its approach, nearly coming to a dead stop as it became parallel with the white touring. Although distracted by the curious onlookers, I drew my attention back to the conversation as Gunner was saying:

"Weaver provided the prototypes to Tinkerer, didn't he?"

Higgins said in a harassed tone, "Well, it must have been

him. It sure as hell wasn't Luther or myself—"

The activation of fire magic gave a sudden jolt to the atmosphere. It crept up my spine, the spell close enough that I could feel the searing heat on my skin and half expected blisters to begin forming. Then the toxic sensation of manufactured magic hit me, and the current of raw energy around us buckled and tore. I turned to the black touring a second time and watched as Gatling Man, sitting in the passenger seat, maneuvered his weapon out the open window, pointed at us with a silver finger, and opened fire.

XVIII

January 1, 1882

"Gunner!"

I didn't even think. I acted on instinct—save Gunner at all costs. I shoved Higgins aside and made a grand, sweeping gesture over Gunner, whose back was to the street. A tidal wave of glittering blue water came up from the frozen ground and created an arc over his body just as the gunfire began. I held my other hand in front of myself as the automobile revved its steam engine and started driving, Gatling Man still shooting even as I brought another shield of water up over myself. The crash and roar of fire bullets hitting magic their elemental opposite was so loud, one could believe an airship had exploded somewhere nearby.

It wasn't until the automobile had reached the end of the block and I had extinguished my own spell that I was able to pick up the bloodcurdling screams among the high-pitched ringing in my ears. I immediately turned to Gunner, but he was okay—more than okay as he raced into the middle of the street, raised his Waterbury, and took shots at the black touring making a successful getaway. When I looked to Higgins, however—

I swore loudly and cast another spell to put out the flames, but by the time they'd dissipated, his anguished cries had ceased and Carl Higgins was dead and burned beyond recognition on the steps of the Magic and Steam field office.

Gunner was shouting from behind me, footsteps pounding the road as he returned to the stolen automobile. "Get in the auto."

"But—"

A door banged shut, the engine bellowed, and Gunner snapped, "*Get in.*"

I stood from my crouch at Higgins's side, turned, and jumped into the passenger seat of the white touring a split second before Gunner spun the wheel and slammed down on the accelerator. "Turn right," I ordered.

Gunner made a hard turn and apologized as we momentarily rode the sidewalk. "Never was a fan of these automobiles."

I pulled my goggles on as the black touring came into view. "No matter what you handle, you look good doing it."

"Now I know you're flirting with me."

"I wasn't certain how to make it more obvious."

"Mind that silver tongue," Gunner replied as he unholstered his Waterbury and shifted it to his left hand.

"Save your bullets," I advised. I scooted in my seat so my back was to the door, reached out to grab onto the rooftop, then said, "Keep me in the auto and I'll show you something I've recently learned tongues can do."

"You're tearing me asunder, Hamilton."

Despite everything, I laughed while hoisting myself up and out to rest my backside on the edge of the automobile's door. Gatling Man was miming my actions, though not quite so gracefully as he struggled to hoist his shoulder weapon out the door and take aim. I raised a hand to the night sky and the raging storm that'd been dogging me, tore a billion volts of lightning from the clouds, and hurled the spell at the gangsters. The lightning met a dozen fire bullets in an explosion of heat and static, and the two competing magics screeched so loudly that the windshield of our auto cracked.

"Keep driving," I called to Gunner when he swerved to avoid a rogue blast of flames.

I raised my hand to the sky again, ignoring the spasm of pain in my nerves as I created a massive, shimmering sphere of water. Its bright, bright blue was like something from a tropical paradise, beautiful, second only to Gunner's eyes. It shifted in and out of itself, like the tides, elegant and smooth around the edges, complementing the wildness of my previous spell. The driver of the black touring made a quick turn onto Broadway at the split in Union Square, but Gunner kept right on them. We passed theatre marquees lit up by my magic as if the water sphere were a steam-powered spotlight, and that's when Gatling Man fired again.

I released the magic and the sphere lunged forward, devouring the bullets midair. But Gatling Man kept shooting, and the burrowing sensation of the manufactured magic was enough to make me feel as if I were losing my mind. At the same time, as I pulled more raw energy from the atmosphere around me to strengthen my spell, I could touch that barrier the refuse of manufactured magic was creating. With every cast of those bullets, the disjoint in the raw currents became a bit more pronounced and that barricade more and more tangible.

My water magic overcame Gatling Man's gunfire and dumped over the automobile like a flash flood. The wheels skidded and the driver nearly overcorrected as they shot past Tenth Street, Ninth, Eighth.... I cast lightning again. The volts shot through the night air, ozone burned, and the magic hit the black touring. Electricity mixed with water and tore steel and brass, obliterated expensive steam mechanics, and decimated the two souls inside. Gunner swerved hard to drive around the explosion, and I nearly overturned right out of the auto.

"I said keep me *inside*," I protested, shimmying into my seat.

"And you need to warn me before you enact that clever trick of yours during a high-speed pursuit," Gunner shot back with just a touch of exasperation in his tone.

I stuck my head back out and looked behind at the wreckage and engulfing inferno growing smaller in our wake. Another half a dozen blocks and a left toward Bowery was when I picked up the distant shrill of a patrolman's whistle and the mechanical wail of a crank alarm. A police-designated prisoner transport automobile came squealing around the corner of Broome as we passed, giving us chase down Bowery. I sat down and yanked my goggles down around my neck.

"Police?" Gunner clarified.

"Never on time and always flirting with the married sister at the party."

Gunner laughed, slow and melodic and thoroughly amused. "Then what do you say we lose them, my dear?"

"You're a bad influence on lawmen, Constantine Gunner."

Gunner was still smiling as he hooked a right turn onto Hester Street, soared down Baxter, and once we'd passed the fork of Canal and Walker, we'd lost the much-slower transport automobile. Gunner parked on the side of the road and climbed out of the extravagant touring, already catching the eyes of several passersby.

A gangly teen in too-short-for-him trousers, with a long nose and cocky smile, came out from under a shop awning, took a few strides in Gunner's direction, and called out, "Oy, sir, want me to watch this machine for ya?"

"He's looking to steal it," I stated nonchalantly as I rounded the rear end of the auto to join Gunner's side.

But Gunner didn't hesitate and tossed the lad a set of steel skeleton keys. "Sure."

The teen caught the ring and flashed a huge, albeit quite skeptical, smile. "Really?"

Gunner unholstered his Waterbury and gave the lad a wink.

"Wait a second… ain't you—?"

"Take good care of it," Gunner spoke over him before he strode for the corner of Baxter and Bayard.

I followed at his side, muttering, "You really do revel in the attention, don't you?"

"I don't mind it."

The storm still blanketed the city as we reached Mulberry Bend. Thunder reverberated loose windowpanes and lightning illuminated the seedy streets that should have been bustling, even at night—especially at night—but my magic had sent the masses inside. Undoubtedly, I will have caused a cascade of new wives' tales, but when I was this angry, the world around me warped and bent and it was just easier to let nature react than to try to contain it inside me.

On the corner of Bayard and Mulberry, between a four-story tenement and a dry foods shop of questionable quality, stood a one-story factory, the overhead sign lit by a single steam lamp reading: *Warner's Quality Medicinal Remedies.* And underneath that: *Factory workers' entrance on Bandit Alley.*

"How apropos," Gunner said, his breath like little plumes of smoke as he spoke.

I snapped my fingers and the lamp's globe shattered, shrouding us in dark. "Bligh knows I'm looking for him."

"Certainly explains our Gatling friend's sudden appearance." Gunner pointed his three-barreled pistol at the hefty chain keeping the front door locked and shot it off.

I grabbed the handle, paused, and then said, "If we survive this, I'd like to discuss… ah… I mean, my birthday is next month."

"Is it?"

"February sixth."

"I'll remember."

"Perhaps we could meet."

Gunner glanced down at me. "It's a date."

I smiled and eased the door open. We both slipped into the facility, unlit save for a bare bulb every dozen or so feet—emergency lighting, not that this was the sort of factory that needed or would even invest in such precautions. There were at least six long tables situated in the main room, down the length of the building, likely where the workers sat all day, filling bottles, applying labels, and packing boxes. After our eyes adjusted to the dimness and not so much as a rat scurried by, we silently crept toward a small-looking room off to the right.

The door had been left ajar. Gunner nudged it with the barrels of the Waterbury, letting it fall open onto a cramped office that Higgins had probably used when he was down at this end of the city. Gunner strode inside, moved around the desk, checked underneath, then went to a closet, although there didn't appear to be anything inside but for a few aprons and drab coats.

I tried the desk drawers—typical stationery and bookkeeping, but I'd need a forensic accountant to really comb the details of those ledgers—then I found a handful of unmarked bottles in the bottom compartment. I selected one at random, shook the clear contents, wriggled the cork free, then winced and looked away as a blinding white light poured out of the head like a dense sea fog.

"The hell is that?" Gunner whispered.

I hastily plugged the bottle again and waved a hand to dissipate the magic vapors. "Aether," I said, my voice low. "Higgins probably took a case at a time from the line, mixed the aether into the syrup himself, then brought it to Grace Gallery to sell under the table." I put the bottle back and shut the drawer. "No indication the front deliveries from Pinkerton's ever came through here."

Gunner shook his head. "I suspect those all went to the warehouse on Hester. Never smart to keep all of your eggs in one basket." He returned to the door and stared out across the work floor. "There's another room on the opposite end."

We stood in the threshold and listened to the building settle, but beyond the natural sounds of weight-bearing pillars sighing and the wind kicking up outside, we were alone. So where was Bligh? Gunner strode across the work floor, sure steps leading the way around supply and tool chests and work benches, until we reached a room that I suspected mirrored Higgins's office, although this door was firmly closed.

As Gunner touched the knob, I wasn't certain which sensation hit me first in that singular second: the nightcrawler magic from the dead and dying mechanical men, squirming under my skin, its intention and origins completely and wholly foreign to me, or one picked up by my physical senses—a *stench*. One I knew well. One I had never been able to forget.

Gunner shifted his weight and looked at me. He smelled it too.

I cast a ball of lightning in my hand and gave him an affirmative nod.

So he cocked his Waterbury, and the manufactured aether activated as Gunner opened the door.

The stink of death and decay was immediate. Gunner brought his forearm up to his nose as he took a step inside the room, but I couldn't move, couldn't follow, couldn't be his backup. The putrid smell of rotting flesh and bone dropped me into the immediate chaos of a field hospital. Men were crying and screaming and vomiting and dying. Doctors used primitive surgical tools on soldiers, hacked off body parts, and nurses discarded the remains into piles stacked as tall as me. Muskets cracked the air, cannon fire shook the ground. A uniformed officer dragged me from the tent and onto the battlefield. I had only wanted to wash my hands. They were caked in dirt and filth and someone else's blood and… I had only wanted to wash them.

"Gillian?"

I startled as if my soul had just reentered the body. The electricity I'd been holding snapped and crackled and melted to the floor like water, leaving behind clean hands. Manicured hands. Palms scarred, knuckles large from all of the breaks, and the left index had healed crooked. These were… my hands—*adult* hands.

I wasn't that boy anymore. I *couldn't* be him anymore. He was suffocating me.

I looked up at Gunner, who was scrutinizing my every shallow breath. "I can't go inside," I whispered.

He simply nodded, came out, forcing me to step back, and shut the door behind himself. "You don't need to."

I was still holding my hands in front of myself, palms up. "What—what was in there? Tell me."

Gunner appeared to be considering his words—weighing the intensity of his description for what I had already pieced together. "The Hester Street warehouse was where Tick Tock was amassing his stockpile of weapons and ammunition."

I nodded.

"But I believe the location where that Sawbones character was building Tick Tock an army of mechanical men was… here." Gunner reached out and gently enclosed my hand with his own. "It appears he hightailed it—very recently. He's left behind considerable evidence."

"Evidence as to who Sawbones is?" I asked.

"If that clue is here, I believe it would require a much more in-depth survey of the room to find."

"Tuffey was right—he's playing God. We can't have Sawbones running free." I touched my neck for the PDD that wasn't there. "Oh… I threw my device at a wall."

Gunner moved his hand to my shoulder and gave it a squeeze. "Let's finish investigating—"

On the opposite end of the factory came a colossal *crash* and *smash*, and we both turned toward the damage as tremors pulsated through the building's frame. An immense ball of fire was already hurtling toward us, consuming my field of vision entirely. I raised an arm to shield us, but my reaction was too sluggish after the resurfacing of those godawful memories, and I was thrown backward into the wall by the manufactured magic. I broke through the plaster and tumbled to a stop somewhere within Sawbones's workroom.

I sat up as another blow shook the floor and Gunner began firing. My sleeves were on fire, and I hastily yanked the winter coat free and tossed it aside. My eyes followed the flames, like a moth, and in the glow, I could make out the fetid discarded body parts. Hands and arms and legs and whole torsos, further surrounded by elemental replacements made of brass and silver and iron. A makeshift surgical table, like what the soldiers had been placed on in the open-air tent, was situated in the middle of the room. And as I stumbled to my feet, my legs all but entirely numb at this point, I could see the table coated in fresh blood, in cogs, in screws, in pressure tubes. The shelves on the walls were cluttered with bottles, vats, and vials—no doubt a plethora of chemicals somehow useful to Sawbones's butchery.

I tripped over myself in my haste to climb through

the hole in the wall, stumbled through the debris, and was immediately sick. I wiped my mouth on the back of my hand and looked up in time to see Gunner run for the cover of a storage cabinet to my right. I jerked my head to the left as the floor shook again and I all but forgot the carnage I'd just scrambled out of.

Because lumbering across the factory was a mechanical creature that not even Mary Shelley could have envisioned while writing *Frankenstein*. He reached at least ten feet, roving forward on heavy iron wheels, not unlike those of Ferguson's locomotive, instead of legs. Before him was a Gatling gun and scope, the barrels still smoking from the previous round of magic, and the gun's levers were operated with terrifying mechanical claws in place of hands, the steam hissing around joints, like it'd been a hasty build and some of the cogs were loose. The monster had a tank of a chest, made from melded elements. Iron and platinum, perhaps, which gave Gunner's Waterbury more of an advantage without any silver incorporated into the build, but his pistol alone wasn't going to save our hides. This atrocity had been built with me in mind, utilizing the least conductive natural elements with also the highest melting point for operating that bastardized fire magic.

The creature had a steam headlamp bolted into its chest, and when it twisted its upper body toward me, I had to raise a hand to shield my eyes. Its iron helmet let out a hiss as fasteners were released and the top flipped back like an accordion—revealing Henry Bligh. His golden hair was in complete disarray, the tip of his nose still blackened from our scuffle earlier in the day, one eye was milky, like an advanced cataract, the other replaced with the face of a pocket watch, and his once-unblemished skin was red and blotchy.

"Bligh. What in God's name have you done to yourself?"

"If it isn't the Bureau's favorite street rat, Gillian Hamilton," Bligh answered, and his voice had gotten deeper, rougher, with almost a metallic tinge to it. "You look surprised to see me, Hamilton."

A sudden sweat had broken out across my chest and underarms as I wrangled with the reality that the body parts strewn about the room behind me, the ones I'd fallen into, *touched*, could very well have been Bligh's.

"Sawbones just got better and better with every build, didn't he? Between the incorporation of a noble element, my manufactured fire, and his quintessence magic, I am *perfect*." Bligh raised a clawed hand, and it rotated in a spectacular three hundred and sixty degrees.

The foreign magic squirming down my spine had a name—*quintessence*.

"Bligh," I tried again, speaking even as my voice shook. "He's turned you into a *monster*."

"That's where you're wrong, Hamilton. Sawbones has turned me into divinity. I am indestructible."

"But your fiancée—"

"Emma Olin is New Money trash. I'm not interested in carrying that albatross around my neck."

"Your family—" But I was cut short when Bligh laughed and fired the Gatling gun at the ceiling and fire began to rain from overhead. I raised my arm and moved it in an arc, a tidal wave crashing into the fire, putting it out, and then the magic water dissipated in smoky, glittering tendrils.

"My father has been withholding a portion of my inheritance," Bligh replied, a smug expression on his disturbed face, "until I was promoted at the Bureau. But so long as you—Moore's golden goose—stood in the way of all the career-making cases, I'd be arresting steam-pilfering scum in the Five Points until I died of old age."

Every incident, every clue, every moment began coming into perfect alignment, like the tumblers of a skeleton key locking in place. I took a step back as Bligh rolled forward on those two massive wheels, the floorboards groaning under the weight. "Did you orchestrate the invention of fire bullets just to one-up me?"

Bligh rolled forward again, but this time I stubbornly held my ground. He stopped several feet short, and with a *ticktock, ticktock*, leaned his upper body closer to me. "Did you know that the mother black lace-weaver spider allows her offspring to consume her alive? That was the idea behind Tick Tock—use a new and mysterious gangster as a way for the Whyos to turn on Driscoll. Allow them to destroy their own gang from the inside out."

"But then you met Weaver?" I countered.

The minute hand of Bligh's clock eye began spinning counter clockwise. "I'll admit this, Hamilton, once you sink those grubby little fingers into something, you're hard-pressed to let go. I didn't meet him. I had the idea to hire an architect and caster team—to tinker with magic bullets as a backup plan to taking Driscoll down. Even if it didn't work, presenting Moore with the evidence of the bullets, something him and every director across the country are terrified of, would mean something for my career."

"But then Milo Ferguson got his hands on some of the prototypes."

That minute hand began spinning faster. "Yes," Bligh ground out. "But even with you involved, let's just say investing in this technology at the jumping-off point would be more lucrative than what my family has amassed in three generations. Partnering with Sawbones is how I closed the gap between plausibility and reality."

"Moore knows," I said, my fists clenched so tightly that it felt as if my knuckles would burst from the skin. "He knows everything. The warehouse on Hester, the shipments from California, that you assisted Gatling Man in Fishback's murder and staged the scene to make it look like a break-in.

What about the one you sent to my home? You planned that too, didn't you? That's why you were so surprised to see me last night. You were celebrating because you thought I was dead."

Bligh's upper lip peeled away from his teeth in a vicious snarl, and that hideous, milky-white eye rolled briefly to the right as my storm outside caused a window to shatter. "Good luck proving any of it without his testimony." Bligh started to right his posture—*ticktock, tick*—

"Moore's alive. I saw to that."

"*Liar.*"

Another window broke and the wind howled. I said, "Sometimes the biggest dangers present themselves in the smallest packages."

Bligh was taken aback, whether about Moore or from my unparalleled skills on display, I couldn't say, but that brief hesitation was all Gunner needed to open fire from where he'd been taking cover. An aether round hit Bligh directly in the clock eye. Springs and gizmos went flying, and Bligh reared back with a roar. His helmet came down over his head, steam hissed as the locks set in place, he maneuvered backward on the wheels, then those clawed hands grabbed the Gatling gun levers. Bligh opened fire, cylinder spinning and barrels pumping out fire spells one after another, after another. Bullets pinged, punctured, ricocheted, and set fire across the entire factory as Bligh followed Gunner across its expanse, only to lose him as my outlaw vanished into Higgins's office.

"Who's your criminal friend, Hamilton?" Bligh questioned. He hammered the doorframe with more bullets, setting the room ablaze.

It took an incredible amount of concentration on my part to push aside the itching sensation of too much manufactured magic in the air just to cast a spell of my own. I shot a hand up, wind screamed through the broken windows, spiraled upward, and tore a portion of the roof off the factory. The rain that had begun assailing the city, glowing a wild blue, rich with energy from the magic atmosphere, came down in torrents inside. I stood before Bligh, one hand pointed toward the office, directing sheets of rain to extinguish the fire, the other moving the water in a circular motion around myself that kept me from being incinerated by Bligh's relentless assault.

He was still cranking the lever when the Gatling gun stopped spitting bullets. Bligh's muffled voice from within his helmet swore, and one clawed hand tore an ammunition pack from his bulky iron-and-platinum right arm. Maintaining the wind and rain, something I could have done under any other circumstance with ease, was taking a much more conscious commitment, as every time I grabbed for more raw energy, I had to push through that newly created barrier—a thick, gooey sort of refuse the illegal spells left in the aftermath. It almost felt as if the festering wound in the magical current got torn open a bit more with every bullet shot, and this waste was the atmosphere bleeding a slow death. If what Bligh created, a potentially successful underground business of manufactured magic, wasn't immediately stopped, this barrier was bound to get stronger. It'd make casting a challenge, not only for me, but for the weakest or newest members of the magic community. There was no way to say what damage this could do to our bodies in the long run, let alone the planet, but I knew—even without the facts, without the data—it would be devastating.

"If you'd done one iota of work in the last three years, Bligh, you'd recognize a face from our rogues' gallery."

Bligh's helmet rose as he looked up from trying to fit the new ammunition cartridge into the Gatling gun. "What?"

Gunner strode from the office just then, flanked by heat and smoke, his face dirty with soot. He raised the Waterbury and said, "You can call me Gunner the Deadly." Then Gunner shot out Bligh's headlight, settling what remained of the factory into darkness, as all of the emergency bulbs had already been destroyed by Bligh's bullets and my magic.

Bligh's torso rocked backward from the hit and the wheels of his roving contraption shifted rather ominously.

"A bit of light, if you will, Hamilton," Gunner called.

I snapped my fingers and lightning cracked and splintered across the sky overhead.

By the sudden illumination, Gunner took aim a second time and fired. I thought he'd wildly missed his target when the three aether bullets ricocheted off Bligh's left arm, but then I realized that Gunner had knocked free another cartridge of ammunition and was now running to collect it. I raised my hands, palms out, and the downpour of rain ceased. It held suspended around us, glowing like a billion fireflies on the first summer night. Gunner turned, Waterbury holstered and a massive metal cartridge that housed the rounds for the Gatling gun in both hands.

"Get down!" I shouted.

Gunner must have had a flashback to Shallow Grave, because he didn't question me. Instead, he dropped the ammunition, threw himself to the floor, and covered his head.

I pulled my hands back and the rain mimicked the motion. Each water droplet elongated until it resembled a needle several inches in length, completely surrounding Bligh from every angle. Bligh, in return, struggled harder to get the new ammunition set into the cylinder, no easy task with metal claws for fingers, and opened fire on me just as I directed the water magic to go on the offense. I reached further into the surrounding atmosphere, the viscous waste now past my wrist, my forearm, until I was elbows-deep, tearing energy to fuel my spell as the rain assaulted Bligh. Every fire bullet eradicated by my magic sent an aftershock through my body, and if I'd not been encased in flesh, surely my skeleton would have been shaken apart. The rain drilled into Bligh's armor, but even with a spell the elemental opposite of fire, the combination of platinum and this unknown quintessence magic kept me from landing any lethal hits.

"Take cover," I called to Gunner before I released the spell and ran back to Sawbones's workroom. I froze in the doorway as the rotten stink assaulted my senses again, but I managed to take a breath without the immediate need to vomit and plunged deeper into the dark, enclosed space. I tripped over a severed arm and stepped in something that *squished*—skinned flesh at best and some sort of innards at worst.

Snap.

Snap.

Snap.

I was choking on bile by the time I reached the far wall slovenly arranged with all of the mysterious bottled liquids. I cast a small ball of lightning, the electricity bouncing in my hand as I read the scrawled labels. The problem being presented to me was that my water magic couldn't easily eradicate the manufactured fire because Sawbones had reinforced Bligh with goddamn platinum. Platinum didn't easily melt like brass, nor did it hold a current the way silver did. And his armor was so thick that even Gunner's aether bullets were having little effect. Before my own magic would be superior in a one-on-one match, I'd have to reduce the effectiveness of Bligh's platinum armor.

Sawbones had clearly kept chemicals on-hand in order to bend and ply his body parts to suit the weapons being shipped in from California. Which made sense, considering each mechanical soldier would be custom, from the one who fell off my balcony, to McCarthy, to Bligh himself. And that meant Sawbones *had* to have had a solvent to use on platinum. I was thinking of the story Higgins told me before his untimely death—of the poison woman and her Aqua Tofana—when I saw it in the back, its label curled and discolored:

Aqua Regia.

It'd been a while since I'd studied my Latin declensions, but *regia* was from the associative term *domus regia*. A home or dwelling; pertaining to a king.

Royal water.

Noble element.

I grabbed the bottle, the orange solution sloshing as I raced back to the factory floor in time to see Gunner run and dive between the wheels of Bligh's apparatus, causing Bligh to almost fire the Gatling gun on himself.

"Come out from under there," Bligh bellowed, rolling back and then forward, trying to catch Gunner without cover so he could shoot several rounds directly into the top of his head.

"Bligh!" I shouted, raising the bottle up and over my head.

He swiveled in my direction. His claws cocked the levers of the Gatling gun. Then he fired.

I smashed the bottle of Aqua Regia on the floorboards, and before it could seep into the wood, I forced the liquid to merge with the storm—used every ounce of raw energy I could pull from the tangles of magic around us—and by sheer brute force, intertwined the Aqua Regia into my water spell so the corrosive elements rained down atop Bligh and his suit of platinum armor. My hands glowed a cobalt blue. The violence kept deep inside me was awake, roaring like a lion, hurling itself against my ribcage to be let free. I had so much magic within me that excess light was streaming from my fingertips, rolling down the sides of my face and neck like sweat.

I was incandescent.

Bligh was screaming as the rain ate through his armor. Pockmarks in the metal began to show, and vapors wafted upward as the Aqua Regia came into contact with platinum, the achievement further fueled by my merciless magic. His fantastical roving vehicle began to crack along its axis, and Gunner, still underneath and shielded from the chemicals mixed into my rain, quickly shot a succession of aether rounds into the floorboards. One of the wheels fell into the caved-in floor, keeping Bligh stuck and at an angle so the mechanics didn't smash Gunner. Bligh's clawed hands let go of the Gatling gun levers and fought to remove his helmet in a sort of blind panic. But then an ominous snap rang out and the armor, bolted onto the wheels and gun about the waist, fell apart and Bligh crashed backward.

I waved one hand and the rain ceased. I watched a moment as Bligh, his armor crumbling with every move, dragged his legless, massive girth along the floor. He reached a broken claw upward for his gun, and Gunner took several steps back while pointing his Waterbury at Bligh. I snapped my fingers and a glittering sphere of water formed before me, growing bigger and bigger, silent as it twisted and turned on itself. Then I shot my hand forward, and the blast hit Bligh so hard, he went flying across the factory, slammed into the front door we'd entered, and dropped into a heap of mechanical garbage.

The storm subsided outside.

The factory was still.

Gunner and I were both breathing hard. Soaking wet, freezing, but alive.

Black spots filled my vision, and when I took a step, I felt as if someone else were controlling my legs. I stumbled into the broken wheels, gripped the treads, and held my other hand toward Gunner. "Help me," I whispered.

Gunner strode toward me, holstered his weapon, and

made to pick me up.

"N-no. Bligh. I need to make sure."

"Gillian—"

"Please."

Gunner wiped wet hair from his face before reluctantly nodding. He offered his arm for support and carefully led me across the torn-up flooring. We reached Bligh, his armor hardly a step up from scrap metal now. I kicked a portion of it, and it echoed like a tin can skittering along an empty cobblestone street. Bligh didn't move.

I let go of Gunner, drew closer, and peered down. His helmet had been tossed several feet away, and his body, severed by Sawbones at the collarbones, had fallen out of the armor and lay on the ground, his mouth agape and trying to gasp for air. All of the quintessence magic and pneumatic tubing that'd kept him alive inside the suit was gone and destroyed, and now all that remained of his physical form was slowly dying.

"*Christ Almighty.*"

Gunner gently took my elbow in one hand as he unholstered the Waterbury. "I'll handle it."

As far as chivalry went, in that moment, I could think of no better example. Gunner was a knight in shining armor.

"Thank you." I didn't look at Bligh again. Instead, turned and began to walk away.

Gunner fired one round.

And then everything went dark.

XIX

January 4, 1882

The bedroom window was frosted over in sinuous opaque curves and lines that were sure to inspire the next artistic movement somewhere in Europe. The room had a cool, bluish glow about it, even though I was fairly certain it was close to lunchtime. I stretched my legs and dug my toes into cold sheets near the foot of the bed. Gunner's pocket watch lay open on the stand to my back, its gentle *ticktock*—so different from that of Henry Bligh's—would have lulled me to sleep if not for the murmur of conversation in my parlor.

I touched the second pillow, dragged my fingertips along the stitching, smoothed my palm along the bedding. I couldn't feel the cloth. I turned my hand over and studied the latticework of scarring. It stood out, bright white against my already pale complexion. Shifting a bit on my side, I tugged back my sleeve and rubbed my index finger against the tendons of my wrist—the sensation a reminder that I was still alive.

The front door opened. A few more words were

exchanged. Then it shut.

I looked over my shoulder as Gunner appeared in the bedroom doorway. "What'd he say?"

Gunner took a few steps inside and sat on the edge of the bed. He leaned over and briefly stroked the newest gray streak on my head. "Moore said he's been temporarily relieved of duty."

I sat up in a rush. "He *what*?"

"He said that D.C. arrived today, and they've taken over the investigation after grievances raised by Frederick Bligh. It seems that a federal agent neck-deep in underground gang activity isn't the main concern, but that Moore approved Henry's murder."

"Moore didn't—"

"Of course he didn't," Gunner said. "But Old Money is involved, and even the FBMS isn't immune to their protestations." He stroked my hair some more. "Moore wanted to warn you that D.C. will be coming to interview you, but because you broke your PDD the other night, he had to wait until he was able to slip out of the office to tell you."

I felt the blood drain from my face and extremities, and a long ago but never forgotten terror wash over me. I felt as if I were stuck under a sheet of ice, drowning, sinking into the dark water below….

"My dear?"

"You have to go."

"Gillian—"

"*No*. Don't argue with me." I shoved the bedding back and stumbled to my feet, cold air nipping at my bare ankles and toes. "D.C. coming here… they're the head of the Bureau."

"I'm well aware of what D.C. implies," Gunner said, shifting where he sat to look at me. "What's going on?"

I paced to the window, stopped, walked away, then went back. "D.C. here… investigating Moore and his report… what did he tell them? Did he skirt the truth about you? About me? Or did he put all of it in writing?" I felt my chin quiver as I said to myself in a hushed voice, "The truth."

The bed creaked as Gunner got to his feet.

I touched the glass pane with my hand and the frozen mural melted away to reveal the comings and goings of Twenty-Seventh Street. A cherry-red automobile was just pulling to a stop on the side of the road, steam vapors billowing in the cold air. Two men in expensive winter coats climbed out and were greeted by my doorman, Dawson. I shifted to get a better angle on the scene and watched as Dawson nodded and made a general gesture toward my window. One of the men tilted his bowler and looked up.

I took a step back, but he'd seen me. "Jesus Christ. They're already here." I spun toward Gunner. "You need to go *now*."

"No," Gunner said adamantly. "Not until you tell me what's going on, Gillian."

"My name's *not* Gillian Hamilton," I cried, and for a singular second, I was free. No more half-truths. No more outright lies. No more undermining my own worth and skill so that I didn't raise any red flags. I was finally, simply, me. The monster. But then I met Gunner's expression, so excruciatingly human in his uncertainty and inevitable hurt that had I had a gun, I'd have done myself in then and there to bring this nightmare of a life to an end.

"What is your name?" Gunner asked, very quiet.

I spared the window one last look, felt the fear of that little boy return, welling up inside me, then said to Gunner in a shaky voice, "Simon Fitzgerald—I'm the Butcher of Antietam. And they've finally found me."

Gillian Hamilton and Gunner the Deadly return in:

The Doctor
(Magic & Steam: Book Three)

C.S. Poe is a Lambda Literary and two-time EPIC award finalist, and a FAPA award-winning author of gay mystery, romance, and speculative fiction.

She resides in New York City, but has also called Key West and Ibaraki, Japan, home in the past. She has an affinity for all things cute and colorful and a major weakness for toys. C.S. is an avid fan of coffee, reading, and cats. She's rescued two cats—Milo and Kasper do their best to distract her from work on a daily basis.

C.S. is an alumna of the School of Visual Arts.

Her debut novel, *The Mystery of Nevermore*, was published 2016.

cspoe.com

ALSO BY C.S. POE

SERIES:
Snow & Winter
The Mystery of Nevermore
The Mystery of the Curiosities
The Mystery of the Moving Image
The Mystery of the Bones

Magic & Steam
The Engineer
The Gangster

A Lancaster Story
Kneading You
Joy
Color of You

The Silver Screen
Lights. Camera. Murder.

An Auden & O'Callaghan Mystery
(co-written with Gregory Ashe)
A Friend in the Dark

NOVELS:
Southernmost Murder

NOVELLAS:
11:59

SHORT STORIES:
Love in 24 Frames
That Turtle Story
New Game, Start
Love Has No Expiration

Visit cspoe.com for free slice-of-life codas, titles in audio, and available foreign translations.

Join C.S. Poe's mailing list to stay updated on upcoming releases, sales, conventions, and more!
bit.ly/CSPoeNewsletter